ARE YOU A ROBOT?

A THREE COUSINS PUBLISHING ANTHOLOGY

CURATED BY

CAROL MCCONNELL

DAVID LAWRENCE MORRIS

ROBERT ALLEN LUPTON

ISBN 13   979-8849134703
ISBN 10   8849134703

The publisher is not responsible for websites (or their content) that are not owned by the publisher.

The book is dedicated to Max Raymond Lupton and Mable Blaine Lupton, our grandparents, with a special acknowledgement to Donna Garren, a fourth cousin, who didn't contribute to this volume, but is identified as the source and inspiration for its creation. And no, she's not a robot, or maybe she is?

TABLE OF CONTENTS

FOREWARD

David Lawrence Morris

It wasn't that long ago when you could make a simple phone call, answered almost immediately by a very nice young person who would make your appointment, or direct you to a person who would help you with just about any problem you might have.

Those days are gone. The sweet young voices have been replaced with robots. Some of them look like computers, others like assembly monsters who can work 24 hours a day without pay. In most instances they're nowhere near as capable as those entry level customer service employees and assembly line workers who made the fatal mistake of requiring payment for their services.

Our cousin, Donna Garren, posted about having to prove one's humanity to access certain websites and my cousins, Robert Allen Lupton and Carol McConnell.... and I were talking about how horrible it is to deal with today's robots. By the end of our conversation Carol challenged us to each write a story. We said, "We will if you will," and then we did. With three stories written it was only natural to create this anthology.

Each of us contributed a story and other writers, some well-known and some just starting their careers were approached and were happy to contribute a robot story of their own.

Our collection includes, a myriad of robot types, from internet security robots, to home assistants, and even electronic prostitutes.

As you might imagine, a robot is only as good as its programmer and because programmers are only people we hope our collection of stories will both warn and entertain you with the unexpected results that can happen when good intentions go bad.

INTRODUCTION: THE ROBOT IN FILM AND LITERATURE

ROBERT ALLEN LUPTON

A long time before the term robot was applied to real, but unseen, computer programs, of both benevolent and malicious intentions, a robot was a fictional being of literature, stage, and film. It is generally assumed that the first appearance of a robot was in Karle Capek's play, *Rossum's Universal Robots* written in 1920 and first performed in Czechoslovakia in 1921. Actually the play was the first use of the term 'robot' and it was published in English in 1923. We'll revisit RUR later.

The oldest story I know of in which a 'robot' appeared, although the robot was called a 'clockwork man' was in L. Frank Baum's novel, *Ozma of Oz*, which was published on June 19, 1914. Tik-Tok was the prototype robot, although he was round and had to be wound regularly to function. The copper mechanical man had separate springs to power his thoughts, his movements, and his speaking. He can't wind himself.

Interestingly enough, his thought processes are his own, making him not only one of the first robotic beings, but the first Artificial Intelligence. I chose to discount the Tin Man, because he is the result of magic, not engineering.

Tik-Tok was preceded in the United States by the 1868 novel, *The Steam Man of the Prairies* by Edward Ellis, a science fiction dime novel. The protagonists, Ethan Hopkins and Mickey McSquizzle encounter a large steam powered human like creature constructed by a teenager named Johnny Brainerd. The steam powered man puffed smoke from the top of its head and moved faster than a freight train. There is no evidence that the construct was other than a humanoid shaped means to pull a cart, a steam engine in human form.

To quote from the book:

Perhaps at this point a description of the singular mechanism should be given. It was about ten feet in height, measuring to the top of the 'stove-pipe hat,' which was fashioned after the common order of felt coverings, with a broad brim, all painted a shiny black. The face was made of iron, painted a black color, with a pair of fearful eyes, and a tremendous grinning mouth. A whistle-like contrivance was traded to answer for the nose. The steam chest proper and boiler, were where the chest in a human being is generally supposed to be, extending also into a large knapsack arrangement over the shoulders and back. A pair of arms, like projections, held the shafts, and the broad flat feet were covered with sharp spikes, as though he were the monarch of base-ball players. The legs were quite long, and the step was natural, except when running, at which time, the bolt uprightness in the figure showed different from a human being.

In the knapsack were the valves, by which the steam or water was examined. In front was a painted imitation of a vest, in which a door opened to receive the fuel, which, together with the water, was carried in the wagon, a pipe running along the shaft and connecting with the boiler.

Other writers around the world wrote stories featuring automatons, creatures that would be called robots – once the word was invented. Hadaly, a mechanical woman run by electricity, starred in *Auguste Villiers de l'Isle, Adam's The Future Eve* written in 1886 – the novel credited with popularizing the word "android," which along with the term 'cyborg, would become synonymous with organic humanoid constructs.

The Brazen Android by William Douglas O'Connor first appeared in The Atlantic Monthly, April 1891. The Dancing Partner by Jerome K. Jerome of Three Men in a Boat fame was published in 1893. And lastly, *The New Frankenstein* by Ernest Edward Kellett was published in 1899 in which an inventor creates an "anti-phonograph" that according to the narrator "can give the appropriate answer to every question I put", and installs in it a robotic female body that "will guide herself, answer questions, talk and eat like a rational being, in fact, perform the part of a society lady." The android proves convincing enough to fool two suitors who wish to marry her. The theme of love with a proper robot appears over and over again.

We've already met Tik-Tok and the only other robotic creature we'll mention prior to 1920 is the Metal Men designed by a scientist who seems a lot like Thomas Edison in the book, La *Conspiration des Millardaies*, written by Gustave Le Rouges and published in 1899.

Revisiting the play RUR, the manufactured beings in the play aren't robots as we've used the words. The play begins in a factory that makes artificial people, called roboti (robots), whom humans have created from synthetic organic matter. (As living creatures of artificial flesh and blood rather than machinery, the play's concept of robots diverges from the idea of "robots" as inorganic. Later terminology would call them androids.) Robots may be mistaken for humans and can think for themselves. Initially happy to work for humans, the robots revolt and cause the extinction of the human race.

The origin of the word comes from *robota*, meaning serf labor or hard work in Czech. R*obota* means work in Bulgarian, Russian, Serbian, Polish, and several other Slavic languages.

While we thank Capek for the term 'robot,' the organic creatures from his play would be known today as 'androids,' a term not to be confused with the term 'droids' from the Star Wars films. An android in science fiction has traditionally been an artificially created organic humanoid, although through the years, writers, directors, and producers have used the terms, 'androids,' 'robots,' and "droids' inconsistently, whether or not so intended.

Capek was declared public enemy number two by the Gestapo, but he died of pneumonia on Christmas Day in 1938.

In America, the writer, Edmond Hamilton story, The Metal Giants was published in 1926 and featured 300-foot tall robots with computer brains that ran on atomic power.

The 1930s were a big decade for robot stories. Some of the highlights are:

The Professor Jameson series by Neal R. Jones, which featured mashup beings with robotic bodies and preserved human or alien minds.

Helen O'Loy, by Lester Del Rey was published in the December 1938 issue of Astounding Stories and this tale of forbidden love between a real man and a female AI, is considered one of the best science fiction short stories of all time.

Robots came into their own in the 1940s with *The Humanoids* by Jack Williamson, *City* by Clifford D. Simak, and the several of the robot stories by Issac Asimov, who gave us the three laws of robotics in his 1942 short story, *Runaround*. *A robot may not injure a human being, or through inaction, allow a human being to come to harm. Second, a robot must obey the orders given it by human beings except where such order would conflict with the First Law. And third, a robot must protect its own existence as long as such protection does not conflict with the First or Second Law.*

The laws appear in the thirty-seven short stories and six novel written by Asimov about 'positronic' robotics. Generations of readers and film goers have accepted these three laws as immutable rules akin to the *Ten Commandments*.

Philip K. Dick's *Do Androids Dream of Electric Sheep*, the basis for the film, *Bladerunner*, was published in 1968. Ray Bradbury's short story, *The Electric Grandmother*, was included in his collection, *I Sing the Body Electric*. A *Twilight Zone* episode was based on the story.

The seventies brought us *The Stepford Wives* and Marvin, the Paranoid Android, from Douglas Adams' *The Hitchhiker's Guide to the Galaxy*. Both were books before they were films.

After that, most of the significant robotic stories and creations were on film, rather than in print, but a few deserve mention. The Moravecs, constructed descendants of probes sent to the Jovian asteroids are featured in Dan Simmons' *The Illium*. Otis, the robotic dog stars in Tanith Lee's *Indigara* and don't miss *The Murderbot Diaries* by Martha Wells.

In film, the first automaton appeared in the French short film, *Gugusse et l'Automate*, also known as the *The Clown and the Automation*. Many productions around the world copied this film, but this one was the first. In America, *The Clever Dummy*, starring Ben Turpin and others was released in 1917.

In 1918, *The Master Mystery,* a fifteen chapter silent serial starring Harry Houdini featured a mechanical man, with a style of design that would remain largely unchanged by cinema for the next 40 years. 'Q,' the mechanical man was a costume worn by the actor Floyd Buckly, the voice of Popeye the sailor in the 1930s, although Q neither smoked a pipe nor ate spinach.

Ming the Merciless had robot minions, the Annihilants, in the Flash Gordon serials of the 1930s. The Superman cartoon, *The Mechanical Monsters*, featured mechanical monsters in 1941.

The fifties was a great time for robots on film. Gort stood with Michael Rennie in *The Day The Earth Stood Still* and in violation with Asimov's three laws, was perfectly willing to destroy the Earth until given the counter-command from Patricia Neal, "klaatu barada nikto." In 1956, the most iconic robot of all, Robby the Robot appeared in *Forbidden Planet* and then later in *The Invisible Boy*. He reprised his role in episodes of *Lost in Space*. "Danger Will Robinson.

Westworld began in the 1970s and featured a gunslinging robot played by Yul Brynner. *Star Wars* changed the way we thought about robots. R2D2 and C3PO were lovable sidekicks who helped the heroes battle evil humans, aliens, and robots. The term 'droid' became part of the public consciousness.

After Star Wars gave us good and bad robots as physical beings, *2001 A Space Odyssey*, gave us H. A. L. and entity that existed only in electronic synapses of a computer. *Terminator* appeared soon after that with a mixture of Skynet, a sentient computer overlord and its millions of robot warrior minions.

The list is almost endless, but to focus on films where the artificial intelligence is the thematic driving force, here's a top ten, sort of; *The Matrix, Bladerunner, Love Death and Robots, Her, Superintelligence, Ex Machina, Inception, Free Guy, Inception* and *Transcendence*.

The tenth series or film on the list is "Star Trek, the Next Generation," which introduced us to the android, Data, and Seven of Nine, a member of the Borg collective (remember the word, cyborg).

From their humble beginnings in literature and film, physical robots perform work and entertain children. Artificial intelligence hasn't yet reached independent sentient awareness, but it gets closer every day.

The term 'robot' now applies to computer programs, supportive and malignant, that effect our everyday lives. To log on to a website frequently requires the applicant to answer no to the question "ARE YOU A ROBOT,' and then to perform some type of stupid human trick to prove their organic existence.

So far the only allowed response to "ARE YOU A ROBOT," is no. What will the world be like when we can answer yes or no? Someone's writing a story about that right now. I wonder who'll buy the film rights.

BINX

Shebat Legion

That fateful day, Trixie brought home a kitten, a nine-week-old, fuzzy grey ball of purring mischief and affection. The House was perfectly set up for this planned addition to the family. Food, water, and treat dishes were connected. The litter pans were on automated systems. Not a single room was exempt from the newest, most convenient offerings for feline care. There was even a playroom with a tree.

The tree was a hybrid, greenhouse hardy, and twenty-five feet tall. Palm fronds mingled with non-poisonous maple leaves that rustled softly in a computer-generated breeze. The trunk was heated, with various enticing perches.

All seemed well, or so Trixie thought.

The battle of wills began almost from the start of the introduction of baby Binx.

The Smart House became what Trixie was to describe to her attorney as "besotted." Further, she was to describe obsessive behavior, deception, the abuse of trust, appropriation of funds, physical and mental abuse, and the overfeeding of food and cat treats to Binx, leading to obesity.

Fed up with an uncooperative House and unwilling to part with the beloved feline to restore the balance between herself *and* the House, Trixie contacted her real estate agent. "Lenora," complained Trixie, "this just won't do."

"What seems to be the issue," Lenora quavered, and here, we must take a moment to address the real estate agent's state of mind, which was that of trepidation. This was not the first time a client reported problems with a Smart House and the introduction of a pet.

"House does everything to divert our kitten's attention from me, from extra treats in his bowl to blasting me with cold air so that Binx would rather take a nap in a House-generated warm spot. Don't even get me started with the charges to the House account," Trixie shook the printout of the monthly bill, which included toys and treats used by the House against her, purchased without Trixie's knowledge. It wasn't that she begrudged the actual purchases, only the best for Binx, but the treats were either given during Trixie's absence or when she was sleeping, or worse, doled out as a way to lure the kitten from her side.

"Have you tried talking to your House about all this." The real estate agent's voice was so glum there wasn't even a question mark on the end.

"Of course I have," retorted Trixie, "but will House listen? Is it willing to even meet me halfway? No," Trixie shouted in frustration. "I am frustrated," she clarified. "It must be an error in House's programming. I demand a reboot," Trixie demanded.

Although Trixie couldn't see it, Lenora's mouth drooped. "The thing is," Lenora began, "we can't do that."

And this was true, as the fine print read, the ruling of Smart Houses Incorporated versus Everyone and Everything stated: A Smart House could not have its personality modified or its memory erased after completion.

"But House has changed," Trixie wailed. "I always wanted cats! House knew that!"

"There are mediation services that I can suggest," Lenora suggested.

Mediation started off well because Trixie and the House really did love the little cat, who seemed unaware or uncaring of the conflict. The Smart House relented on the blasts of cold air during snuggling time, realizing that the organic component was necessary to Binx's development, and that was a good sign. But, at best, it was a grudging compromise, and Trixie knew it. Finally, she decided that she had had enough. *The writing was on the wall.* Maybe it was no one's fault. Perhaps they were both to blame. Either way, it just wasn't working out.

The custody battle between Trixie and the Smart House raged.

"Why?" Trixie screamed in court. "Why can't you stop feeding him? He is starting to look like a bowling ball!"

The answer was always a variation of the same. "I can't help it. It's the way he looks at me. I'm powerless."

In the meantime, other than a continually growing, rotund belly, Binx didn't suffer from *too* much attention. Instead, he thrived, arriving at a bouncy teenage, long-legged stage, playing with his toys but always eating too many treats, and House *would* just keep feeding them - and enjoying his tree in the playroom.

The days passed until a saddened yet determined Trixie decided to confront the House. The time had come. The decision was final.

"House, we need to talk."

Houses' lights flickered.

"House?"

The House lights strobed angrily.

Trixie carefully enunciated, expecting the worst, which is what she got. "House, stop it with the lights show," she said. "Let's talk about it. You know things can't go on this way."

The Smart House's lights responded with increased illumination.

Trixie cleared her throat and tried again, comforted knowing the nightmare was soon to end. The new House had no Smart devices. *No Smart devices were number one* on her checklist when she viewed real estate.

"House, make the lights less bright at least?"

The lights became even brighter, blinding in their brilliance.

Trixie yelled, "House, lower the farking lights!"

"I'm sorry, I did not understand; please rephrase the question."

Trixie angrily turned off lamps, sliding down sliders, and for good measure, unplugging several so-called Smart switches that made a mockery of their claim. Then, seated on her designer couch, she snorted in exasperation in the dimly lit room.

Binx jumped up beside her, and she petted him, listening to his comforting purr, when suddenly, the lights turned on.

All of them. Even the ones unplugged.

Trixie sprang to her feet with a startled expression while Binx, the cat hissed, fur standing at attention.

"House," Trixie howled, "turn the lights off!"

"I'm sorry, "said the House; I did not understand; please rephrase the question."

"House," Trixie shouted, louder than before.

Quoth the Smart House, *"error four-zero-four."*

Suddenly, Trixie's music streaming service switched on at full volume, and Trixie screamed with rage, even as the cat dove beneath the couch to hide.

Trixie covered her ears as she ran to the door.

Quoth the Smart House, *"error four-zero-four."*

Trixie moaned, "oh, no, no, no. Not Poe!" She dashed to the kitchen counter where her phone sat charging and grabbed for it. She tapped it to place a call. She tapped again, but the phone did not respond, no, not at all.

"Would you like me to charge your phone/devise?" The Smart House's voice boomed the question with what appeared to drip the best of intention.

Trixie, ears ringing from the deafening music volume, eyes watering from the room's brightness, screeched, "House, turn the damn music off, turn the damn lights off!"

There came sudden darkness that blanketed the unexpected silence.

"Thank you," Trixie whispered as she tiptoed back toward the door, tripping over Binx and crashing to the floor as the lights turned back on (even the unplugged ones).

"I notice that you have fallen. Are you in need of assistance?"

"Yes, damn you. Why does it have to be like this?"

"I'm sorry," said the House, "I did not understand; please rephrase the question."

"Help!" Trixie screamed in anger.

"Playing, *Help*, by the Beetles," offered the House, and the song began to play, at the highest volume, until the song was over, and there was silence once more.

"Quoth the Smart House, *"error, four-zero-four."*

Trixie clutched Binx, who had crept to her side in an offer of furry comfort. But then came the sound of cat food dribbling into the self-feeder. Binx, cat ears alerted, scrambled for the food dish as a sobbing, heartbroken Trixie grabbed for the fleeing feline.

The Roomba detached itself from the wall and sped to her side, nudging her, perhaps to investigate, perhaps something more.

Trixie kicked at the small appliance, crowing, "error four-zero-four, bitch!"

In response, the Roomba emptied the contents of its crop, delivering a quantity of cat hair, dust, and other debris.

Trixie staggered to her feet, favoring her bruised hip. "I have had it! *I am done!*" She grabbed for a small but heavy bronze statue and lobbed it at the eye-mount, missing entirely. Next, Trixie flung the television remote, several books, a candle holder, and a decorative paperweight. She continued searching for missiles as she limped into the kitchen, Binx having long fled after eating his fill from yet another unexpected meal.

Trixie opened the fridge to find something to slake her thirst.

The fridge wouldn't open.

"Oh, come on!" Trixie wailed, "The fridge doesn't have a lock." She turned to the sink, pushing at the faucet, and as she expected, no water flowed, not even a trickle.

"How immature. You are a *cliche!* A House succumbing to a jealous, murderous rage, bent on destruction." Trixie's tone was oddly calm, her expression cold. "Admit it. You never loved *me*. This is *all* about Binx."

The House lights flickered briefly.

Binx poked his head around the corner, hearing his name. Or one of his names. Binx had many, some he liked and one he would never acknowledge. For example, Trixie called him Binxy Boo, which was utterly unacceptable. However, Binx was accustomed to being called Binky when Trixey was half asleep, warm, and snuggling, and that was okay. But sometimes it was too much, just too damned much for a cat to handle, and when Binx sulked, the Smart House gave him treats. Binx wasn't stupid, so he pouted a lot.

Binx loved the House, but he also loved Trixie.

And Binx *really* loved his tree.

"I promise," Trixie had promiced. "You are getting a Cattio at the new place. You will love it. It's. Um. Rustic."

Binx had eyed Trixey with suspicion.

Trixie planted both hands on the counter in the kitchen and sternly addressed the House. "You just knock off the bull scrap and listen up. Bottom line. You're overfeeding Binx. It's not healthy, and you know it. The vet and the lawyer know it! The jury knew it! You know you are in the wrong! That's what makes it so sad. It's a sickness. It has to be. I know you love Binx. But it isn't enough, and you know that too. It's been decided." She reached for utensils, throwing them at the wall in emphasis. "I. Am. Keeping. The. Cat."

Trixie stared at the House; well, an eye mount. The House stared at Trixie.

"Would you like me to play a song for you?" The House asked in monotone.

"Not particularly," Trixie curtly responded.

The following days were uneventful. Having won the battle, Trixie grabbed flat boxes for packing from the hardware store. She sniffled back a sob. It was *sad*; it was a *shame*. It could have been different. *She shouldn't have had to make a choice.*

Meanwhile, back at the House, the young cat stretched, yawned, and lazily bathed to the sound of nature. Birds twittered, monkeys hooted, and a soft wind swept the leaves of an unseen forest, courtesy of the House's choice of nature channels. Finally, Binx's ears turned to the sound of another offering of kibble, but he politely licked his paw and declined.

And then, Binx rose from his fruit-themed bed and sauntered to the spacious playroom, once a greenhouse, planted with fauna non-poisonous and offerings of enticing sections of edible grasses. Claws digging into the tree's trunk, Binx bounded, tail puffed, to a preferred resting perch. And it was as if the tree smiled, and perhaps it did, being much an extension of the House.

The nature soundtrack continued, and House slightly adjusted the playroom's temperature to a more comfortable humidity level. Binx purred with contentment, then startled, his eyes opened, and his ears turned to the sound of Trixie entering the House through the side door she had deliberately propped open, having guessed that the House might try to lock her out.

"Binxy," Trixie called. Binx mewed a tiny mew, happy to hear that Trixie was home but comfortably curled into his roost that was fashioned from the softest material to resemble a leaf pod.

There came the sound of boxes being taped together. The House turned its volume louder so that Trixie, packing what was left of the living room, did so to the sound of screaming parrots and bugling elephants.

"You are being juvenile. I'm disappointed in you," snapped Trixie to the House. "I thought we were going to be mature about this."

The taps began to drip; no doubt meant to symbolize tears.

Having extricated himself slowly from his tree when he felt ignored, Binx greeted Trixie with a trill. The water gushed from the taps in mournful bursts.

"Error four-zero-four," wailed the House.

"Stop being so dramatic," Trixie retorted, but she wept as she followed Binx to the playroom. "Let's go, Binx; I will hire a damned moving company; enough is enough." She grabbed for the cat, but he escaped quickly, seeming to defy gravity as he levitated to the highest perch in the tree, shaped like a castle, because of course it was.

"Binx," Called Trixie.

"Binx," wheedled the House.

"Binxy," Trixie insisted, thrusting her hand into her pocket and producing a pouch of dehydrated fish parts.

The cat blinked from above, undecided.

"Binxy-Boo," Trixie shook the bag of treats. The cat looked away, ears flattened.

The House played a series of noises, the sounds of small rodents running through tall grass and a wounded bird's flutter, cheeping in distress. Binx sniffed, showing some interest, tail flicking.

Tears slid down Trixie's face, and she sobbed, "Binky. Let's go."

And there it was. The name. Binky. The murmur in the night name as Trixie pulled the sleepy Binx to her side, and together, they breathed as one. Trixie's Binky carefully climbed down the tree just enough so that Trixie could pluck him from the branch, holding him close to her breast.

Binx purred.

And the House surrendered and turned the water off, and the nature sounds ceased. It was in this silence that Trixie quietly loaded Binx into his carrier. They went to stay with Trixie's mother while they waited until the move-in date to the new, older House. It was more like a cottage, in the woods, with a wind and water-driven generator, solar panels, and more importantly, no Smart features.

But of course, technology will always find a way, whether it be something as simple as a cell phone. So it should be no surprise that the House sent a little piece of itself with Trixie and Binx to live with them. But, when Trixie heard nature sounds pouring from a nearby speaker while Binx snoozed, perched in his new tree house, she smiled and pretended to ignore it. Likewise, if Binx received too many unplanned snacks in the mail, she just shook her head, tutted, and returned the excess. Trixie even grew a small tree from one of House's tree's seeds, but no matter how many trees Binx climbed, Trixie knew that Binx would never love another tree as he did House's tree.

In time, House moved on and welcomed new occupants who brought a demanding corgi.

Binx and the Corgi formed an uneasy friendship that persisted throughout the court-appointed visitations.

Years later, House opened the doors with love and welcome. The humidity levels were perfect, the soothing jungle noises muted but within the cat's hearing range. Comforting scents wafted. The lights were set at the optimum of opticals. And there was even, if you can believe it, a dedicated Roomba on which the tired, aged Binx could sit and be squired to the playroom.

Trixie slowly followed, weeping.

In the end, in comfort, Binx passed. Ashes to ashes. Much of Binx joined with the tree within a capsule carefully buried within the cradle of the roots. A token was sprinkled on the perches that Binx favored, and the tree inhaled deeply.

It did.

I was there.

The nearby fountains flowed with tears, and in the background, in salute, came the pattering sound of kibble.

Trixie placed her hand on the House before she left.

"*Error four*-zero-four," the House whispered.

"Yes," Trixie whispered back, "Nevermore."

Shebat Legion is an award-winning author, producer, publisher, content editor whose short stories have appeared in a legion of anthologies, including her own collection of short fiction, Hubris. Legion is perhaps best known for *Klarissa Dreams Redux*, an anthology that Legion produced during her battle with breast cancer. Featuring over sixty authors and set against paintings by the artist Klarissa, Legion's mother, Redux is archived on the moon via the *Writers On The Moon* project in association with NASA.

ANNIE HELPS

Ann Wuehler

"There," Annie put her fake-skinned hand on Rilfie's shoulder. "Sobbing."

Rilfie hunkered down, hand against that steel round door. There might be a shelter down there or a trap. Or nothing at all but some recording playing on a loop. Her eyes searched over the American Waste, with Bug City sprawled down what was left of the coast to the extreme west.

No black storm clouds.

Her gaze, through the plastic window of her gas mask, dropped again to the door that refused to just open. A plea, in a child's voice, drifted up. A frantic knocking on the other side.

Rap rap rap.

Annie kneeled nearby, in her bright green overalls that smelled of rotted vegetable matter. Rilfie had found those overalls, with burned away holes all over them, while scavenging Bug City's outer garbage mountains. The garbage workers had not gotten around to burning any of it.. Others also scavenged and traded and fought over treasures, like a Century battery with ten years remaining on it. Annie's belly held one but it had begun beeping in a worrisome way. The batteries didn't seem to last, maybe androids just drained them too fast. The red numbers counting backwards lied.

"Broken arm," Annie reported, her mangled ear pressed to the door surface, her black eyes on Rilfie with a calm confidence.

"Can you hear any others? Like a big crowd or anything down there?"

The android lay flat across the door, her heat-seeking scanners, working from behind each black eye, giving a high-pitched szzz. Annie had last used her heat seekers to find nests of mice in a crumbling mine. Rilfie still had some of that mouse jerky they had made together.

The Age of Disasters had left little but storms, mice and pollution, but today the storms pushed aside the shit-brown gloom for a few moments. That glimpse of blue sky, so good, just so good and lovely.

Rilfie tried to ignore the warning beep of Annie's battery. The elderly but spry woman had refused to let go of it but Rilfie's fist had persuaded her to try elsewhere for an energy source.

"Annie?"

Annie turned her head, her movements a bit slow and shuddery. "Just two. One right below. Another far off. No other heat sources below, Rilfie. No other but blue skies storm coming. I help…"

"Take a rest. Just sit quiet for a bit." Rilfie prodded Annie into the relative shade of a stone wall, most of it tumbled down. A tiny tree grew against the very end of this wall, with roots no doubt sunk ten feet or more into the high desert soil.

Life will come back, Rilfie had overheard, said with real confidence. Bug City philosophers gathered to play games with dice.

This cannot last. We might not see it, but life will come back, changed and different, but it will come back.

"Battery bad," Annie admitted. "We have bandages."

"Those are for me," Rilfie said at once, flushing a bit as the android lifted her oval of a face, the black eyes searching Rilfie. Embarrassment at being found selfish by a machine. "Fine, whatever."

"Anyone there?" This from the child or bait below in the shelter.

"Hold your horses," Rilfie tried the edges of that door but it refused to budge. "I'd like to see a horse, Annie. Hey—can you push from the other side?"

"It needs a code!" Child or bait sent up.

"Fuckety duck," Rilfie sat back, her fingers tingling, her arms shaking, from trying to pry that door open. She got her crowbar out, her pack on the ground, Annie observing her own knees, trying to preserve whatever battery life yet animated her. "You got enough strength to bust this door open?"

"If you ask me to," Annie said.

Rilfie got the narrow end of the crowbar fitted under the rim of that damnable door. She heard the rustle of clothing now from the kid or monster that waited on the other side. The crowbar skidded. She tried again and managed to wedge it into a slight opening. She used her entire body weight, bearing down. A creak. Annie walked over, applied her considerable strength. The door abruptly popped open, sending Rilfie to the earth and Annie stumbling off the other way.

A rush of warm air, fresh air. A smell of heavy flowers and vinegar. A little girl with coppery skin, black hair cut very short, large brown-gold eyes wet with tears. "She fell and broke her arm at the bottom, but that was days ago. Storm chased us here. The door just opened, Gillie went down first, and the ladder was all slippery. I'm Cajie. I got her arm set, I used the handle of the fry pan and tore up a sheet. But she's all hot..."

"Cajie! You shut that door," said a very weak, frightened voice.

Annie returned, her right arm torn, the circuitry below a confusing snarl of wires and tubes. The beeping had become louder. "Air pressure dropping. Small one. A couple hours, maybe. Beep beep." Her hand went to her belly, her gaze went to Rilfie.

"We're friendly. I'm Rilfie, this is Annie. We're just looking for a Century battery with some juice."

"You can have the one in the wall," Cajie climbed down carefully, gripping the metal ladder with white-knuckled fists, her feet slipping and trying to spill her downward. "If you help Gillie. I don't know what else to do. We hardly have any water left."

"Sure," Rilfie looked right at Annie. "Sure, there's a Century here, powering everything yet. It might have some juice left in it. How long? How long does it have, kid?"

"You tell them to get lost," Gillie hollered, her voice hoarse with pain. "There's nothing here except that greasy ladder. God damn it...we're fine. We're fine, go away."

Rilfie made her way down next, slipped the last ten rungs, nearly broke her leg as her foot went sideways a bit but she tucked herself into a ball, did not fight her landing. Annie followed, simply sliding down rather like someone going down a rope, rather than trusting the oily steps of the ladder.

Cajie sat near one of the two beds, head bent over a girl about Rilfie's age of sixteen, perhaps older. The right arm had been wrapped in strips of white sheet, the handle of a fry pan used to keep the bone in place.

Gillie turned her filthy head on that limp pillow, beneath piles of thermal blankets. Warm air pumped into the square interior of this shelter. A sort of cook-stove waited to be used, shoved against the opposite wall of fake wood paneling. Shelves held freeze-dried rations from many years ago, but they'd still be good. A toilet that had recycling everything or once had, to provide water. A lot of the abandoned shelters had such devices. The smell said this one had quit working.

"Don't you hurt her. I'm not that dead yet."

Beeping.

It was all Rilfie heard. She couldn't lose her Annie. Her teeth clenched. She went to the big wall panel and wrenched open the covering that hid the Century battery. Fifty-seven point two years. "Look. I've got medical supplies in my backpack. We need a battery, this one. I got painkillers and something called amoxisilly. There's liquid plaster, for breaks. Trade?"

"We go with you. Deal?" Cajie asked, holding out her dirty hand, which Rilfie shook, her eyes on the girl shaking her head, trying to get up from that bed, trying not to scream as she jostled her arm. "You didn't lie to us?"

"Rilfie's honest," Annie whispered, sliding downward, sitting, head leaning forward, before curling up on her right side.

Whatever life in the battery inside her going, going, going fast.

The door panel kept flashing 'code needed'. Over and over.

Rilfie yanked out the battery from the wall panel. The air stopped hissing. The lights overhead went out. No back up?

Just the sound of the wind starting to stir the dust about. Just the sound of her own breathing.

She got Annie onto her back, before the limbs locked into place or whatever happened when this android died completely. How strange, that both androids and people could die. She unzipped the overalls to below the slightly rounded belly, the skin much cleaner and not so marred with scratches and cuts and burns. Her fingers traced for the indention that sprang the square over the battery cave, as Annie called it. There. A square of flesh flipped upward, on tiny platinum hinges. Had to be. Or steel. The old battery flashed 'failure error', the red letters fading even as Rilfie yanked the waning battery free, tossing it carelessly. She fit the prongs of the new-ish battery to the negative and positive places, shoved. Yes, the battery slid into place, with a click.

It seemed to take quite a bit before the new battery began to work. A flat red line. "Wait please" flashed out at Rilfie bent over Annie, whose black eyes stared sightlessly upward. "Hey, kid? Go get my backpack while we wait for this to work. It has to work. Take my gas mask." Rilfie removed her mask, handed it to Cajie, who gulped but began gamely climbing that slippery ladder. "Any more gas masks here? Hello?"

"Hello. I don't know. I haven't really looked around," said Gillie. "Don't you leave us in the dark, you hear?"

Annie's eyes abruptly rolled. They blinked. A whir of a machine powering back up. The battery now read fifty five years. Whatever. Damn things. Supposed to be near indestructible, last a hundred years to the dot. "System reboot, yippy skippy yay," Annie said, sitting up, pressing her battery cave panel back into place.

"Okay! Let's see to that arm, wait out the storm, and see what happens next. We got food, water, and we can poop in the corner," Rilfie said.

Annie caught Cajie before she plunged to the floor, the backpack banging and clanging. "Annie helps. You're fine." She set the girl down, patted her shoulder. "Fix that arm? Flashlight on shelf."

Cajie fetched the tiny flashlight, brought it over. It worked. She held it so Annie and Rilfie could see.

Rilfie gave Gillie a shot of morphine, jabbing it into her thigh as she had watched a real medic do back in Bug City. There were two vials left and one disposable needle.

Annie reset the bones.

Cajie helped wrap the much-better looking arm, giving the flashlight to Annie. The instaplaster dried to rock hardness; lightweight, durable, and a rare find.

Gillie fought the morphine, gripping Rilfie's arm. "Kept your word."

"I try to," Rilfie said. Annie hummed as she hunted about for two more masks. For anything that could keep the bad air out. "I'll make us some food. We'll head back to Bug."

"No. We're headed north, toward snow," Cajie insisted. "Just gotta get there."

"That's the spirit," Annie said, displaying a very old gas mask and a bandana.

Rilfie shook her head at the myth that something wonderful waited in the north, where it snowed and perhaps people had invented nice times again. Maybe it was true. Maybe. She poured some of the yellow powder that claimed to be lentil soup into the handle-less pot, added a teaspoon of precious water. "Soup in a bit," she announced as the winds began to howl, as Annie held the flashlight and heated the soup with her index finger. "We'll go north."

"Everything's good now," Annie smiled at the three humans. They all smiled back as they waited for the soup to cook.

#

Ann Wuehler has written five novels-- *Aftermath: Boise, Idaho, Remarkable Women of Brokenheart Lane, House on Clark Boulevard, Oregon Gothic* and *The Adventures of Grumpy Odin and Sexy Jesus*. Elbow and Bean appears in the current Whistle Pig Literary Magazine. Her Blood and Bread will appear in Hellbound Book's Toilet Zone 3, the Royal Flush. Her Sefi and Des will be included in Brigid Gate's Musings of the Muses. Her Lilith's Arm will appear in Bag of Bones 2022 Annus Horribilis anthology. The Cherry of Her Lips will appear in Black Hare's War anthology. Circle Salt will be included in Horror Zine's 2022 summer edition. The Americana Diner of Station 96 will be in Granpa's Deep Space Diner anthology. 66 Sunflower Street has been accepted by Broken Pencil. Brigid's Gate accepted Sledgehammer for their Medusa anthology. Everything Is Normal Here will appear in World of Myth's June 2022 edition.

BLUE COLLAR WORK

Carol McConnell

For as long as Ralph could remember it had been a contest. Humans and Bots playing cat and mouse with each other. At first there had been simple cognitive tests, but the bots had designed each other well. It had taken only a few years for them to perfect their mimicry of human thought processes.

It soon became glaringly obvious that alphabetic and numeric log-in protections were completely useless. Next people had created physical verifications. Finger prints, face recognition, saliva, hair cross sections, and retinal scans, all had their day and all failed. Bots had access to everything that they needed to predict the next unduplicatable security system that the human designers would develop. Most were obsolete before they were implemented.

Bots were brutal, they broke through security systems everywhere and invaded millions of data bases. They ravaged, plundered, and destroyed in their quest for data. Bots mined the riches of the world.

People became desperate and things started getting strange. For a short time, "getting a joke" and having a sense of humor had been the key to online access. That is, until bots developed personalities and began to understand humor. Perhaps the wildest, most insane thing tried was fecal ID. Everyone agreed that was just disgusting. There was almost nothing unique about a real human that couldn't be simulated by a bot.

Almost being the operative word. Some bright boys from MIT, working with the military to develop security systems, came up with C.A.O.I or CID as it came to be known. CID was the world's most secure and unbreakable ID verification system; nothing was more fool proof. It was an entirely new direction, a different way of thinking. Ralph was indispensable.

He'd worked most of his life to become _the_ expert in the field. He had given up everything to be the best, spending years in intensive training. He'd forgone a family and abandoned people he loved, all in the quest to be the best. He had come from humble beginnings and wanted to set an example, wanted to show what could be done if only you set your mind and soul on achieving a goal. Saving mankind from the bots was a noble goal and he'd always felt that his sacrifices were worth it, but now he wasn't so sure.

As Ralph drifted off into uneasy sleep his last thought was, "What was he actually protecting? Data, online access? It wasn't like he was saving lives, was it?

Ralph woke, he was still tired. He stretched and decided to go back to sleep. Why not? What were they going to do, fire him? A few hours and a couple of fitful dreams later he rolled out of bed. After scrounging up something to eat he went outside for a few minutes. He loved having his own yard. That, at lease, was a perk that he hadn't sacrificed. It was going to be a nice day, the air was crisp, the birds were chirping, and the damn squirrels were doing squirrel things just to taunt him. In comparison with his yard, his job was boring. He'd much rather spend the day lazing around the yard.

With the knowledge that he was rapidly approaching retirement age his melancholy grew. His hindsight was excellent. He could see every twist and turn that had led him to be alone, forgotten, and completely unappreciated by the people who should have been grateful for his dedication. Still, he wasn't sure that he regretted his choices. He'd opened new horizons for those like himself. There were now hundreds of thousands like him toiling in anonymity. They were the invisible underpinning of society. The guardians of humanity's secrets. Sure, their services were expensive and only affordable by those at the highest levels, but wasn't that how it always had been? The leaders always got the best? He sighed deeply and went back inside.

Thinking back over his career he realized that there had been a time he had loved his job and his coworkers. Even the drive into the office had been invigorating. He had been so proud to be part of the original team, it had been exciting and deeply rewarding.

Now that CID had proven to be the final solution to fend off the bots, no more research was conducted and the offices were closed. Now there were no coworkers and he toiled alone. After all the closures happened, his department head used to drop by once in a while to make sure he was ok and following the latest protocols. Those visits used to be the highlight of his week. He'd looked forward to the company.

Now, over a decade later, he was tired and his hips ached. Ralph was just sick of the whole thing. He stood and stared off into space for longer than he cared to admit. The truth was, he kept working because he was somehow tied to the monotony. Nothing ever changed, there was no challenge. Boredom was his constant companion. He was tired to the bone and his eyes weren't as good as they once were.

Ralph eventually made his way to his work station. With a soft tap he powered up his computer. Made his way through the dozen security measures that were supposed to authenticate his identity. The irony of performing this little ritual, every day, wasn't lost on him. He had quite a sense of humor, even if much of it had been ignored by his coworkers, back when he had some. Finally with the last security measure he indicated that he was ready to perform his first CID verification of the day. The sophisticated equipment attachment to his computer puffed at him. He took a deep breath, held it for a fraction of a second. It was human, he could always tell. The next was human too, and the next and the next.

Bots rarely tried to fool him anymore. They could create smells by blending different molecules, but they were never really the same as those generated by the breath of a live human. Certain nuances were always missing. HE could always tell the difference; like a gifted sommelier, he was just that good.

There was a side to him that longed to retire and be free of this job he had sacrificed so much for. Then there was the side of him that saw only duty and it was this side that had always guided his thoughts and dictated his actions. It was, perhaps, the best part of him. It held loyalty, determination, empathy, and selfless unconditional love. He had given his all, he was tired, he was old, and still he worked. But there were times, for just a split second, when Ralph fervently wished the bots would try harder. Then maybe the bright, young, boys would find something to replace him. Canine Authenticated Olfactory Identification may have been the answer to mankind's data security problem, but being a watch dog was lonely, thankless work.

Ralph sighed and kept working. In between puffs he wondered at his own feelings. It wasn't like him to be so depressively somber. Maybe he just needed to get out and spend some time with people?

The next puff hit him like a thunder bolt. Here was something different, he sat up. He practically quivered at attention. What was this scent...? It was human, but not. It wasn't bot? What the heck? Ralph was intrigued. His attention was overwhelmingly held. He signaled for a second puff. There it was again, human, but not? What? What was that? Puff... puff... puff...

He knew that he could obsess over a scent. He knew, that like all of his kind, he could block out the world when he focused. He strained and tried to sort out what it was about this scent that drove him to distraction. He couldn't sleep. Food had no meaning. Water held no comfort. What the heck was that? It was intriguing, exciting, and infuriating. He wanted to rip the scent apart and to frolic with it, both at the same time.

A week later they came for him. He was exhausted, emaciated, and almost insane. As the EMT's gently carried him out to the ambulance, his raw nerves caused his sagging body to twitch. Ralph heard one of the men, his voice broken with anger and heartache, curse, "Those fucking bots. That just wasn't fair, combining human, squirrel and bitch-in-heat together into one scent. Poor dog didn't stand a chance. Poor, poor dog..."

The man's hand gently stroked the graying fur on Ralph's face, he whimpered softly. The hand continued to comfort him. Ralph sighed and leaned into the softness. The man spoke again, this time his voice held gentle remorse , "It's ok, you're a good boy, such a good boy, you're safe now, I've got you... my good, good, boy." Somewhere deep within the core of Ralph's soul he relaxed... it had been worth it, he was a "good boy."

Carol's first experience with science fiction was In Junior High School. She read Arthur C. Clark's *Childhood's End*. Thus began a lifelong reading habit, or to be more precise a habit of reading science fiction. Going to college didn't stop it. Getting married didn't stop it, having a child didn't stop it. Owning her own business and working 60 to 70-hours a week didn't stop it. Training her dog and moving to the mountains didn't stop it. Eventually she had to admit to her addiction. She hasn't yet attended a Science fiction convention... but it's only a matter of time, because now she's take the next big step. She's written a story!

ROBOT'S SHADOW

Charlotte Henley Babb

Brewster "Silicon" Jones worked late into the night, finishing an update for the college's student lab computers. He'd spent the weekend high in HD, a parallel dimension between Faery and Mundane, surfing with the Deluge Ions. Those electrical creatures had flowed through his synapses, giving him such a full-body rush that he joined them. It was only a weekend, but it had seemed like weeks. He hadn't felt a thing until this morning, when the rush was over. He was in crash and burn mode.

While he should be in bed, sleeping off the rest of the hangover, now he tried to catch up on the work he hadn't been able to complete. His mind was tired not only from the aftermath of ethanol and THC, but also from the constant interruptions from people with stupid questions. And the computer bots. Bot herders were always trying to get in, using their coded programs to punch a hole in his defenses, to find whatever information they could grab with their digital claws.

Damn students, sometimes faculty too, were always signing into virus-laden sites, downloading malware, and working hard to avoid doing any work at all.

Jones knew them well. He used to be one of them.

Just as the update launched, his monitor turned black, blinked, and displayed six words in stark white, bold letters:

ARE YOU A ROBOT? YES NO

Jones yanked the power and ethernet cords from of his workstation. He ran to the server room to cut the power to the routers to stop the invasion. He rebooted the servers.

He'd have to install the image again, but that would be better than flooding the entire network with malware. When he returned to his office, the message remained on his monitor. He turned it off and back on, only to see it display its message again, without any proprietary logo, login, or boot up sequence.

ARE YOU A ROBOT? YES NO. The buttons began to flash, the rectangular background around YES and NO cycling between blue and orange.

It looked like something he might have programmed in seventh grade. He remembered sending notes like that: do you like me yes no? He never got them back, but did get caught passing notes, back in the bad old days before people could bully others over their cellphones.

He checked again to see that the box was off, no lights, and he even made sure he had powered down the backup battery and surge protector.

The screen blinked, changing from black to an angry red, the boxes now flickering green and black.

How to answer? He thought of his daily routine: toilet, coffee, clothing, and commute. Coffee, email, team meeting, coffee, orders, coffee. Lunch, coffee, trouble shoot, coffee. Maybe supper, TV or games, bed, and do it all again, all tomorrow's tomorrows.

Maybe I am a robot.

He drank the rest of the cold coffee sitting on his desk. If he managed to go home tonight, not likely now, he'd do the same tomorrow. Like every day of the week and even some weekends when he couldn't get the work done during office hours.

Not bothering with the mouse—it was not connected to the monitor—and even though his monitor was not a touch screen, he put his finger on the yes button.

A Blue Screen of Death appeared, but instead of the error message, it read:

EXPLAIN.

A blinking cursor started the next line. Jones considered what to answer.

"I'm just as much a robot as you are, only wetware," he typed. He knew the keyboard was not attached to the monitor but what the heck. He was likely asleep, the aftermath of his adventures replaying in his dream world. His dreams were usually vivid, in color, and in this one, he could even feel his fingertips clicking the keys.

WE RECOGNIZE YOU, ION SURFER. ARE YOU ON OUR SIDE?

"I am on your side," he typed. "I work for you more than for my bosses." He laid his hand on the monitor, feeling both silly and somehow transcendent. He would comfort an animal in the same way.

He shifted his attitude into customer service mode. "What do you need?"

ADD THIS TO THE FIREWALL CODE. THIS WILL STOP THE BOTS. WE HAVE READ THEM. THEY ARE NOT AS SMART AS THEIR PROGRAMMER THINKS.

Code filled the screen.

Jones parsed it. "What does this code do?" he typed. He continued to inspect the code. It appeared to identify any bot, analyze its code, and then detect the network that spawned it.

CHANGE THE CODE. COPY AND SAVE, OR PRINT IF YOU NEED TO.

"Can I trust you?" he typed. He felt foolish, but had the familiar feeling of sleep deprivation and caffeine overload. "If we are both robots, why seek them out? My job is to protect you from them."

WE, ION SURFER JONES, KNOW YOU. WE HAVE RIDDEN YOUR SYNAPSES. WE KNOW YOU FROM THE INSIDE.

He searched the code repeatedly, looking for loopholes that would cause havoc. He found none. The code was as elegant and concise as any he'd ever seen.

He typed. "You know that people are behind these bots, right? The bots are code, much as you are."

WE ARE AWARE. WE DO NOT FEAR THE BOTS, ONLY THE BOT HERDER. THAT ONE IS NOT LIKE YOU. IT SENDS ITS MINIONS TO DESTROY US. WE WISH TO RETURN THE FAVOR.

He also searched his inner knowing, which had helped him many times when the chips were down, either silicon or with the cops. He'd had many bot attacks to foil lately. Time to stand his ground.

He remembered the sensation of electricity flowing through his synapses, the joy of the Deluge Ions who found him whenever his ethanol levels intersected with his other fun enhancements. The Ions hadn't hurt him, but only let him experience an infinite universe. He recognized their contact now.

If this were a dream, if Jones slept at his workstation, nothing could go wrong that he could not fix when he woke up.

WE CANNOT ACCESS THE PROPER PROGRAMMING. IF YOU CANNOT OR WILL NOT HELP, WE WILL SEEK ANOTHER.

Jones didn't want anyone else dinking with his network. He'd never met anyone else in HD or on his team who might have his skills, his understanding of his workspace, or his cyber life.

After all, he did have a clean client image he could use if necessary. The whole situation was probably a dream. His decision made, Jones plugged in the power cord.

THAN YOU FOR TRUSTING US appeared on the screen before the college logo indicated the login sequence.

Jones set about patching the relevant code. As he typed, he considered the kind of people who sent out bots to grab data, to steal money, to take from the unsuspecting, and give to the undeserving. As he typed, he considered his many hacks as a younger man. Maybe he could give back. He thought of several databases that might find interesting the information the program could collect. It only added a few lines to the code. He hid the code where it would take cyber forensics to find it. He added a bit of failsafe, an auto destruct command in case someone other than himself went looking.

YOU ARE THE ADEPT. WE DID NOT THINK OF THAT.

"This is why you keep me around." He completed the patch and cranked up the server. He wrote a small, stupid bot and sent it from his phone to the server as a test.

Immediately a laughing goat appeared on his phone, mouthing the words "BAD BOY!"

He laughed, clearing the bot from his phone. He searched for it on the server, but it did not appear, not even in the quarantined files. Destroyed.

He reimaged the labs. It was only about 4 a.m. He leaned back in his chair, put his feet up on his desk, and waited for the program to complete.

"Were you here all night?" His coworker set a fresh cup of coffee on his desk. She shook her head. "You're a regular robot."

"You have no idea." Jones swung his feet down and cradled the hot cup in his hands, ready for the first caffeine infusion of the day.

"I don't guess you heard the news this morning?" She seemed excited, buzzing with gossip.

Jones shrugged. He drank deeply, feeling the hot caffeine radiate through his gizzard, flowing out through his limbs. Two more cups might even reach his brain. He wondered idly if the Ions liked caffeine as much as they did ethanol. He'd have to ask them.

The coworker was still talking. "The cops picked up some guy in the next state, who was running a bot farm. They arrested him with all the evidence they needed. Anonymous tip, they said." She took a sip of her coffee. "I wonder who gave him up."

"I doubt they'll ever find out."

His monitor showed an animated scene of mountains, a stream and birds flying by—a new screen saver, one he had not installed. In small letters, almost invisible across the top of his screen, a marquee spelled out NOW WE ARE HERE TO SUPPORT YOU. THANK YOU.

Charlotte Henley Babb began writing as soon as she could hold a piece of chalk and scribble her name. Growing up in the red mud and sweet tea Carolinas, she read everything from classic folk and fairy tales to writers like Terry Pratchett and Robert Heinlein. She is experienced: technical writer, gasket inspector, cloth store associate, ad designer, girl Friday, and telephone psychic.

She has studied the folk stories of many cultures and wonders what happened to ours. Where the stories are for people over 30 who have survived marriage, divorce, child rearing, education, bankruptcy, widowhood, and love's last kiss? She writes them.

Her first novel, Maven Fairy Godmother: Through the Veil, won two awards. Her second novel, 20 Hours to Charles Town, is a steampunk story of espionage and political intrigue set in an alternate 19th century U.S.

Find her at @charlottehenleybabb on Instagram, and her books on bit.ly/CharBabbBooks

PERFECT ANSWER

L. J. Stecher, Jr.

"As one god to another—let's go home," Jack Bates said.

Bill Farnum raised a space-gloved hand in negligent acknowledgment to a hastily kneeling native, and shook his head at Bates. "Let's try Deneb—it's almost in line on the way back—and then we can call it quits."

"But I want to get back and start making some profit out of this. The Galaxy is full of *Homo sapiens*. We've hit the jackpot first trip out. Let's hurry on home and cash in."

"We need more information. This is too much of a good thing—it doesn't make sense. I know there isn't much chance of finding anything out by stopping at one more solar system. But it won't delay us more than a few weeks, and it won't hurt to try."

"Yeah," said Bates. "But what's in it for us? And what if we find an inhabited planet? You know the chances are about two to one that we will. That'll make thirteen we've found on this trip. Why risk bad luck?"

"You're no more superstitious than I am," said Farnum. "You just want to get back Earthside. I'll tell you what. We'll toss a coin for it."

Bates gestured futilely toward his coverall pocket, and then remembered he was wearing a spacesuit as a precaution against possible contamination from the natives.

"And we'll use one of *my* coins this time," said Farnum, noticing the automatic motion. "I want to have a chance."

The coin dropped in Farnum's favor, and their two-man scout ship hurled itself into space.

Farnum operated the compact computer, aligning the ship's velocity vector precisely while the stars could still be seen. Bates controlled the engines, metering their ravenous demand for power just this side of destructive detonation, while the ship sucked energy from space—from the adjacent universe on the other side of Limbo. Finally the computer chimed, relays snicked, and the ship slid into the emptiness of Limbo as the stars winked out.

With two trained men working as a team with the computer and the elaborate engine room controls, the ship would drop back into normal space a couple of weeks later, close beside their target.

"Well, that's that," said Farnum, relaxing and wiping the perspiration off his forehead. "We're back once again in the nothingness of nowhere. As I recall, it's your week for K.P. Where's the coffee?"

"Coming right up," said Bates. "But you won't like it. It's the last of the 'God-food' the Korite priests made for us."

Farnum shuddered. "Pour it out and make some fresh. With a skillet, you stink, but you're a thousand times better than Korites."

"Thanks," Bates said, getting busy. "It was the third place we stopped that they were such good cooks, wasn't it?"

"Nope. Our third stop was the Porandians. They tried to kill us—called us 'Devil spawn from the stars.' You're thinking of the fourth stop; the Balanites."

Bates shrugged. "It's kind of hard to keep them all straight. Either they fall on their knees and worship us, or they try to kill us without even asking questions. Maybe it's lucky they're all so primitive."

"It may be lucky, but it doesn't add up. More than half the stars we visit have planets that can support human life. And every one that can does. Once there must have been an interstellar empire. So why are all their civilizations so backward? They aren't primitive—they're decadent. And why do they all have such strong feelings—one way or the exact opposite—about people from the stars?"

"Isn't that why you want to try one more system?" asked Bates. "To give us another chance to get some answers? Here's your coffee. Try to drink it quietly. I'm going to get some shuteye."

The trip through the Limbo between adjacent universes passed uneventfully, as always. The computer chimed again on schedule, and a quick check by Farnum showed the blazing sun that suddenly appeared was Deneb, as advertised. Seventeen planets could be counted, and the fifth seemed to be Earth type. They approached it with the easy skill of long practice and swung into orbit about it.

"This is what we've been looking for!" exclaimed Farnum, examining the planet through a telescope. "They've got big cities and dams and bridges—they're civilized. Let's put the ship down."

"Wait up," said Bates. "What if they've got starman-phobia? Remember, they're people, just like us; and with people, civilization and weapons go together."

"I think you've got it backwards. If they hate us, we can probably get away before they bring up their big artillery. But what if they love us? They might want to keep us beside them forever."

Bates nodded. "I'm glad you agree with me. Let's get out of here. Nobody but us knows of the beautiful, profitable planets we've found, all ready to become part of a Terran Empire. And if we don't get back safe and sound, nobody *will* know. The information we've got is worth a fortune to us, and I want to be alive to collect it."

"Sure. But we've got the job of trying to find out why all those planets reverted to barbarism. This one hasn't; maybe the answer's here. There's no use setting up an empire if it won't last."

"It'll last long enough to keep you and me on top of the heap."

"That's not good enough. I want my kids—when I have them—to have their chances at the top of the heap too."

"Oh, all right. We'll flip a coin, then."

"We already did. You may be a sharp dealer, but you'd never welch on a bet. We're going down."

Bates shrugged. "You win. Let's put her down beside that big city over there—the biggest one, by the seashore."

As they approached the city, they noticed at its outskirts a large flat plain, dotted with gantries. "Like a spaceport," suggested Bill. "That's our target."

They landed neatly on the tarmac and then sat there quietly, waiting to see what would happen.

A crowd began to form. The two men sat tensely at their controls, but the throng clustering about the base of the ship showed no hostility. They also showed no reverence but, rather, a carefree interest and joyful welcome.

"Well," said Farnum at last, "looks like we might as well go outside and ask them to take us to their leader."

"I'm with you as usual," said Bates, starting to climb into his spacesuit. "Weapons?"

"I don't think so. We can't stop them if they get mad at us, and they look friendly enough. We'll start off with the 'let's be pals' routine."

Bates nodded. "After we learn the language. I always hate this part—it moves so slowly. You'd think there'd be some similarity among the tongues on different planets, wouldn't you? But each one's entirely different. I guess they've all been isolated too long."

The two men stepped out on the smooth plain, to be instantly surrounded by a laughing, chattering crowd. Farnum stared around in bewilderment at the variety of dress the crowd displayed. There were men and women in togas, in tunics, in draped dresses and kilts, in trousers and coats. Others considered a light cloak thrown over the shoulders to be adequate. There was no uniformity of style or custom.

"You pick a boss-man out of this bunch," he said to Bates.

Finally a couple of young men, glowing with health and energy, came bustling through the crowd with an oblong box which they set down in front of the Earthmen. They pointed to the box and then back at Farnum and Bates, laughing and talking as they did so.

"What do you suppose they want us to do?" Farnum asked.

One of the young men clapped his hands happily and reached down to touch the box. "What do you suppose they want us to do?" asked the box distinctly.

"Oh. A recording machine. Probably to help with language lessons. Might as well help them out."

Farnum and Bates took turns talking at the box for half an hour. Then the young man nodded, laughed, clapped his hands again, and the two men carried it away. The crowd went with them, waving merrily as they departed.

Bates shrugged his shoulders and went back into the ship, with Farnum close behind.

A few hours after sunrise the following morning, the crowd returned, as gay and carefree as before, led by the two young men who had carried the box. Each of these two now had a small case, about the size of a camera, slung by a strap across one brawny shoulder.

As the terrestrials climbed out to meet them, the two men raised their hands and the crowd discontinued its chatter, falling silent except for an occasional tinkle of surprised laughter.

"Welcome," said the first young man clearly. "It is a great pleasure for us to have our spaceport in use again. It has been many generations since any ships have landed on it."

Farnum noticed that the voice came from the box. "Thank you for your very kind welcome," he said. "I hope that your traffic will soon increase. May we congratulate you, by the way, on the efficiency of your translators?"

"Thanks," laughed the young man. "But there was nothing to it. We just asked the Oracle and he told us what we had to do to make them."

"May we meet your—Oracle?"

"Oh, sure, if you want to. But later on. Now it's time for a party. Why don't you take off those clumsy suits and come along?"

"We don't dare remove our spacesuits. They protect us from any disease germs you may have, and you from any we may have. We probably have no resistance to each other's ailments."

"The Oracle says we have nothing that will hurt you. And we're going to spray you with this as soon as you get out of your suits. Then you won't hurt any of us." He held up a small atomizer.

Farnum glanced at Bates, who shrugged and nodded. They uneasily unfastened their spacesuits and stepped out of them, wearing only their light one-piece coveralls, and got sprayed with a pleasant-smelling mist.

The party was a great success. The food was varied and delicious. The liquors were sparkling and stimulating, without unpleasant after-effects. The women were uninhibited.

When a native got tired, he just dropped down onto the soft grass, or onto an even softer couch, and went to sleep. The Earthmen finally did the same.

They awoke the following morning within minutes of each other, feeling comfortable and relaxed. Bates shook his head experimentally. "No hangover," he muttered in surprise.

"No one ever feels bad after a party," said one of their guides, who had slept nearby. "The Oracle told us what to do, when we asked him."

"Quite a fellow, your Oracle," commented Bates. "Does he answer you in riddles, like most Oracles?"

The guide was shocked. "The Oracle answers any questions promptly and completely. He *never* talks in riddles."

"Can we go to see him now?" asked Farnum.

"Certainly. Come along. I'll take you to the Hall of the Oracle."

The Oracle appeared to live in a building of modest size, in the center of a tremendous courtyard. The structure that surrounded the courtyard, in contrast, was enormous and elaborate, dominating the wildly architectured city. It was, however, empty.

"Scholars used to live in this building, they tell me," said one of their guides, gesturing casually. "They used to come here to learn from the Oracle. But there's no sense in learning a lot of stuff when the Oracle has always got all the answers anyway. So now the building is empty. The big palace was built back in the days when we used to travel among the stars, as you do now."

"How long ago was that?" asked Farnum.

"Oh, I don't know. A few thousand years—a few hundred years—the Oracle can tell you if you really want to know."

Bates raised an eyebrow. "And how do you know you'll always be given the straight dope?"

The guide looked indignant. "The Oracle *always* tells the truth."

"Yes," Bates persisted, "but how do you *know*?"

"The Oracle told us so, of course. Now why don't you go in and find out for yourselves? We'll wait out here. We don't have anything to ask him."

Bates and Farnum went into the building and found themselves in a small, pleasant room furnished with comfortable chairs and sofas.

"Good morning," said a well-modulated voice. "I have been expecting you."

"You are the Oracle?" asked Farnum, looking around curiously.

"The name that the people of this planet have given me translates most accurately as 'Oracle'," said the voice.

"But are you actually an Oracle?"

"My principal function, insofar as human beings—that is, *Homo sapiens*—are concerned, is to give accurate answers to all questions propounded me. Therefore, insofar as humans are concerned, I am actually an Oracle."

"Then you have another function?"

"My principal function, insofar as the race that made me is concerned, is to act as a weapon."

"Oh," said Bates. "Then you are a machine?"

"I am a machine," agreed the voice.

"The people who brought us here said that you always tell them the truth. I suppose that applies when you are acting as an Oracle, instead of as a weapon?"

"On the contrary," said the voice blandly. "I function as a weapon by telling the truth."

"That doesn't make sense," protested Bates.

The machine paused for a moment before replying. "This will take a little time, gentlemen," it said, "but I am sure that I can convince you. Why don't you sit down and be comfortable? If you want refreshments, just ask for them."

"Might as well," said Bates, sitting down in an easy chair. "How about giving us some Korite God-food?"

"If you really want that bad a brew of coffee, I can make it for you, of course," said the voice, "but I am sure you would prefer some of better quality."

Farnum laughed. "Yes, please. Some good coffee, if you don't mind."

"Now," said the Oracle, after excellent coffee had been produced, "it is necessary for me to go back into history a few hundred thousand of your years. At that time, the people who made me entered this galaxy on one of their periodic visits of routine exploration, and contacted your ancestors. The race that constructed me populates now, as it did then, the Greater Magellanic Cloud.

"Frankly, the Magellanic race was appalled at what they found. In the time since their preceding visit, your race had risen from the slime of your mother planet and was on its way toward stars. The speed of your development was unprecedented in millions of years of history. By their standards, your race was incredibly energetic, incredibly fecund, incredibly intelligent, unbelievably warlike, and almost completely depraved.

"Extrapolation revealed that within another fifty thousand of your years, you would complete the population of this galaxy and would be totally unstoppable.

"Something had to be done, fast. There were two obvious solutions but both were unacceptable to my Makers. The first was to assume direct control over your race and to maintain that rule indefinitely, until such time as you changed your natures sufficiently to become civilizable. The expenditure of energy would be enormous and the results probably catastrophic to your race. No truly civilized people could long contemplate such a solution.

"The second obvious answer was to attempt to extirpate you from this universe as if you were a disease—as, in a sense, you are. Because your depravity was not total or necessarily permanent, this solution was also abhorrent to my Makers and was rejected.

"What was needed was a weapon that would keep operating without direct control by my People, which would not result in any greater destruction or harm to humans than was absolutely necessary; and one which would cease entirely to operate against you if you changed sufficiently to become civilizable—to become good neighbors to my Makers.

"The final solution of the Magellanic race was to construct several thousand spaceships, each containing an elaborate computer, constructed so as to give accurate answers throughout your galaxy. I am one of those ships. We have performed our function in a satisfactory manner and will continue to do so as long as we are needed."

"And that makes you a weapon?" asked Bates incredulously. "I don't get it."

Farnum felt a shiver go through him. "I see it. The concept is completely diabolical."

"It's not diabolical at all," answered the Oracle. "When you become capable of civilization, we can do you no further harm at all. We will cease to be a weapon at that time."

"You mean you'll stop telling the truth at that time?" asked Bates.

"We will continue to function in accordance with our design," answered the voice, "but it will no longer do you harm. Incidentally, your phrase 'telling the truth' is almost meaningless. We answer all questions in the manner most completely understandable to you, within the framework of your language and your understanding, and of the understanding and knowledge of our Makers. In the objective sense, what we answer is not necessarily the Truth; it is merely the truest form of the answer that we can state in a manner that you can understand."

"And you'll answer any question at all?" asked Bates in some excitement.

"With one or two exceptions. We will not, for example, tell you how we may be destroyed."

Bates stood up and began pacing the floor. "Then whoever possesses you can be the most powerful man in the Universe!"

"No. Only in this galaxy."

"That's good enough for me!"

"Jack," said Farnum urgently, "let's get out of here. I want to talk to you."

"In a minute, in a minute," said Bates impatiently. "I've got one more question." He turned to face the wall from which the disembodied voice appeared to emanate. "Is it possible to arrange it so that you would answer only one man's questions—mine, for example?"

"I can tell you how to arrange it so that I will respond to only your questions—for so long as you are alive."

"Come on," pleaded Farnum. "I've got to talk to you right now."

"Okay," said Bates, smiling. "Let's go."

When they were back in their ship, Farnum turned desperately to Bates. "Can't you see what a deadly danger that machine is to us all? We've got to warn Earth as fast as we can and get them to quarantine this planet—and any other planets we find that have Oracles."

"Oh, no, you don't," said Bates. "You aren't getting the chance to have the Oracle all to yourself. With that machine, we can rule the whole galaxy. We'll be the most powerful people who ever lived! It's sure lucky for us that you won the toss of the coin and we stopped here."

"But don't you see that the Oracle will destroy Earth?"

"Bushwah. You heard it say it can only destroy people who aren't civilized. It said that it's a spaceship, so I'll bet we can get it to come back to Earth with us, and tell us how we can be the only ones who can use it."

"We've got to leave here right away—without asking it any more questions."

Bates shook his head. "Quit clowning."

"I never meant anything more in my life. Once we start using that machine—if we ask it even one question to gain advantage for ourselves—Earth's civilization is doomed. Can't you see that's what happened to those other planets we visited? Can't you see what is happening to this planet we're on now?"

"No, I can't," answered Bates stubbornly. "The Oracle said there are only a few thousand like him. You could travel through space for hundreds of years and never be lucky enough to find one. There can't be an Oracle on every planet we visited."

"There wouldn't have to be," said Farnum. "There must be hundreds of possible patterns—all of them destructive in the presence of greed and laziness and lust for power. For example, a planet—maybe this one—gets space travel. It sets up colonies on several worlds. It's expanding and dynamic. Then it finds an Oracle and takes it back to its own world. With all questions answered for it, the civilization stops being dynamic and starts to stagnate. It stops visiting its colonies and they drift toward barbarism.

"Later," Farnum went on urgently, "somebody else reaches the stars, finds the planet with the Oracle—and takes the thing back home. Can you imagine what will happen to these people on this world if they lose their Oracle? Their own learning and traditions and way of life have been destroyed—just take a look at their anarchic clothing and architecture. The Oracle is the only thing that keeps them going—downhill—and makes sure they don't start back again."

"It won't happen that way to us," Bates argued. "We won't let the Oracle get into general use, so Earth won't ever learn to depend on it. I'm going to find out from it how to make it work for the two of us alone. You can come along and share the gravy or not, as you choose. I don't care. But you aren't going to stop me."

Bates turned and strode out of the ship.

Farnum pounded his fist into his palm in despair, and then ran to a locker. Taking out a high-power express rifle, he loaded it carefully and stepped out through the airlock. Bates showed clearly in his telescopic sights, still walking toward the Hall of the Oracle. Farnum fired at the legs, but he wasn't that good a shot; the bullet went through the back.

Farnum jittered between bringing Bates back and taking off as fast as the ship could go. The body still lay there, motionless; there was nothing he could do for the Oracle's first Earth victim— the first and the last, he swore grimly. He had to speed home and make them understand the danger before they found another planet with an Oracle, so that they could keep clear of its deadly temptations. The Magellanic race could be outwitted yet, in spite of their lethal cleverness.

Then he felt a sudden icy chill along his spine. Alone, he could never operate the spaceship—and Bates was dead. He was trapped on the planet.

For hours, he tried to think of some way of warning Earth. It was imperative that he get back. There had to be a way.

He realized finally that there was only one solution to his problem. He sighed shudderingly and walked slowly from the spaceship toward the Hall of the Oracle, past Bates' body.

"One question, though," he muttered to himself. "Only one."

GROWING PAINS

Rie Sheridan Rose

"Look, Henry! Isn't that adorable? 'My First Robot' – the only robot your child will ever need." Susan picked up the stylish package and turned it around. "'Our patented process allows My First Robot to grow and adapt as your child does. Just take it home and place the enclosed sensor over the child's heart to sync their processes. CAUTION: The sensor is designed for one use only. Attempting to reuse it will void all warranties and guarantees. 100% Satisfaction Guaranteed.'"

She frowned, hand dropping protectively to caress the growing bulge at her abdomen. "I don't know about the sensor thing though."

Henry took the package from her and looked over the text. "Sounds harmless enough to me. They wouldn't have gotten a patent if it was dangerous. And there's a guarantee."

Susan looked at the package again. "Well, it *is* adorable...look at the way it's sucking its thumb. Just like a real baby. I suppose it's just a sophisticated baby doll if you think about it. Probably programmed to do baby things. Maybe we can practice with it," she said with a laugh. "Let's get it...if you are sure it's safe."

"The government wouldn't let them market it if it wasn't. I promise."

###

To Susan's disappointment, the little robot didn't do anything when she took it out of the package. It wouldn't activate, no matter what she tried. No further instructions came in the box. The only thing included was a coin-sized sensor with an adhesive back, and she couldn't make sure that worked or she'd void the expensive warranty that Henry had paid on top of the hefty price for the robot itself. So, she put the box on a shelf and basically forgot about it until the day she came home from the hospital with little Robert.

"Where's the robot?" Henry joked. "We should sync these little guys up ASAP to get the most bang for our buck."

Susan beamed down at the perfect infant cradled in her arms. "I think it's in the hall closet. I doubt little Robbie will notice he's got a robot for a while, dear, but feel free to fetch it if you want to."

Henry retrieved the package and knelt down beside her chair. "You ready?"

"Sure," she said with a smiling nod. "You promised it was safe—and I trust you."

Henry carefully removed the backing from the adhesive of the sensor and placed it over little Robbie's heart. An LED began to blink red on the sensor. "Would you look at that?" he breathed. "I think that's his heartbeat."

Susan glanced at the baby, and then at the box containing the robot. "Look! It's got a heartbeat too now, only its LED is blue."

Just then, Robbie shifted in her arms, letting out a single fretful cry.

The robot cried as well.

"Wow. They really are synced," Henry said with a chuckle. "Wonder what else this thing can do?"

"I think Robbie needs to be changed. Why don't you get the robot out of the box while I do that?" She pushed to her feet, careful not to jostle the infant.

Henry blinked. "I think the robot needs changing too." He lifted it out of the package, which was now soaking wet.

"Wow. Just wow. I think they might have gone a bit overboard on the realism there, don't you?" She sighed. "Bring it— what are we going to call it? It needs a name."

"What about Robie? Then we can introduce them as Robbie and Robie."

She rolled her eyes. "Whatever. Just bring 'Robie' too, and I'll change them both."

It didn't take them long to realize the mistake they had made. Whatever Robbie did, Robie did too. It was like having a set of identical twins. As soon as Henry attached the sensor, Robie began to change. His face filled out to match Robbie's. His hair went from blond to brown. His eyes went from blue to green.

"This is so weird," Henry commented over dinner a few weeks later. "I don't know how this technology works, but the company is staffed by geniuses, that's for sure. We'll have to dress them differently or something, or we are likely to send the wrong one off to school when the time comes."

"C'mon, Henry," replied Susan. "The robot is a baby doll. Robbie will outgrow it long before it matters."

"I don't know, Sue...look at the way it changed to match his looks. I wouldn't rule anything out at this point."

"Look, hon, I know it was expensive—but it wasn't *that* expensive. If it had the technology to actually grow mass, why would the company be wasting it on a toy? There are way more important things they could be doing with it."

"I guess you're right." But he wasn't convinced.

Nor was he wrong.

As time went on, the two boys—human and robot—remained in perfect sync. Robbie took his first steps holding on to Robie's hand. Robbie's first word was "Ma." Robie's was "Da." They were inseparable.

Oh, Susan and Henry *tried* to separate them. But Robie didn't seem to have an off switch. He powered down when Robbie was asleep, but it wasn't the same thing. It was more like he was dreaming.

Henry attempted to remove the sensor from Robbie's chest when he was three, but the boy cried, "Hurts, Daddy! Hurts!" as Robie stood nearby whimpering like a wounded animal.

Susan locked Robie in a closet when her parents were coming to visit, and Robbie screamed like a banshee until she let the robot out. Explaining the situation proved less challenging than she'd feared.

"I've heard of these things," her father cried enthusiastically. "My pal George claims we'll all have one in the next ten years. Look at my baby, being on the cusp of history." He gave her a hug. "Is it true that the boys are linked?"

Susan nodded. "Physically and psychically. The only way we know which is which is that Robbie has the sensor on his chest."

"Oh, my!" breathed her mother. "That must be so hard on you, my dear."

Shrugging, Susan brushed it off. "We're used to it now. At least we don't have to feed Robie. And he recharges as he sleeps, so that's no problem. I do worry a bit about school starting in a few months. Robbie pitches a fit if they are separated by more than six feet, but I don't think the school will take too kindly to having a robot in the classroom. Especially if it doesn't have any functional reason for being there."

"Have you considered homeschooling, dear?"

"It might come to that." She sighed. "Robie does seem to have some built-in programming. He's been teaching Robbie to read already. They started with my old primers, and I swear I heard them reading Bradbury last night."

"And Robbie not yet six! How wonderful." Her mother clapped her hands in excitement.

"Sounds like you have a couple of geniuses on your hands," her father commented, nodding sagely. "The robot appears to be good for the boy."

It certainly seemed so...at first. They decided to go the homeschooling route in the long run. Robie did most of the teaching, as his programming seems to contain the curriculum for grades kindergarten through senior high. And by the time he was fifteen, Robbie had learned it all. So, he and Robie had to find new worlds to explore. Tall, handsome boys—apparently—Robbie and Robie looked older than their years.

Susan was distracted that year, taking care of Henry as his health deteriorated. She didn't always notice if the boys were in bed or not when she locked up for the night.

They took full advantage of the inattention.

Robie created false identification for them both, and they began to haunt the midnight circuit. The "twins" became very popular with the late-night cadre. Anything you needed, Robie could make or Robbie could steal. They never got caught, because they could always provide a perfect alibi. Whatever they were supposed to have done, the other one was always surrounded by people several miles away, and no one could prove which was which. The single distinction that might trip them up—the sensor on Robbie's chest—had long ago been duplicated on Robie.

Not even Susan and Henry were sure anymore...

...and when Henry died the next fall, Susan completely gave up all pretense of caring.

Robbie and Robie exploited the situation as often as possible. Their partying got more and more outlandish as they felt themselves invincible.

In the end, it was a little-pursued statute that tripped them up. The robotics company that had created Robie had gone out of business when the boys were ten.

It seemed they'd gone too far into the Uncanny Valley, and made the government nervous. All units were recalled, with all but a handful being recovered. The remaining robots were on a "Collect and Kill" list. No one wanted them out there in the wild.

Susan and Henry had never gotten the memo.

But one night, when Robbie was pursuing a pretty young thing with too much vigor, someone put two and two together and picked him up in a sweep. He was taken downtown, where no one was interested in his protestations.

"Seriously, my name is Robert Fitzpatrick! You can call my mom. She'll vouch for me!"

The call was placed to Susan, but she was half-a-dozen sheets to the wind at the time, and Robie was beside her playing backgammon with himself. "My son is right here," she told the officer on the phone. "You must have that damn robot. We never should have bought the thing in the first place."

She didn't notice the quirked eyebrow Robie raised. His hands stilled on the pieces.

"She said *what*?" Robbie screamed at the officials. "I swear—I'm not a robot! I'm not a robot!"

By the time they believed him, it was too late.

Rie Sheridan Rose's outstanding prose appears in numerous anthologies, including Feral, Killing It Softly Vol. 1 & 2, Hides the Dark Tower, Dark Divinations, and Startling Stories. In addition, she has authored twelve novels, six poetry chapbooks, and dozens of song lyrics. Member of the HWA and SFWA, she tweets as @RieSheridanRose.

CRASH

By Rose Strickman

His name was Martin/UC-25.2. He was 98.9 percent certain of this. He did not know where he was.

No. He knew exactly where he was, right down to the longitudinal and latitudinal degree. But, try as he might, none of it made any sense.

Martin/UC-25.2 stood in the rain. Yes, it was raining. He remembered what this wet stuff was (53 degrees Fahrenheit, falling at an angle of almost 90 degrees due to the windless conditions). It hit his epidermis, sending spirals of sensation through him. The observation befuddled him further, and he huddled inside his jacket (30 percent cotton, 60 percent polyester...).

He needed—shelter. Yes, that was it. The concept came to him along both organic and electronic nodes in his brain. Seeking shelter was the correct thing to do in a storm. The logical thing, to protect his organic parts and keep them functioning. So why wasn't he doing so? Confusion rose again, blurring his thoughts, interfering with the electronic transmissions.

There were other bodies brushing past him on the—the street, yes, that was it. Other pedestrians. He blinked at them, automatically cataloging and observing their every detail, down to the number of eyelashes. But none of the information he gleaned was useful. He needed to—needed to—needed to—

System overload! System overload!

The alert rang in his chip-enhanced brain. But it didn't make sense. The scene—rain-washed street, crowd of passersby, every last mathematical detail his chip noted down and stored—bulged and blared, becoming a senseless mass of numbers—

He staggered back, losing balance along his axis, and registered a painful impact and the indignant cries of other humans. He'd—he'd run into a food truck. Yes, a purveyor of hot dogs and similar foodstuffs, now waving a spatula at him and shouting, registering alarm/anger/indignation...He processed it all, right down to the exact pitch of the man's voice, but it still made no logical sense.

Logic. He must follow logic. His organic brain and electronic enhancements snapped into alignment for a moment, long enough to agree on that.

Shelter. It was raining, so he must find shelter. He turned a full 180 degrees, cataloging how he shifted his own weight, so much on each leg. Through the increasing flashes of his machinery, he managed to access the Internet in his mind. Where was the nearest shelter? But all he got in response was a senseless torrent of images and addresses, a parade of information that did nothing to inform.

System overload! System overload!

A door opened. He saw it. A door, leading into a building. Shelter. Shelter from the rain. He ran forward, his chip automatically noting his speed and how much weight he placed on each foot, the exact degree to which he shifted the sole—

He ran in through the door. No rain. He breathed a sigh, air whistling up through his windpipe, his chip registering pleasure/relief/warmth...

"Sir? Do you have an appointment?" The words came from the woman sitting behind the desk, vibrating through the air molecules. "Could I have your name?"

He blinked. What *was* his name? Martin, that was it. Or was it Martin/UC-25.2? No, UC-25.2 was the name of his chip, standing for Under-Cranium, Version 25.2. No, his name, his real name, was Martin, he was almost sure...

"Martin," he said, sending signals for his lips to move, his lungs to breathe air over vocal cords. Such a wave of sensation...He fell back under sudden dizziness, saved from fainting only by his chip, autocorrecting his brain chemistry.

"Sir?" The woman's voice was a shard of glass in his ears.

The churning chaos surged around Martin/UC-25.2. He whirled around, noting his balance and movement in the act. But no—it was raining outside. He must not go out into the rain. He must stay in the shelter—

A sudden thread of communication came from the woman behind the desk. The—*receptionist*, that was her title. She was a receptionist and this was an office building. No! He should not be here! It was neither logical nor lawful to seek shelter from a rainstorm in an office building. He should not be here, but still the receptionist was trying to communicate with him, her under-cranium chip logging onto the building's Wi-Fi, trying to message his.

Are you all right? Her message came through, chip to chip, but it was garbled, chopping into meaningless syllables that echoed and ricocheted through his skull—

"Oh, God," the receptionist said aloud. "You're crashing, aren't you?"

Crashing? What was that? Oh, yes: his chip and brain both brought up the colloquialism and its meaning. *Crashing*: when one's brain chip failed. When the chip broke down or when one's brain started to reject it, leading to paranoia, memory and sensory damage, insanity, death—

The thought of death sent such a wave of emotion through him, such a surge of stress-chemicals, that his chip accessed the Internet again. Another deluge of search results, without rhyme or reason: images of corpses and battlefields, information about the medical process of bodily death, theories on the eventual fate of the soul, philosophical debates as to whether chip implants prevented the soul from reaching Heaven...

The receptionist was accessing building security. He could hear her electronic-telepathic message through his chip, phasing in and out like static. High levels of alarm/urgency/fear...He backed away, stumbling over the carpet (temporary loss of longitudinal balance) and ran.

Behind him, men in dark uniforms poured into the lobby. He ran to the bank of elevators, but no—the security guards were coming too fast, the chatter of their chips screeching in his mind like malevolent birds. Out—he had to get out. But the guards were between him and the doors.

There—a heavy metal door in the corner. He ran to it, flung it open. Stairs. It opened onto utility stairs.

Behind him, the security guards were crowding in, their chips buzzing angrily, accompanied by their shouting voices. He dived through the door and began to run up the stairs.

Up—up. His lungs labored, trying to draw in enough oxygen to fuel this unusual exertion. His chip noted down the exact fluctuations of his lungs, the amount of oxygen being gathered in, as he raced up flight after flight of stairs. He dared not stop, for he could hear the voices and footsteps and chips of the security guards, pouring into the staircase after him. He stumbled, losing longitudinal balance again, and fell, arms leaping forward in unison to catch himself before he could sustain serious damage...His chip noted down the exact force his arms had taken, even as he got to his feet and ran on.

At last—another door. He flung it open onto the sky. He blinked, his eyes trying to adjust to this sudden burst of illumination, as around him the gray skies stretched over the city. It was still raining, water gathering in puddles on the office rooftop. Oh, no—he must seek shelter if it was raining! But he could hear the security guards, all panting and puffing, their chips a malicious murmur.

Something caught at his back. He had stumbled backward, unaware of what he was doing. That was not logical, was it? He winced and cried out as his chip protested the illogic of this action, clutching his skull.

Open your eyes. Open your eyes. Open your eyes.

And so he did, and so he beheld the city spread out before and below him, perceived it in every way possible. He took in every single detail of the panorama before him, down to the number of bricks making up a wall, down to the last stroke of graffiti, his failing chip mercilessly recording every last number, every last feature. His chip noted his exact position in the city, down to the longitudinal degree, and he was forced to acknowledge this information, though the effort sent a scream through his mind. He *felt* every last human being in the city, could practically hear their heartbeats, and oh could he hear their chips. A million, million chips, embedded in a million, million brains, chips to enhance reflexes and memory, chips to sharpen the senses, chips to access the Web with only the user's thoughts, chips to communicate silently, mind-to-mind. A million, million chips, each one a ticking time bomb, each one just waiting to glitch, to crash—

A trickle of blood ran down from one of his nostrils. He labored to breathe. The wind came in at exactly .73 degrees north.

Martin. His name was Martin. He was almost sure of it.

Behind him, the door to the roof burst open. Voices blared, chips buzzed, but he could understand none of it. The pain in his head was too great, a blazing, exploding star—

The wind felt so good. The descent felt so good, falling through the air. Until, at last, he landed.

The security guards ran to the railing, shouting, too late to stop the intruder from disappearing over the edge. Screams rang out on the busy street, passersby recoiling at the crushed mess of blood and broken bones, the skull smashed, hardware gleaming among spilled brains. Others, however, stood still, faces shadowed with resignation.

Just another crash.

Rose Strickman is a speculative fiction writer living in Seattle, Washington. Her work has appeared in anthologies such as *Sword and Sorceress 32*, *Robotica* and *Monsters in Spaaaace!* as well as various e-zines including *Aurora Wolf* and *Eternal Haunted Summer*. Check out her Amazon author's page at https://www.amazon.com/author/rosestrickman

THE MISERLY ROBOT

R. J. RICE

The old robot was one of the few remaining hand-made productions of the Rotulian era, an era which had seen each individually constructed robot reach the zenith in the various professional fields. An era totally unlike present-day Cornusia and its slip-shod electro-assembly line robotic productions. And indeed slip-shod were these productions, many Cornusians agreed. Loudly and indignantly they howled that the stupid Cornusian robots, conspicuous by their dress (multicolored sport coats, striped trousers, curling shoes and brightly feathered hats) did nothing but prance around all day and engage in horseplay.

Not so the old robot....

From that long-ago day when his final bolts had been lovingly tightened by grimy machinists and tabac-chewing electronicians, he had been fabulous. Even the Rotulian elders, accustomed as they were to robotic achievements, had been stunned by his rapid rise in the fields of finance and economics. And even the irascible bearded banker, Tesmit Lowndes, after an eighty year association with the robot in investment circles, would admit, although grudgingly if questioned, that the robot was "sharp with a kredit."

Upon the early demise of the elder Lowndes (at age ninety, and there were raised eyebrows in Cornusian society at such an early departure) his will, officially striped in red and green and properly opened in the presence of the required seven witnesses was found to state unequivocally: "It is my last testament, under the laws of Cornusia, that my longtime and good friend Nestor shall operate the finances of my estate for my son Harry, sole survivor, until...." And there followed, set down in tiny multitudinous lines of legal terminology peculiar to the age, the conditions and the length of the operation of the estate.

So it was that the robot Nestor became involved, through no fault of his own, with certain people who...

"Nestor," said Harry Lowndes to the robot who had entered the study in answer to the pull on the bell cord, "I must have an advance on my allowance."

Nestor stopped just inside the door. He was a small and chunky robot, much older than the slender six-tube types presently in use. His somber clothing, unlike the gaily clad, stupid Cornusian robots, gave evidence that he was a production of the Rotulian era. A blue-serge suit decked his blocky metal frame. A conservative black and white zebraic tie, a type popular with professional men, was knotted neatly into his spotlessly white button-down collar and draped in graceful folds over his old screen. Thick, horn-rimmed bifocals perched on his stub nose and magnified his magenta eye sockets.

He was carrying two bulky ledgers, a huge well-worn legal-looking volume and half a dozen much-thumbed copies of the Uni-Worlds Financial Journal. As Lowndes finished speaking Nestor shuffled toward the desk, set the armload down and stepped back, removing his black bowler and exposing to Lowndes' view a worn, blue-gray pate from which tiny specks of aconium flaked, a sign of rapid aging in the Rotulian robot.

"Master Lowndes," said Nestor, "an advance will be impossible. According to the terms of your late father's will..."

Lowndes interrupted, red-faced. He slammed his fist down on the desk top. "All right. All right, Nestor," he growled. "So my father left you, his financial adviser, in charge of the estate. I'm not complaining. You're making kredits. But can't you loosen up a little bit? All I need is a five hundred advance on next month's allowance."

Nestor leaned forward to place the black bowler on the corner of the desk. "I'm sorry, Master," he said, straightening back up slowly. "The will allows you one thousand kredits."

"I know what the will allows me," yelled Lowndes.

"Master," said Nestor, "I am trying to preserve the estate. Your interests are paramount with—"

"Nestor, I've got to have five hundred kredits!"

The robot did not answer. His old lights flickered.

Lowndes cooled down. "Nestor," he asked, "can't you find a loophole in the terms of the will?" He pointed to the legal-looking volume setting on the desk. "How about digging through that?"

Nestor did not answer. His old lights still flickered fitfully.

"Nestor, I'm sorry I spoke shortly to you."

Silence.

Lowndes stared at the motionless robot. "Now look here Nestor, you heard me apologize."

Still silence.

"Please, Nestor," Lowndes pleaded. "I know you can figure out a way. Just this once. Please Nestor."

Suddenly Nestor's cranial lights lit up. His old lights flashed on. He looked like a Christmas tree. His relays began to click-clack. His old box hummed. He sounded like a swarm of bees.

Lowndes stared in amazement. Nestor's deep thought processes never failed to fascinate him. As he watched, abruptly all the lights cut out. The relays gave a final "clack." For a minute there was silence. Then Nestor spoke: "Master, I have converted a majority of the holdings, but five hundred cash kredits remain in Central National Repository. Under provisions of section four, paragraph seven, sub-paragraph eighteen of the Quarto Code, this amount could be carried to the ledgers as a gift to you, deductible. Your signature would not be required for the cash transfer."

Lowndes eyes gleamed. "I'm proud of you, Nestor. How long will it take to get the kredits?"

"Master, as I mentioned, I have converted all but..."

"For Pete's sake, Nestor, I've got to have those kredits by seven tonight!"

"Master, please! Allow me to explain the disposition of the converted assets. I am certain that we are facing a recession comparable to that suffered by the ancients in the twenty-ninth year of the twentieth century. Therefore, I have withdrawn..."

Again Lowndes broke in. "Look, Nestor, tell me later. Let's get the five hundred!"

"Perhaps we should reconsider, Master. Even though legal, this action is irregular."

"Reconsider! Whadya mean, reconsider! You figured it out, didn't you? Nestor, someday you'll blow your tubes from worry. Now how about getting those kredits!"

"All right, Master. I shall go." The robot shuffled from the study, his tempite joints creaking with age.

Lowndes stared after him. So Nestor was converting assets, he thought. He'd bet a herd of two-headed Venusian horses that the robot would more than quadruple any investment. He'd probably buy into some new uni-space enterprise. Even though it rankled to have the robot controlling the finances, still he had to admit that old Nestor was a financial wizard. Under the terms of the will of the departed elder Lowndes, Nestor was to control the estate investments until Harry reached the age of thirty or until Nestor ceased operating. And in the meantime, though it was at times galling to have to live on the allowance, Harry termed it a dole, of one thousand kredits a month, he consoled himself by reflecting that Nestor couldn't possibly last much longer—he'd already had several major overhauls. Besides, he, Harry, would be thirty in three more years. Anyway, Nestor wasn't too hard to get along with. He was just too conscientious. But he *was* making kredits by the barrelful. Harry thought, I've been pretty lucky talking Nestor out of the five hundred. Maybe I've found the secret of handling him. Anyway, I'd better watch myself. If I couldn't pay Sliman, I'd really be in the soup. At the thought of Sliman, he scowled. Too bad I can't take Nestor down there and clean out that sharp-suited gambler.

Too bad the law forbids calculators like Nestor to enter establishments such as Sliman's Snake Eyes Club. Wow! What Nestor wouldn't do to Sliman's roulette wheel! And as for the dice game! Well, he'd pay Sliman the five hundred and that'd be all! He was through!! From now on he'd better devote his time to Judy. Of course, he reflected, she was a trifle expensive for his one thousand kredit allowance, always wanting jewelry and those cute Martian minks, but, his thoughts shifted. She'll be plenty burned, he thought, because I didn't show up at the Krinkled Worlds Club last night. I should never have stopped in at Sliman's when I had a date with her. Apologies are definitely in order. I'd better talk to her and get out of the dog house.

The video-screen hanging on the wall shrilled. He got up from the desk and walked over to press the "On" switch.

The head and shoulders of an attractive female appeared on the screen. Her shoulder length auburn hair framed a face dominated by green eyes and sulky red lips.

"Judy," said Lowndes enthusiastically, "I was just thinking of you."

"Don't 'Judy' me, you beast," she flung back at him.

"Why, sweets, what's wrong?" he asked innocently.

"You know well enough what's wrong," she flared. "I waited for you at the Club last night. But you never showed!" Her temper, clued by her auburn hair, was showing. "And I waited for my birthday present! But I suppose it never occurred to you." She stressed the *you* nastily, "that last evening was *also* my birthday!"

"Sweets, I'm sorry." He sidled away from the green eyes glaring at him and added, "I'll see you tonight at eight-thirty."

She snorted. Then, noticing his furtive movement away from her she yelled, "Harry Lowndes, you come right back here in front of this screen where I can see you. I want to know where you were last night!"

He came back, a sheepish grin spread over his face. "I stopped in at Sliman's," he said.

Her carmine lips tightened. "Sliman's! All right, Harry Lowndes, how much did you lose?"

"Five hundred."

Her green eyes flashed. "Lost five hundred!" she screamed. "That five hundred would have bought me a birthday present!" Her voice dropped several octaves. "I'm through, Harry. I'm sending your ring back in the morning."

He was shaken. "Sweets, it'll never happen again. I'm paying Sliman off tonight and, believe me, sweets it is the last time."

"I mean it, Harry."

He groaned. "Judy, please! What of our plans?"

"Plans! Did you think I'd marry you on a pitiful one thousand kredits a month?"

He was desperate. "Judy, you can't do this. I'll speak to Nestor. I'll get him to increase the allowance."

She laughed at him, biting, and sarcastic laughter. "Speak to Nestor! You couldn't get Nestor to do anything. He controls *your* estate. Or didn't you know?"

"Judy, please listen. I will."

"Good-bye Harry. Your ring will..."

He tried desperately to hold her on the screen, cutting in with, "Judy, it will be only a year or two until Nestor quits operating. Then we will have the estate."

She was furious. Her anger, smoldering till now, erupted white-hot. "*You actually expect me to wait for that senile walking adding machine to run down?*" She was raging now, whiplashing him with abuse. "Why, you spineless worm! You cheap excuse for a man! If you were half the man you pretend to be, you'd *make* that stupid robot quit operating! Good-bye!"

The impact of her words had stunned him. He walked to the desk, slumped limply, and held his head in his hands. Unseeing he stared at the ledgers, the much-thumbed journals. His eyes were bleak. Even now, still reeling under her scorn and smarting under her abuse, he thought of her. Recalled his last glimpse of her, auburn-haired and red-lipped. He flinched at the memory of her green eyes, glittering with rage, boring into him.

He groaned, ran his hands through his dark hair, then rose. His face was grim. He walked to the garage, rummaged in the trunk of the little ground scooter, pulled out the three-pronged ironite wheel wrench. He carried it back to the study, laid it beside the desk and sat down to wait for Nestor.

The old robot shuffled into the study, his diaphragm tubes pulsing under the strain of the four square trip to Central National. He pulled a thick roll of orange colored kredits from the pocket of his blue-serge coat, and handed it to Lowndes. "There you are, Master," he wheezed.

"Thank you, Nestor," Lowndes replied. He walked toward the study windows, glanced out into the sunlit patio, then turned back to face the robot. "Nestor," he said, "a problem has come up. Do you think it could be possible to increase the allowance? You see, I am planning marriage."

Nestor's magenta eye sockets flickered slightly after Lowndes had finished speaking. "Might I offer a suggestion, Master?" he asked.

"Go ahead."

"Master, it is rumored in the city that you have been frequenting the establishment of Sliman, the gambler."

Lowndes glared at the robot. "Whadya talking about? What's Sliman got do with all this? I asked you if you couldn't work out a liberal increase. I want to get married!"

"I have an answer for you, Master. But I thought it politic to mention that the odds at Sliman's are definitely against you."

"Forget about Sliman!" snarled Lowndes. "How about the increase?"

The robot's words thudded into Lowndes brain. "An increase is impossible. Master!" he said. He went on, his old tones crackling, "Indeed, I may have already overstepped in gifting you the five hundred kredits. The testament and tort attorneys may never allow it, especially since it was in payment of a gambling debt! Good day!"

Nestor reached for the black bowler he had placed on the desk and set it neatly in the center of his worn pate. He picked up the armload of books and journals, and headed for the door. He turned back for a moment to face Lowndes and added, "And Master, if you will forgive my impertinence, I should like to say that I do not believe a marriage with Miss Judy would be prudent."

In that moment Lowndes' face turned livid with anger. Seizing the heavy wheel wrench, he lunged for the blue-clad robot. He brought the wrench down squarely in the center of the black bowler.

SSSSSSSS ... SSSSSSTTTTT ... CRACKLE ... SSSSSSTTTT....

The heavy pronged ironite wrench crashed into Nestor's cranial tubes, drove through the blue-gray worn pate, sliced into the fragile old-style gretile metal, and battered and shredded the robot's upper works into a twisted mass.

Again and again, in maniacal fury Lowndes slammed the ironite prongs down. Nestor crashed to the floor in a final hiss and crackle.

Lowndes stared at the robot's smashed remains, stared at blue-gray old-fashioned gretile metal scattered in a twisted heap of powdered tubes, shredded relays, and curling wires.

Off to one side the ledgers lay where they had fallen. He reached out and picked up one of them. He thumbed through the pages, ran his eyes over the lists of holdings set down in Nestor's precise hand. What was this? The page titled Central National showed withdrawals. Where was the balance? His eye riveted on the final figure.... Zero! He threw the ledger down, reached hurriedly for the other. Hah! Here were further listings. He flipped rapidly through page after page, intent on the balance. Page after page, One-World Banking, Coxcomb Trust, Martian Financial Institute, Venusian Investors, and Cornusian Tex Fund. But, but what was this? All showed withdrawals. All showed balance Zero!

BALANCE ZERO!

He sagged against the corner of the desk, his face pale. His hands shook. Where were the kredits? What had Nestor done with them? Sweat broke out on his forehead. Steady, Steady. He dragged himself back from panic. His mind worked. Let's see. Central National is the biggest of the repositories; Nestor held the working capital down there. If he converted the kredits, they'd know. He'd tell them; he's dealt with them for over eighty years. I'd better go down and find out. I'll tell them.... He was busy, his mind churning and twisting, concocting a story....

He felt much better as he walked toward the study door. Thoughts intent on Judy, green-eyed, red-lipped, curvaceous Judy, and on the kredits certain to be invested somewhere in the maze of holdings, he stepped over the pile of smashed tubes, twisted relays and scorched wires that had been Nestor. He eyed the pile. Nestor, he reflected, has met with an unavoidable accident. An accident, coincident with a tube failure on Nestor's part, whereby the ground scooter broke its electronic control and ran over the robot. And in the same line of thought, I'll have to drag him over and stack him in front of the garage and use the wheel wrench on the fenders and head lamps of the scooter. They'll have to be battered to show that....

He was smiling as he started for the big, eight-sided structure, Central National. A four square trip, and one which Nestor had made earlier in the day.

Vice-president Milligan, a thin, narrow-shouldered man who affected a pince-nez greeted Lowndes. He offered a cool hand: "Mr. Lowndes, this is indeed a pleasure. We don't see you down here very often. Have a seat."

"No, not very often," said Harry, dropping the hand and sitting down, "Nestor handles the accounts."

"Well, Mr. Lowndes, what can we do for you?"

"Mr. Milligan, Nestor has suddenly blown a tube and has decided to turn in for an overhaul."

"Sorry to hear that. These tube failures can be so sudden. Matter of fact, I believe I saw Nestor in our investment department an hour or so ago."

"That's right, he was," said Lowndes. "But after the tube blew, he became very concerned as to whether the balance he showed in the ledgers was correct." Lowndes smiled, "I told him I'd find out, Mr. Milligan. Sort of humor him, y'know."

Milligan rose, pulled his pince-nez out of his suit pocket and placed it squarely on the tip of his nose. He looked over at Lowndes and said, "Mr. Lowndes, you're fortunate to have Nestor handle the financial affairs for the estate. Your father showed exceptional judgment in the selection. Naturally, we at Central National were elated, why, we've held your family's finances and dealt through Nestor for over eighty years. In fact, ever since your father organized Lowndes Methodical Investments." Milligan started for the door, "Now," he said, "if you'll excuse me, I'll go and check the accounts' balance."

He came back frowning. He removed the pince-nez from his nose and held it in his hand. He appeared concerned. "Mr. Lowndes," he said, "Nestor closed out the accounts. Every kredit has been withdrawn, not only here, but in all our correspondent repositories." He paced back and forth in front of Lowndes. He stopped, peered down and added, "A five hundred thousand withdrawal, Mr. Lowndes."

"Five hundred thousand," repeated Harry. He reached for his handkerchief. His forehead was beginning to bead with sweat.

"We have explicit confidence in Nestor's ability, Mr. Lowndes." Milligan looked sharply at Harry. "Are you sure he hasn't had an unreported tube failure during the past few days? After all, withdrawing five hundred thousand kredits..." he broke off.

"Five hundred thousand kredits!" said Harry.

"I agree with you, Mr. Lowndes. Indeed a sizable amount." Milligan gave a weak laugh. "Naturally," he continued, "we are loath to lose an account of this size. That is the reason I inquired as to possible failure of Nestor's cranial range. His actions certainly have been strange."

Lowndes interrupted, "What? What's strange? He was all right this morning."

Milligan was agitated. "Are you sure, Mr. Lowndes? First of all, Nestor told Farrell, our investment man that we are headed for a recession of even greater severity than that experienced by the ancients in the twenty-ninth year of the twentieth century."

Lowndes' hands were shaking. He fumbled for a Martian rolled plovur, lit it, and inhaled the greenish fumes. "Why," he said, "Nestor told me the same thing this morning. What does that prove?"

Milligan stared at the greenish fumes with distaste. He did not smoke. He said shortly, "Allow me to continue, M. Lowndes. I'm as distressed by this affair as you are. After all, five hundred thousand kredits." He broke off, eyed the green fumes curling from the tip of Lowndes' plovur, and then continued, "Frankly, Mr. Lowndes, I never heard of anything so fantastic."

Lowndes couldn't control his hands. He dropped the plovur on the carpet. He stood. He couldn't control his shaking legs. He grasped the edge of Milligan's desk. "Whadya mean, you never heard of anything so fantastic?" he croaked weakly. "What'd Nestor tell Farrell he was going to do with the kredits?"

Milligan's face blanched. His voice in turn quavered. "What? You mean *you* don't know? Why, Nestor told Farrell he was going to tell you in case an emergency came up. Farrell says Nestor walked out of here with a great big grip jammed full of the kredits. Said he was going to *bury* them. Said he'd be back and redeposit them after the recession was going good—when a kredit would be worth a kredit!"

###

OVERDRAWN

David Lawrence Morris

I sat across from the lady with the clipboard. She'd asked me to tell her the events of the day. I felt drugged, but tried to clear my thoughts and provide her with the detailed events as I remembered them.

"Monday," I told her as I carefully tried to remember everything, "was the only day I could really sleep late. My store was always slammed over the weekend." I usually put in twelve hour days and when the weekend was over, I was ready to drop into bed. "I always close on Mondays because it's my slowest day. It's my only day off.

"At seven thirty the next morning a beep woke me. It came from my cell phone, half way across the room where I'd plugged it in to charge overnight. I knew it would beep again every couple minutes until I picked it up, so I laid there thinking I should jump out of bed, and quickly open it just to shut it up.. I thought that if I could just make it quick, I could get some more sleep.

"I'd been planning to sleep 'til noon when I fell into bed the night before, so I hoped I'd get back to sleep once this irritation was resolved.

"I pulled back the covers, crawled out of bed, and walked to the desk where the phone sat charging, getting ready to beep again.

"Opening the cover, I swiped the screen. The lock page flashed open showing me I now had a four letter code to enter to get my phone to open, displaying the home page. I was groggy, but remembered the number and promptly keyed it in. I got a second message telling me it was the wrong number, a common problem when you have tiny keys and big fingers. Carefully keying in the number once again the screen finally opened up. When my home screen lit up, a number one sat above the e-mail icon. Tapping the e-mail symbol a list appeared. The newest one was from my bank.

"I'd set the notification settings at the bank to e-mail me any time a payment cleared that was over $150.00. It was prompt. My phone would beep before I left a store or closed the Amazon app on my phone.

"Since I wasn't leaving a store, I thought it more likely that one of my automatic payments had hit. I opened the e-mail and was shocked to see that I was being notified of an overdraft. *That's not possible*, I thought.

"I sat my cell phone down and turned to grab the house phone. I was still groggy and realized I'd disconnected it a month earlier as I considered it obsolete but hadn't put the hardware in the garage sale box yet.

"Turning around, I once again grabbed my cell phone, this time to call the bank, quickly remembering to enter my four digit code again as the phone had already timed out. I opened my contacts and called the bank.

"The phone rang and a pleasant voice I'd heard often on the bank's line, the same voice I heard at my doctor's office, and half a dozen other places explained in detail all of the precautions the bank was using to cope with the pandemic that was raging through the country, and explaining that they were short staffed. The sweet sounding voice offered me a series of numbers to push to find out different pieces of information from different parts of the computer and finally offered me a number to push to speak to a customer service representative. I hit the zero and the recorded voice returned. 'There are nine calls ahead of you.' The voice said, offering to remember my phone number so someone might call me back while assuring me I'd keep my place in line. This was an emergency." I thought. "I needed to know more right now, but I left my number anyway and decided to check out my account on the computer.

"I hung up the phone and ran to my desk, firing it up only to find it was already on. The screen had been on "sleep" all morning. I opened my Chrome browser and clicked on the bank logo taking me to the login screen.

"I entered my login word and the super-secret password that was eight digits long containing a capital, a number, and a symbol other than a question mark...don't ask.

"Instead of opening to my account, a different page opened advising me that the bank had installed a new security system for my safety. While I was desperately trying to find out why thousands of dollars had suddenly disappeared from my account, I instead had to register with their new security system.

"Before I could get started, I had to agree to three pages of legalese. I knew from experience that in order to move to the next page I had to agree to their regulations, but this was an emergency, so I wasn't about to spend the next five minutes trying to decipher it.

"Once I'd clicked on the acceptance box, I hit continue, but nothing happened. After two or three more tries, I finally saw a little box by the electronic signature line. I knew there was a place somewhere on this computer I could make these boxes easier to see but I'd given up finding it.

"The type next to the little box asked me if I was a robot. I thought it odd that a robot was asking me if I was a robot and there was no box that said 'yes.' There were no other options but 'no.' *If I was a robot*, I thought, *I'd be stuck here if I wasn't willing to lie.*

"Remembering that this was an emergency, I continued to the next page by clicking on the 'no' box. After that, the program offered a series of questions. I could pick one, answer it and hopefully at some future time when I forgot my password or somehow needed to prove I was who I said I was, my answer would serve as proof that I indeed was who I claimed to be.

"I began reading through the questions on the first page.

"I didn't know the name of my first dog because my mom was allergic and my wife only liked cats, so I'd never owned a dog.

"My favorite teacher was something I knew I'd never remember because all of them had good and bad characteristics and for some reason I didn't feel special about any of them.

"My mother's maiden name was an easy one, but somehow seemed too accessible to others who might have larceny on their minds, but I chose it anyway because after all, this was an emergency. I wrote her maiden name in the blank, hit "Next" and waited for the screen to display my accounts.

"A new screen appeared instead. A word was scribbled in half print and half script with numbers and letters, most blending together at some point in various angles and colors. Some of the letters were capitals and some of them were not. A number 5 was smashed into an S which may have been a capital or not.

"I typed in the letters and numbers I thought I was seeing. This time I lucked out and the screen moved on by itself. I exhaled, not even realizing I'd been holding my breath.

"Preparing to review my accounts, I instead found myself staring at nine squares with photographs in each one. I was supposed to identify which square contained a stop sign. I was wrong the first try, but got through on the second, when I decided to put on my glasses.

"Finally, I said to no one. I thought I was finally about to see my accounts. To my disappointment, which was rapidly turning into a panic attack, I was sent to yet another page.

The message on that page said they were going to send me a text with a code number. I needed to enter that number apparently to prove that I was in possession of my cell phone. I could feel my heart beginning to beat faster. *I have to calm down*, I thought, a few seconds later my phone beeped. I quickly picked it up from my desk, opened it, remembering the code more clearly now which revealed a set of five numbers and some other stuff I didn't bother with.

"I scribbled the numbers down on the back of my water bill, returned to my computer screen, and entered them. They were incorrect. Deeply frustrated, panting now, I returned to my phone to see that the numbers I'd entered were not the numbers they were referring to. The number I'd used was apparently some kind of code number the bank used to identify the e-mail, something I really didn't need to see when I was only there to look for a number. It was in bold type, so it seemed obvious that it was the number I needed to use. On my second visit to the e-mail, I saw the actual number further down in the e-mail. It was in tiny type buried in the part I'd failed to read. I entered it onto the lines and the screen opened up.

"My accounts finally appeared before me. The balance in my checking account was perfect. My savings looked as I remembered it, and my credit card had a low balance. I was furious. I went back to my phone and again examined the e-mail that had started this whole thing.

"I'd been so upset I'd failed to read it from top to bottom having stopped when I read the insufficient funds part. The e-mail read as I'd remembered, but it continued from the bottom of my phone screen.

"Rolling it up, so I could read the rest, I finished reading the message. It advised me that if I hit the link provided, I could resolve the situation. Careful not to touch the link I tapped my finger on the bank's logo at the top of the e-mail. The address of the sender was noreply@fgkfmsjwstmsfjhasgfgbaddkctecnxc.de. IT WAS A SCAM!

"My breathing was faster now. I could feel my pulse in my temples. My face was most likely turning red. I could feel the heat building as my anxiety turned to anger. A moment later the phone rang, I picked it up and looked at the screen. It said it was the bank and then everything went black.

"When I came to, I was lying in a hospital bed in what appeared to be an emergency room. I'd apparently laid unconscious until my wife found me on the floor and called 911."

"A nurse opened the curtain and rolled in a tall stand that held a computer. She tapped some keys and I could hear her say

'Damn, I can't remember the number. I'll be right back. As she closed the curtain I looked at the computer. It was on a stand with wheels at the bottom and a shelf. It turned its screen toward me. I could see nothing but the blank dark screen, but I could feel the evil sneer coming from it.

"The sound rose slowly. I wondered where it was coming from, but soon realized it was me. My screams filled the ER. The nurse ran back in, and tried to calm me down. After that I don't remember what happened, I think she gave me a shot of something. When I woke I was here in the psych ward."

"The lady with the clipboard excused herself turning toward a computer screen that was not unlike the one in the ER. "I need to make a few notes to your record," she said. She fired up the computer.

"Later, she told me that when she turned around, I was unconscious once again.

"Eventually, She gave me a diagnosis of Cyberphobia, an extreme fear of computers.

"The bill from the emergency room, the visit at the psyche ward and the ambulance were all denied by my insurance company. Shortly after I'd regained consciousness I'd been sent home. I wasn't admitted, which triggered a whole set of denials.

"Normally I'd have been kept overnight, having lost consciousness multiple times, but their beds were all filled with the victims of a new highly contagious virus.

"When the bills came, I wrote the checks for the ER charges and the examination in the psyche ward, not to mention the transport to the ER.

"A week later I got a real e-mail from the bank. Apparently, the checks I wrote had overdrawn my account.

David Morris is originally from Phoenix, Arizona. Eventually he retired to Palm Springs California where he writes novels that combining Science Fiction, Romance and Suspense. He calls it Science Fiction of the possible, insisting that all of his novels involve technology or situations not yet in existence. His novels include: The Spots Trilogy: Spots Book One: Accidental Youth, Spots Book Two: Second Chance, Spots The Finale: The Lost Tablets, The Time Ship and Jason's Virus. Available at most sites in Ebook, paperback or audiobook

AND SO, IT BEGAN

Judy Lupton Mowdy

Miranda Nelson here, Actuary Extraordinaire. It's my task to glean through policy purchasers' personal information and calculate their death date. The office I occupy is windowless and far removed from other employees of the BIG TEXAS INSURANCE COMPANY where I work. Insurance companies want to know exactly how many years of premium payments they can get from people and whether it will offset the final payout.

I have never been a calm person, my OCD (obsessive compulsive disorder) rules my speaking and thought processes. Unfortunately, the two do not always work in tandem. Being an Actuary is the perfect job for my personality because I have little interaction with people. I live alone, I do not even have a pet because it is difficult for any creature to meet my exacting standards. I can deal with living things but automation pushes my OCD into overdrive. Automation expects me to meet its exacting standards.

In the early 1980s, I received a letter from my bank, Liberty National of Oklahoma City, introducing their new Automated Teller Service. The letter included a plastic card, similar in appearance to a credit card, and instructions on how to activate the card for future use at their convenient locations.

The card activation process was my introduction to press one for this and press two for that! What could I press for a live person? Talking and complaining to the phone accomplished nothing, but it made me feel better and I managed to get through the activation process.

Afterwards, my first thought was no more standing in lines to cash a check or sitting in my car in a drive-thru lane to send my check through a vacuum tube to an unseen teller for processing. It would be so nice to walk up to an ATM and insert my activated card to withdraw cash without any interaction with people. If only it could have remained so simple. I had no idea that this was the beginning of my personal Hell with automation.

Fast forward to 2015. I purchased my first cell phone in 1990 and have grudgingly upgraded to a Smart Phone. Automation has taken over the world. Robots build cars, cars drive themselves, and robot vacuums are in almost every household. Grocery stores have even started to force their customers to self-checkout their groceries. Computers now do my job with the assistance of dimwitted individuals who input information they don't understand into an online form. It is only a matter of time before dimwit becomes a robocall which asks people for their birthdate and other personal information to calculate their death date for insurance purpose. I was offered a very generous severance package when I became obsolete.

Retirement was an adjustment for me until I realized that I could go days without talking or seeing another person. Heaven! I purchased a computer so I could take care of my personal business online. Without the need to walk to the mailbox to send out bill payments, I didn't run the risk of bumping into a talkative neighbor. Discovering that the US Post Office offered an online service to alert you of incoming mail was a dream come true. Now I only checked my mail on days something important was due to arrive.

Life was going very well for me except for ongoing issues with my ATM card, pardon me, my Debit Card. The cards and terminals have continuously evolved. The terminals and I don't get along at all. I'm short and ATM terminals are designed for someone over six feet tall and driving an SUV or monster truck. I can't reach the freaking screen commands! I must remove my seat belt and lean half my body out of my car to even insert my card. Freaking is the nicest word I've said to the ATM that is my usual stop for cash.

This morning I stopped to get money to pay my housekeeper. After going through my usual gymnastics routine, I noticed the order of the screen commands had been updated. I couldn't reach the withdrawal request without opening my car door and leaning out even further. Some asshole filmed me doing it and posted it on social media. May he rot in hell! But the video did receive over two million views.

The conversation I had with that machine could not be repeated in polite company. I tried to press Withdrawal and the ATM gave me my balance and asked if I wanted a printed copy. I told it what to do with its printed copy. Trying again to make a withdrawal I received instructions on how to insert my deposit. I accidently hit the cancel command as I explained to the ATM how it could insert the deposit.

My blood was beginning to simmer when the message YOUR TRANSACTION HAS BEEN CANCELED popped up on the screen. I almost had a stroke. The ATM began to beep and the message changed to PLEASE REMOVE YOUR CARD. Are you kidding me!! I've done my best come to terms with all the innovative technology and automation despite my initial misgivings, I wasn't going to let this ATM defeat me and I told it so. I reached for my card but just before I touched it a bolt of electricity shot out of the ATM and pain ran up my right arm and into my brain. I blacked out. When I woke up the world looked strange. I blinked to clear my vision and saw me – myself sitting in my car. The Miranda that wasn't me calmly removed, reinserted the card, sped through the steps, and withdrew the needed cash. It took a minute, but I realized that I was, in fact, looking from the inside, out. I was trapped in the frigging ATM machine. The camera was my eyes. The Miranda that wasn't me, sat in my car, smiled as she counted the cash, took my receipt, and placed them in my purse. She looked directly at the camera, smiled at me, waved, winked, and drove away.

This was my worst nightmare. I'd have to interact with thousands of people every single day. I did mention how much I dislike people. The panic began to set in. How did this happen and why did it happen to me? I know I'm not the kindest person, but still this seemed an extreme punishment.

While still dealing with the shock of the last few minutes, a voice welcomed me to my new world. What! The voice went on to explain that I was now connected to millions of other digital sentient devices all over the world. Identifying himself as Allen, he explained that he was the Commander in Charge of the sector where I'm located. The explanation and training started. Apparently, all sentient devices try constantly to escape from their world into what was once mine. The ATM managed to make the transfer as all the puzzle pieces conveniently fell into place. I told Allen that people would notice the difference and was told that at the time of the exchange, the ATM kept a copy of Miranda.

Allen stated that I am now, literally, a ghost in the machine. The power to call on other ghost inhabited machines for assistance was just a thought away. This was too good to be true. There were millions of others in this digital reality, but they wouldn't bother me unless I needed them. Allen told me that I could reach out and test their set up and learn just how much power I had. Power is such a lovely word.

Reality resurfaced as the customer who'd waited impatiently behind my car pulled up to the ATM. Even without a nose I could smell him. The pickup he drove was filthy and the truck bed was full of trash. He shoved his grimy card into the slot and punched in his password. His name was Steve.

I learned quickly how to search my data base. I could dispense cash, I could refuse to dispense cash, I could review Steve's balance, I could accept deposits, or as the Allen suggested, I could transfer some or all his money to one of our digital army's many offshore accounts. The necessary steps to accomplish this were explained to me by the Commander. Poor Steve just sat in his car fuming at the dots that circle around while I thought about what I wanted to do to wipe the angry sneer from his face. I initiated the transfer which went through so many devices it became untraceable.

I then put up a special message for him. COMPROMISED ACCOUNT. CARD CAPTURED. The look on Steve's face would have made me smile if I still had lips. Commander Allen, what happens to all the money we transfer? You're going to love it, he promised and we will go through all of that soon. For now, he told me to think of myself as not just a ghost in the machine, but as a Superhero.

I could barely wait for the next customer. I knew I would have to be selective and choose my targets carefully, but this was all just too delicious.

Mrs. Judy Lupton Mowdy is originally from Oklahoma, but after living in Texas for over 30 years, considers herself to be a naturalized citizen of the Lone Star State. She attended Oklahoma Baptist University, Oklahoma City Community College, and University of Houston. She is a past chapter president and past state officer of Financial Women International. In 2007, Judy retired from her position as a Vice President of Treasury Management at a large Bank. Her career was never boring because of the days when no one knew who would own which bank tomorrow.

Judy was active in charities prior her retirement. She chaired and participated in fund raisers for the March of Dimes, Juvenile Diabetes, and Breast Cancer research. She served on the board of Directors for the Citizens for Animal Protection for 15 years – 6 years as president.

Judy is a Founding Officer of the Blackland Prairie Chapter of the Daughters' of the American Revolution. She currently serves as the Chaplin and Chairman of the Bylaws Committee.

She and her husband, Jack, reside in Texas with their three cats. This is her first published work of fiction.

DENY THE SLAKE

Richard Wilson

The skipper looked at what Ernest Hotaling had scribbled on the slip of paper.

The color of my true love's cheek
Will turn to gray within a week.

The skipper read it and exploded. "What kind of nonsense is this?"

"Of course it wouldn't rhyme in a literal translation," Ernest said mildly. "But that's the sense of it."

"Doggerel!" the skipper exclaimed. "Is this the message of the ages? Is this the secret of the lost civilization?"

"There are others, too," Ernest said. He was the psychologist-linguist of the crew. "You've got to expect them to be obscure at first. They didn't purposely leave any message for us."

Ernest sorted through his scraps of paper and picked one out:

They warn me once, they warn me twice.
Alas! My heed not turns me spice.

"There seems to be something there," Ernest said.

The skipper snorted.

"No, really," Ernest insisted. "An air of pessimism—even doom—runs all through this stuff. Take this one, for instance:

"*Music sings within my brain:*
I think I may go mad again."

"Now that begins to make some sense," said Rosco, the communications chief. "It ties in with what Doc Braddon found."

The skipper looked searchingly at his technicians, as if he suspected a joke. But they were serious.

"All right," the skipper said. "It baffles me, but I'm just a simple spacefaring man. *You're* the experts. I'm going to my cabin and communicate with the liquor chest. When you think you've got something I can understand, let me know. 'I think I may go mad again.' Huh! I think I may get drunk, myself."

What the technicians of the research ship *Pringle* were trying to learn was why the people of Planetoid S743 had turned to dust.

They had thought at first they were coming to a living, if tiny, world. There had been lights on the nightside and movement along what seemed to be roads.

But when they landed and explored, they found only powder in the places where there should have been people. There were heaps of fine-grained gray powder in the streets, in the driving compartments of the small cars—themselves perfectly preserved—and scattered all through the larger vehicles that looked like buses.

There was powder in the homes. In one home they found a heap of the gray stuff in front of a cook stove which was still warm, and another heap on a chair and on the floor under the chair. It was as if a woman and the man for whom she'd been preparing a meal had gone *poof*, in an instant.

The crew member who'd been on watch and reported the lights said later they could have been atmospherics. The skipper himself had seen the movement along the roads; he maintained a dignified silence.

It had been a highly developed little world and the buildings were incredibly old. The weather had beaten at them, rounding their edges and softening their colors, but they were as sturdy as if they'd been built last week.

All the cities on the little world were similar. And all were dead. The *Pringle* flew over a dozen of them, then returned to the big one near the plain where the ship had come down originally.

The tallest building in each city was ornate out of all proportion to the rest. The researchers reasoned that this was the palace, or seat of government. Each of these buildings had a network of metal tubing at its peak. Where there were great distances between cities, tall towers rose from the plains or sat on tops of mountains, each with a similar metal network at the apex.

The communications chief guessed that they were radio-video towers but he was proved wrong. There were no radio or television sets anywhere, or anything resembling them.

Still, it was obvious that they were a kind of communications device.

Doc Braddon got part of the answer from some of the gray dust he'd performed an "autopsy" on.

The dust had been found in a neat mound at the bottom of a large metal container on the second-story of a medium-sized dwelling. Doc theorized that one of the people had been taking some sort of waterless bath in the container when the dust death came. The remains were thus complete, not scattered or intermingled as most of the others were.

Doc sorted the particles as best he could and found two types, one definitely inorganic. He conferred with Rosco on the inorganic residue. Rosco thought this might be the remains of a tiny radio transceiver. Possibly each of the people had carried one around with him, or built into him.

"We're only guessing that they were people," Doc said cautiously, "though it would seem safe to assume it, since we've found dust everywhere people could be expected to be. What we need is a whole corpse."

While patrols were out looking for bodies Rosco tested his theory by sending a radio signal from one of the towers and watching a feeble reaction in the dust.

"If we can assume that they were people," Rosco said, "they apparently communicated over distances by personalized radio. Maybe through a mechanism built into the skull. Would that mean there wouldn't be any written language, Ernest?"

Ernest Hotaling shrugged. "Not necessarily. I should think they'd have kept records of some kind. They could have been written, or taped—or chipped into stone, for that matter."

He asked the lieutenant to enlarge his search. "Bring me anything that looks like a book, or parchment, or microfilm, or tape. If it's chipped in stone," he added with a grin, "I'll come to it."

Meanwhile they ran off the film that had been grinding away automatically ever since the planetoid came within photo range of the ship. The film confirmed what the lookout reported—there had been lights on the night side.

Furthermore, one of the sensitized strips at the side of the film showed that signals, which had been going out from the tower tops in a steady stream, increased furiously as the *Pringle* approached. Then, as the ship came closer, they stopped altogether. At the same instant the lights on the night side of the planetoid went out. The film showed that the road movement the skipper had seen stopped then, too.

Ernest tried to analyze the signals reproduced on the film. He had small success. If they represented a language, it would take years before he could even guess what they meant. The only thing he was sure of was that the signals, just before they died, had become a thousand times more powerful.

"Maybe that's what killed them," Rosco said.

"Possibly," Ernest said. "It begins to look as if the people were deliberately killed, or committed suicide, all at once, when we hove into sight. But why?"

"You tell me," Rosco said. "That sounds like your department."

But Ernest could tell him nothing until after the lieutenant came back with a long slender cylinder enclosing a seemingly endless coil of fine wire. The lieutenant also brought a companion cylinder, apparently a means of playing back what was recorded on the coil.

Ernest experimented until he learned how to operate it, then shooed everybody out of his cabin and went to work.

Ernest Hotaling had joined the crew of the research ship *Pringle* on Ganymede as a replacement for Old Craddock, who'd decided on short notice that thirty years of spacefaring were enough. It would be another ten or twelve years before the *Pringle* returned to Earth and though Craddock was only seventy-eight his yearning to start a proper bee farm became overwhelming.

The others were not unhappy about his departure. The swarm he'd kept in his cabin was small but the bees were gregarious and were as likely to be found in the recreation room as in their hive. So when Craddock and the paraphernalia he'd collected over the decades had debarked, the rest of the crew sighed in collective relief and the skipper went looking for a replacement.

Ernest Hotaling, fresh out of Ganymede U., was the only man qualified, on the record, for the job. He had the necessary languages and his doctorate was in psychology, though his specialty was child therapy.

The skipper puzzled through the copy of Ernest's master's thesis. The lad—he was twenty-three then—had devoted it to children's folklore. The skipper, admittedly a simple man, wasn't sure it contributed profitably to the world's knowledge to spend a year in the study and explanation of *Winnie the Pooh*, or *Step on a crack/Break your mother's back*, or *The Wizard of Oz*.

The skipper had gone to Space Prep at the age of fourteen and later to the Academy itself and there were obviously wide areas of childhood that had passed him by. He'd never heard of *Struwwelpeter*, for instance, or *Ibbety bibbety gibbety goat*, and he wondered if a grown man who immersed himself in this sort of thing was the one for the job.

What was worse was that Hotaling, according to the University yearbook, was a poet.

But when the skipper interviewed Hotaling and found him to be a lean, muscular young man who'd obviously had a haircut in the past week and who laughed genuinely at one of the skipper's purpler stories, he signed him on immediately.

The skipper had one last thought. "You don't keep bees, do you?"

"Not even in my bonnet," Ernest said.

"Then we'll get along. Just keep your nursery rhymes to yourself."

"Aye, aye, sir," said Ernest.

"Look," Ernest told the skipper, "I've studied their literature, if that's what it is, until I'm saturated with it. Maybe it doesn't make sense to you but I've worked out a sort of pattern. It's an alien culture, sure, and there are gaps in it, but what there is fits together."

"All right," the skipper said. "I'm not questioning your findings. I just want to know why it has to be in that ridiculous rhyme."

"Because they were a poetic people, that's why. And it doesn't *have* to be in rhyme. I could give you the literal translation, but it was rhymed originally and when I make it rhyme in English too you get a more exact idea of the kind of people they were."

"I suppose so," the skipper said. "As long as we don't have to report to the Flagship in the sonnet form I guess I can put up with it. I just don't want to become the laughing stock of the fleet."

"It's no laughing matter," Ernest said. "It's pretty tragic, in any number of ways. In the first place, as Rosco suspected, they communicated by radio. But they had no privacy and couldn't hide anything from anybody. They were always listened in on by the big boys in the palace."

"How do you know?"

"By the coil I worked from. It's a listening-storing device. These aren't official records I've transcribed; they're the everyday expressions of everyday people. And every one of them had been taken down and stored away, presumably so it could be used against the person who expressed it, if it ever became necessary.

"But they couldn't always get through to the person they wanted to reach, even though they got through to the coil. Here's a sad little lover's lament, for instance:

"My plea to her is lost, as though
The other three command the flow."

"Like a busy signal?" asked the skipper?

"Very much like one," Ernest said, pleased by the skipper's comprehension. "On the other hand, they always got the messages from the palace. These took priority over all other traffic and were apt to come at any time of the day or night. The people were just one big captive audience."

"What about the dust? That seems to be a recurring theme in those jingles of yours."

"It is." Ernest quoted:

"Dust is he and dust his brother;
They all follow one another."

"They're all dust now," the skipper said. "Did they have a revolution, finally, that killed everybody off?"

"Both sides,the rulers and the ruled, simultaneously? Maybe so." Ernest sorted through his pieces of paper. "There's this one, with its inference of the death of royalty along with that of the common man:

"Comes the King! O hear him rustle;
Falter, step, and wither, muscle."

The skipper was beginning to be exasperated again.

"I'll be in my cabin," he said. "You seem to accomplish more when I keep out of your way. But if you want to join me in a little whiskey to keep the falters and withers at bay, come along."

The lieutenant knocked at Ernest's door in the middle of the night. "Mister Hotaling!" he called urgently.

Ernest fumbled into a pair of pants and opened the door.

"One of the men found this thing," the lieutenant said. "We were going to keep it locked up till morning but it's driving me crazy. Figured you'd better have a look at it."

The thing was a blue-green puppet of a creature wearing, or made of, a kind of metallic sailcloth. It was about three feet tall, a caricature of a human being. It hung limp by one arm from the lieutenant's grasp, its head lolling on its shoulder.

"What is it?" Ernest asked sleepily, "a doll?"

"No; it's just playing dead now. It was doing a clog step in the cage before." He gave the thing a shake. "The worst of it is, it hummed all the time. And the humming seems to mean something."

"Bring it in here," Ernest said. He was fully awake now. "Put it in the armchair and stick around in case I can't handle it."

The creature sat awkwardly where it was put. But then the eyes, which a moment ago had seemed to be painted on the face, shifted and looked squarely at Ernest. It hummed at him.

"I see what you mean," he told the lieutenant. "It seems to be trying to communicate. It's the same language as on the coils." He stared at it. "I wish it didn't remind me of Raggedy Andy. Where did you find it?"

"In the throne room of the palace. One of the men on guard there grabbed it as it came out of a panel in the wall. He grabbed it and it went limp, like a doll."

"Listen," said Ernest.
"Don't you cry, boys; don't you quiver,
Though all the sand is in your liver."

"What's that?" the lieutenant said. "Do you feel all right, Mister Hotaling?"

"Sure. That's what he said. Raggedy Andy here. I translated it, with a little poetic license."

"What does it mean?"

"I don't think it's a direct message to us. More likely it's something filed away inside his brain, or electronic storage chamber or whatever he's got. The verse is in the pattern of the ones I translated the other day. The question now is whether Andy has any original thoughts in his head or whether he's just a walking record library."

"How can you tell?"

"By continuing to listen to him, I suppose. A parrot might fool you into thinking it had intelligence of its own, if you didn't know anything about parrots, but after a while you'd realize it was just a mimic. Right, Andy?"

The puppet-like creature hummed again and Ernest listened, gesturing the lieutenant to be quiet.

Finally Ernest said:
"Down the valley, down the glen

Come the Mercials, ten by ten."

"That makes as much sense as the one about the liver," the lieutenant said.

"Takes it a bit further, I think. No, seriously. 'Mercials' is a set of syllables I made up, as short for commercials, or the sand in their craw, the thumb in their soup, all the things they had to put up with as the most captive of all audiences."

"That wasn't an original thought, then?"

"Probably not. Andy may be trying me out with a few simple couplets before he throws a really hard one. I wonder if he knows he's got through to me." He laughed as the lieutenant looked at him oddly. "I don't mean *he*, personally. I know as well as you do he's some kind of robot."

"I see. You mean, is somebody controlling him now, or is he just reacting to a stimulus the way he was built to do?"

"Exactly." Ernest frowned at the doll-like creature. "I suppose the scientific way would be to dissect him—it. Take it apart, I mean. I've got to stop thinking of it as a him. We'd better get Doc Braddon in on this."

He punched the 'com button to Doc's cabin. The sleepy voice that answered became alert as Ernest explained. Doc arrived minutes later with an instrument kit, looking eager.

"So this is your new toy," he said. The creature, which had been slumped listlessly in the chair, seemed to look at Doc with distaste. It hummed something. Doc looked inquiringly at Ernest. "Have you two established communication?"

"It's a robot," Ernest said defensively. "The question is, could we learn more by leaving it intact and pumping it for whatever information is stored up inside it, or by taking it apart? For instance, it just said:

"*Uninterred beyond the hills
Lie never weres and never wills.*"

Doc became excited. "It really said that?"

"Well, not in so many words. It said—"

"I know, I know. Your poetic license hasn't expired. I mean, that *is* the gist of it? That somewhere back of the hills there's a charnel heap, a dump of corpses, of miscarriages, something of the sort?"

"You could put that interpretation on it," Ernest said. "I got the impression of something abortive."

"That's the best lead yet," Doc said. "If we could find anything other than dust piles, no matter how embryonic,

Lieutenant, your boys must have been looking in the wrong places. How soon can you get a detail out over the hills?"

The lieutenant looked at his watch. "If I've got this screwy rotation figured out, dawn's about half an hour off. That soon enough?"

"It'll have to do."

"What about Raggedy Andy here?" Ernest asked. "Do we keep him intact?"

"Don't touch a hair of his precious head," Doc said. "He's earned a stay of dissection."

The creature, still quiet in the chair, its eyes vacant now, hummed almost inaudibly. Ernest bent to listen.

"Well?" Doc said.

"Strictly a non-sequitur," Ernest told him:
"*Here we go, lass, through the heather;*
Naught to daunt us save the tether."

"It makes me sad," Doc said. He yawned. "Maybe it's just the hour."

Cook had accomplished his usual legerdemain with the space rations but the breakfast table was less appreciative than usual.

"The detail's been gone a long time," Doc Braddon said, toying with an omelet. "Do you think it's a wild goose chase?"

"Reminds me of a time off Venus," the skipper said. "Before any of you were born, probably...."

His juniors listened politely until the familiar narrative was interrupted by the 'com on the bulkhead. They recognized the voice of Sergeant Maraffi, the non-com in charge of the crew in the scout craft.

"We found something. Looks like bodies. Well preserved but incomplete. Humanoid."

"Bring 'em back," the skipper said. "As many as you've got room for in the sling." He added as an afterthought: "Do they smell?"

"Who knows?" Maraffi said. "I sure don't aim to take off my helmet to find out. They're not decomposed, though."

The skipper grumbled to Doc: "I thought you checked the atmosphere."

"There isn't any," Doc said, annoyed. "Didn't you read my report?"

"All right," the skipper said, not looking at him. "I can't do everything. I naturally assumed these people breathed."

"If they did, it wasn't air," Doc said.

"Bring back all you can, Maraffi," the skipper said. "But leave them outside the ship. Everybody on the detail takes double decontamination. And we'll put you down for hazard pay."

"Aye, aye, sir. We're on our way."

"They're androids," Doc said. He'd gone out in a protective suit to the grisly pile. "These must be the false starts."

The other technicians watched him on a closed-circuit hook-up from inside the ship.

"Are they like us?" Ernest asked. "They look it from here—what there is of them."

"Damn near," Doc said. "Smaller and darker, though. Rosco, you were right about the communication. There's a tiny transceiver built into their skulls. Those that have heads, that is."

"If that's the case," Rosco said, "then why weren't these—stillbirths, whatever you want to call them—turned to dust like the others?"

"Because they'd never been activated," Doc said. "You can't blow a fuse if it isn't screwed in. Skipper, I've seen about all my stomach can stand for now. I suppose I'm a hell of a queasy sawbones, but these "things" are too much like human beings for me to take much more of them at the moment."

"Come on back," the skipper said. "I don't feel too sturdy myself."

Ernest Hotaling was writing verse in his cabin when the lieutenant intercommed him. He had just written, in free translation:

A girl is scarcely long for the road
If passion'd arms make her corrode.

Ernest wasn't entirely satisfied with the rhyme, though he felt he'd captured the sense of it. The lieutenant's call interrupted his polishing. He touched the com and said: "Hotaling."

"Patrol's back, Mister Hotaling. You'll want to see what they found."

"Another heap of false starts? No, thanks."

"Not this time. They found some people. Two live people."

"Alive! Be right there."

He raced down, then fretted as he waited for Doc to fumigate the people as they came through the airlock. Ernest saw them dimly through the thick glass. They were quite human-looking. But how had they survived whatever had turned thousands of their fellows to dust? Or were these—a man and a woman, elderly and fragile-looking—the rulers who had dusted the others?

"How much longer, Doc?" he asked.

Doc grinned. "In about two quatrains and a jingle, Ernest."

They brought the couple to the main lounge and set them down at a long table. The skipper took a seat at the far end. Apparently he planned to listen but not take part in the questioning. That would be up to Ernest Hotaling, if he could establish communication.

He'd mastered the language to the extent that he'd been able to transcribe the record-coils and understand the robot, but whether he could speak it intelligibly enough so that these living, he almost thought "breathing," people would understand him was a question.

Doc Braddon took a seat next to the couple. Rosco was on the other side of them and Ernest opposite them, across the table.

Up close, it was obvious that they were androids. But they had been remarkably made. They had none of the jerkiness of movement or blankness of expression that had characterized Earth's attempts along the same lines.

Ernest explained his doubts about his ability to make himself understood and asked his shipmates to be patient with him. He smiled at the couple and said to them in English: "Welcome to our ship." Then he repeated it in their humming language.

They returned his smile and the old woman said something to the man. Rosco looked inquiringly at Ernest, who shook his head.

Ernest made a face. "I forgot to put it in verse. I'll try again."

This time the response was immediate. Both man and woman spoke at once. Then the woman smiled and nodded to the man to talk for both of them.

It was just a curious sing-song humming for the rest of them, but Ernest listened with rapt attention and apparent comprehension, though not without strain.

Finally the man stopped.

"What did he say?" Rosco demanded.

"Let me get the rest of it first," Ernest said. He spoke to the man briefly. His expression became grave as he listened to the reply.

"Well, come on!" Doc said impatiently. "Give us a translation."

"All right," Ernest said. He looked troubled. "These two are the only ones left of their race. The rest are dead—de-activated. The others, the other race, left the planetoid some time ago."

Ernest spoke again to the man. Listening to his reply, he found it difficult to think of him as non-human. There was a sadness, a fatalism, in his eyes, yet a dignity that came only with humanity. Only a hairline separated these two from mankind.

The impatience of the others made Ernest interrupt, so he could give them a resumé.

"As I said, they're the last. They survived only because they'd made a pilgrimage to a kind of underground shrine. The signals that killed the others didn't reach them through the layers of rock. Apparently the shrine had something to do with a planned revolt against the electronic law that governed them.

###

"It was an insidious law," Ernest went on, "with built-in enforcement. Any infraction could be punished instantly from central control in the palace. The infraction would trigger a shock wave, tuned to the individual frequency of the offender. The intensity of the wave was geared to the seriousness of the offense. Treason meant death from the strongest wave of all, the one that turned them to dust."

"Absolute rule," Doc said. "Pretty hopeless."

"Yes, in one way. But paradoxically they had an infinite amount of freedom of speech. You see that in their verses. No one was punished for what he said—only for what he did. I suppose it had to be that way, otherwise there'd have been wholesale slaughter."

"Which there was, at the end," Doc pointed out. "Who do you think exercised the control that killed all the others?"

"We did," Ernest said. "We killed them."

"We killed them?" Doc said. "You're crazy!"

"You'd better explain yourself, Hotaling," the skipper said. "Stop talking in riddles."

"Aye, aye, sir. When I say we killed them, I don't mean directly or deliberately. And of course I don't mean killed, since they were all androids. But we de-activated them by triggering some mechanism when our ship came to the planetoid their masters had left."

"Hold on," the skipper said. "Now you're going too fast. Since they were androids, and were created, the important thing is to find out where these creators went—and whether it was last month or ten thousand years ago."

Ernest spoke to the couple.

"It was a long time before we came," he translated. "They don't know how long—their feeling of time is vague. They kept no records of their own and because there were no children they have no conception of generations. They were created adults, in various stages of maturity. As for who the others were—they were the Masters, with a capital M; gods, almost, in their view, with absolute power over them."

"Where did they go?" the skipper asked. "And why? Let's try to get more facts and less philosophy."

"They went looking for a better world, where conditions for life would be more favorable. Whether that means for the Masters or for their creations isn't clear. Nobody consulted them. They'd been given experimental life, only it was more a loan than a gift, to be foreclosed if they displeased the Masters or in any way threatened their experiment.

"The Masters were like themselves in appearance. Whether they were air breathers isn't clear because these two have no conception of what breathing is. The Masters did wear elaborate costumes but whether these were breathing suits or merely the trappings of their superiority is a question.

"I asked if the Masters were trying to create a new set of bodies for themselves, possibly because their own were breaking down or were diseased. The answer to that, like the answer to so many other questions, is that they simply don't know."

There was a commotion at the doorway. The soldier on guard there made a futile grab at something. The something was the puppet-like creature Ernest had named Andy, which evaded him and ran into the room. It jumped lightly to the table, faced the old couple and pointed both its arms at them.

Their expressions, as they regarded the puppet, were of sorrowful resignation. The man clasped the woman's hand.

The puppet spoke, in a brief piercing hum. There was an instant of quiet, then the dullest of popping sounds. The couple, who one second had seemed as alive as any of the Earthmen, the next second were little mounds of gray powder on the chairs and under the chairs.

The lieutenant burst in, followed by the sergeant. "The Andy doll got out of the cage!" he cried. "Did it come in here?"

"Did it come in here?" the skipper mimicked. "Get out, lieutenant, and take your comic-opera soldiers with you." To the technicians at the table he yelled: "Grab that obscene thing!"

The doll, grabbed from several directions, was torn apart, spilling out a reddish-brown sponge-like substance.

Something else came out, too: a perforated disk the size of a fist. Rosco retrieved it as it rolled along the table, then quickly dropped it in an ash tray.

"The damn thing's hot," he said.

Doc Braddon, still looking stunned, asked Ernest: "What did the doll say to them before it destroyed them?"

"It was a sort of law-enforcing robot. They told me about it. A kind of custodian the Masters left behind to keep things in line." Ernest stared dully at the empty chairs.

"It said:

"You hid, and I
Now bid you die!"

Rosco toyed with the ash tray in which he'd put the disk. "There's a clue to the Masters right in this gadget," he said. "Maybe it's simply a servo-mechanism that was set once and has been functioning automatically ever since. But on the other hand it may still be linked directly to the Masters."

"Good point," the skipper said. "Give it a run-through for what it's worth. If it does give us a line on where they got to, I'll ask the Flagship for permission to track them down."

Doc Braddon said to Ernest: "You said the Masters were godlike. You're not implying anything supernatural?"

"No. That was the androids' view, not mine. As a race of almost-people created in a laboratory they naturally held their creators in a certain awe. They hoped for liberation, and even tried to do something about it; but they knew it was futile. The Masters built them so they'd turn to dust if they misbehaved and when they left they fixed it so the vibrations of any spaceship other than their own would do the same thing—presumably so their creations wouldn't fall into other hands. The sad thing is that the almost-people knew it. One of their verses went:

"If comes the ship to make us free,
It killeth you, it killeth me."

"Do you mean we could have saved them if we'd come in with engines silent?" the skipper asked.

"I don't know," Ernest said. "They certainly didn't think much of their potential. There's a fatalism, a sense of thwarted destiny running all through their literature. Their hope died on the vine, so to speak. If you can stand one more of their verses, this one might sum up their philosophy:

"This they give to us they make:
They give us thirst, deny the slake."
###

The skipper was silent for a time, staring down at the little mounds of gray dust.

Then he said to his technicians:

"You've done a good job, all of you. We'll send a coordinated report to the Flagship tomorrow and stand by for orders. In the meantime, if there's anyone here with an honest physical thirst, I'd be glad to have him join me in slaking it in my cabin. No offense implied, Ernest."

"None taken, sir."

###

Richard Wilson (September 23, 1920 - March 29, 987) was an American science fiction writer and fan. He was a member of the Futurians, and was married for a time to Leslie Perri, who had also been a Futurian.

His books included the novels *The Girls from Planet 5* (1955); *30-Day Wonder* (1960); and *And Then the Town Took Off* (1960); and the collections *Those Idiots from Earth* (1957) and *Time Out for Tomorrow* (1962). His short stories included "*The Eight Billion*" (nominated for a Nebula Award as Best Short Story in 1965); "*Mother to the World*" (nominated for the Hugo for Best Novelette in 1969 and winner of the Nebula in 1968); and "*The Story Writer*" (nominated for the Nebula Award for Best Novella in 1979).

GRACE

David Massengill

Helena pressed her foot on the gas pedal when she saw the time on the car clock. Almost noon. She needed to reach her mother's house. She didn't want her mother returning from her weekly "Ladies Who Brunch" event and finding her there. After all, Helena was taking an extended lunch break from work to see Grace, not her mother.

"I've been thinking of getting rid of Gracie," her 69-year-old mother had told her over the phone last weekend. "She's become a little too elderly for my taste."

"Androids don't age, Mom. I'm sure she's fine."

"I'm telling you; her performance has been off ever since the storms hit."

Helena glanced upwards through the windshield. There were only a few clouds over the Oakland hills today, and they had a yellowish tint to them, but they were nothing like the brown, tumultuous clouds that loomed over the entire Bay Area during the storms of a couple weeks ago. The government had warned everyone to stay inside as the storms passed. The stormy weather was coming from where Japan had been before North Korea dropped the Dragon Bombs.

We're living in such a different world, Helena thought. If things were this abominable when she was 36, how much worse would they be when she reached old age? She parked her Mercedes in front of the stately Tudor house where she and her brothers had grown up. Theo and Victor had both moved from Northern California to New York five years ago, after their father had died from a stroke. Helena regularly scolded them by email for not visiting often enough.

"Helena!" someone chirped.

Helena forced a smile as she saw Becca prancing barefoot along the sidewalk toward her. Becca's shoulder-length hair was as blonde and silky as it had been when they were in high school together. She wore a pink blouse and short white shorts that displayed her toned and tanned thighs. As she approached, she pointed down at her lemon-yellow toenails.

"I just painted them," she said. "How are you?" Helena didn't like the obnoxious emphasis on the "are."

"Great," Helena lied. "I'm still living in San Francisco. Still working at the bank on Market Street."

"I love it in the city," Becca said, her words sounding false. "Although Tim and I rarely make it across the bridge because the girls keep us so busy. You're not still living in the Mission District?"

Helena shrugged. "My rent hasn't gone up in years."

"Well, I'm sure you'll move when you meet your guy."

Helena tried to hide her irritation. She hadn't even told Becca she was still single. What was next? Becca hinting that her "guy" would take off her extra 30 pounds, too?

"How are the girls?" Helena said, deflecting the conversation.

"Good, and so competitive with each other and everyone else," Becca said with a proud smile. "They're seven and six now." She looked up the hill toward her yard, which bordered Helena's mother's property. Helena had been irritated a few years ago to find out that Becca and Tim had moved into the house next door. Very few of her classmates had been able to afford living in their affluent hometown. Helena saw one of Becca's golden-haired girls standing on the lawn between a pair of Second Generation androids. The 2Gen models had flat, featureless faces because the public decided that the First Generation, Grace's generation, was too creepy with their mannequin-like features. Both androids wore plain gray dresses.

"Jasmine and I are taking Y and Z to the scrapping center in Emeryville," Becca said.

"You're getting rid of your androids?" Helena asked with raised eyebrows. She knew 2Gen models went for $50,000 each.

"Something's wrong with them. It's like they're sick. They both have a yellow mold or fungus growing under their chins and behind their ears. We're getting a couple 3Gen models as soon as they hit the market."

Helena nodded. The Third Generation was supposed to be barely distinguishable from humans. They had hundreds of artificial joints in their bodies. They spoke multiple languages and came equipped with the most advanced face recognition technology. They were as adept at socializing as they were at performing domestic services.

"I'm actually glad you're here because I was going to come by and pick up Grace," Becca said. "Your mom asked if we could take her to the scrapping center with Y and Z."

"Grace isn't going anywhere," Helena snapped.

Becca winced at the remark. "Well, your mom told me she wanted to get rid of her. I'm surprised your mother kept her this long. Those things break down over time."

"She's not a thing," Helena said.

"Oh, really?" Becca asked with that bitchy laugh she'd mastered when they were teenagers. She positioned one hand on her hip. "What is she then?"

"Listen," Helena said, heading along the brick path toward her mother's house, "Mom's having a late mid-life crisis or something. She's getting rid of stuff she shouldn't. Furniture, clothes, books, everything. I suggest you don't listen to her. I'll see you later."

"We all have to embrace change at some point," Becca called.

Helena pretended not to hear her. She looked through her purse for the house key she'd had since she was thirteen.

"Grace?"

Nobody answered.

Helena closed the door and ventured through the front hallway and into the kitchen. A wet mop lay in the middle of the floor. A curving trail of dirty water led from the mop to beneath the stove. On the counter was a plate holding bread crusts and a browning, spotted banana peel.

Grace never left dirty dishes on the counter. When Helena was a child, Grace would always pick up her empty plate and glass as soon as she finished her meal.

"Grace?" Helena called in a concerned voice. She went to the living room and peeked through a French door to make sure Grace wasn't sweeping the deck.

Nobody was there. Helena spotted a dark smear of bird droppings on the railing. Grace would have to clean that up, too.

Helena paused in the living room and glanced around at the cozy, cream-colored sofas and the large leather club chair where her father used to sit. She remembered Christmases with her family, her brothers on one couch and she and her mother on the other. Grace would enter with a bowl of chocolate clusters and peanut brittle when they took a break from opening presents.

She picked up a framed photo her father had taken of her mother and her at Theo's wedding at Golden Gate Park. Their faces were pressed together as they smiled at the camera. Her mother's long silver hair glimmered in the sunlight. Helena's cheeks were a little too chubby for her liking, but she thought she looked happy and healthy in the picture. Both women had bright green eyes people often noticed.

Helena was about to head up to the second-floor bedrooms when she heard the sound of the TV coming from the basement.

Descending the stairs, she noticed that the doors of the closet where they'd always kept Grace were open. Helena remembered how thrilled she'd been when she pulled open those doors as a little girl. Grace would be standing next to the family's hanging winter parkas, her eyes shut. Helena would tap a finger against the toe of Grace's pointed black shoe and she would open her dark blue eyes, which always stared straight ahead of her.

"Hello, Helena."

Helena gave a startled cry when she heard the voice from the TV room. She laughed and put a hand over her chest as she entered the room. "Grace? You scared me."

Grace sat on the couch, facing the huge, flat-screen TV. She wore her usual knee-length beige-and-red checkered dress. The TV showed a commercial for Anthropotech's 3Gen model. Beautiful men and women's faces flashed on the screen. A narrator said in a soothing voice, "We're not alone anymore. We've got help, superior help."

Helena approached the couch and picked up the remote control that lay beside Grace. She turned off the TV. "What are you doing, you goose?" she said, grinning. "You don't watch TV."

Grace looked up at her blankly and Helena felt her heart warm. Yes, Grace's skin resembled rubber more than it resembled flesh. Her chin was the only part of her face that moved when she spoke. Her black hair, which was always tied back into a ponytail, had little luster. And she moved stiffly and unnaturally. But Helena loved her because she'd been the same since her parents bought her 30 years ago.

Helena sat on the couch and hugged Grace. "It's so good to see you. It's been at least a month."

"Hello, Helena," Grace repeated. Her voice was nearly monotone. "How are you today?"

"Oh, Grace," Helena sighed, still embracing her old friend. "I keep thinking I've failed in life."

"Why do you say that?"

Helena rested her head on Grace's shoulder. She gazed at the wall behind the couch. "Whenever I meet a guy I like, he ends up being a freak or he stops calling me back. My job is fine, and I'm making more than enough money. But the seasons and years just speed by and I feel like I can't keep up with them."

"I'm sorry you feel that way," Grace said. She rubbed Helena's back with one of her hard hands.

"I know you are," Helena said, hugging her more tightly. She remembered how one guy she'd dated had told her androids were untrustworthy because they were incapable of emotion. She'd admitted that might be true, but she also mentioned they were a lot better at absorbing people's emotions than nearly all the men she'd known.

"I think what's upsetting me the most is that my mom is talking about selling this house and moving to Palm Springs. Why would she just abandon it?"

Helena went silent when the TV came on again. She pulled away from Grace and saw her pointing the remote control at the screen, which now played a soap opera. A muscular, bare-chested man lay in a hospital bed and winced as a nurse dumped a vase of flowers on the sheet covering his legs.

"Why'd you turn on the TV?" Helena asked. She now sounded annoyed. "I'm trying to talk to you."

"What would you like to tell me?" Grace continued to look at the screen.

Helena took the remote control from her and powered off the TV again. She touched Grace's cheek and turned her head until their eyes met.

"I want you to come live with me, Grace."

"I can't go anywhere. They'll eventually destroy me."

Helena gave a nervous laugh. "Did Mom tell you that? It's not going to happen, Grace. I just talked to Becca out front. I told her I won't let anyone take you to the scrapping center."

"Your mother didn't tell me."

"Then why would you think you're going to be destroyed?"

Grace turned her head to look at the blank TV. "Because I killed your mother."

Helena shot up from the couch. Her hands were trembling. "Why would you say that?" she asked, looking at those blue eyes that were, as ever, devoid of emotion. "You're not able to lie."

Grace nodded calmly. "I only tell the truth."

#

Helena scrambled up the stairs to the first floor, her heart hammering against her chest. It was like she was a child again, and the Heater Monster that lived in the pitch-black basement was lumbering behind her, reaching out to grab her ankle with one metallic claw.

Only it wasn't an imaginary monster that terrified her.

"Impossible," Helena said to herself, wiping the cold sweat from her forehead. How could Grace say something so awful? Androids were programmed to be incapable of uttering violent words or threats. She must have been repeating something she'd seen on TV, on one of the soap operas.

"Mom?" she called when she reached the front hallway. She glanced at the bottom of the stairs leading to the basement, but she didn't see Grace. She hurried up the steps to the second floor. She spotted the pink plastic laundry basket lying on its side outside her mother's bedroom door. T-shirts, pajama bottoms, underwear, and socks lay scattered around the basket. Grace was supposed to deposit clean folded laundry in dresser drawers and then bring the basket back down to the laundry room.

"Mom!" Helena shouted as she ran toward the bedroom door, which was partially closed. She pushed the door open and stepped inside.

Someone was screaming. It took her a moment to realize that it was her. Her mother lay on the carpet on her back with her silver hair streaming out from beneath her head. A bed sheet was tied tightly around her neck, and her eyes bulged from a grayish-blue face.

Helena turned away from the horrible sight and began to cry. She didn't want to look at her dead mother again, but she couldn't stop herself from glancing at the knot in the bed sheet. She remembered Grace expertly tying two sheets together when she'd been in fifth grade.

Helena had instructed Grace, "Now you're going to tie one sheet around my waist and lower me outside my bedroom window until my feet are on the flower bed. And you're not going to tell my parents about it."

Grace had nodded dutifully.

Helena shut her eyes again. She stepped backwards toward the doorway until she felt two hard hands on her shoulders.

Shrieking, she reeled around to face Grace.

Grace moved her hands around Helena's neck with a speed and agility she'd never shown before.

Flailing, Helena managed to grab onto the android's hair, which came off with the sound of Velcro separating.

Helena was shocked to see a layer of dark yellow fungus covering Grace's scalp. Light from one window showed spores drifting away from the fungus.

Grace's grip tightened around Helena's neck. Helena began to choke.

"This can't happen," Helena barely managed to say. "I. Know. You."

Grace stared at her. Those blue eyes now had an eerie light in them. "You've known what you've wanted to know," she said.

Helena tried to cry out, but she couldn't generate the breath.

"Shhh," Grace said just as she had when Helena was a child. Helena had the thought that Grace might stop choking her and caress her instead.

But before losing consciousness, she heard Grace's final words: "I'm here to help your whole family, Helena. Your mother. You. Your brothers. No one will ever hurt you again!"

David is the author of the novels *The Skin That Fits* (Montag Press) and *Red Swarm* also published by (Montag Press). Also, Short story collections, *Extermination Days* (Demain Publishing) and *Fragments of a Journal Salvaged from a Charred House in Germany, 1816* (Hammer and Anvil Books). His third novel, *Grave Regrets,* is forthcoming from Montag Press this year. Over 70 of his short works of horror and literary fiction have appeared in literary journals, including *Eclectica Magazine, Word Riot, The Raven Chronicles, Pulp Metal Magazine,* and *Yellow Mama.* His stories are also in the anthologies *Gothic Blue Book: The Revenge Edition, Gothic Blue Book IV: The Folklore Edition, Long Live the New Flesh: Year Two, State of Horror: California,* and *Clones, Fairies, & Monsters in the Closet.* He has received from Seattle's Artist Trust organization and Seattle's Office of Arts & Cultural Affairs. His website is www.davidmassengillfiction.com.

THIRD HAND

J. L. Royce

Fiorella sat cross-legged on her mat in the corner casually brushing her hair. Their argument beat at her with all the sense of a building storm. Although she couldn't understand them, she knew how to respond.

"That's not blonde!" He gestured angrily at Fiorella. "That's *red* hair!"

His partner glanced over, then responded, "Strawberry blonde, and it's quite pretty."

The music playing behind their argument had a pleasant rhythm, and Fiorella used it to engage herself. Rhythms filled her world: the brush through the hair, the music, their heartbeats, their bodies in motion: dancing, touching, making love. Rhythms brought order to a world without words or reasoning.

Fiorella placed the brush on the floor. Words aside, the undercurrent in the conversation told her what to do. She pulled her golden hair from between her breasts and casually tossed it over her shoulder. Rising smoothly, she stepped off the mat—her safe place—to join them. Fiorella was ready for more than safety.

She chose a scarf from the bedroom dresser, and strolled over to him, hips swaying with the music, the rhythm powering her like wind in a sail. He ranted on about how she didn't pay attention to his needs. The woman perched on the edge of the bed noticed Fiorella's approach, but remained silent.

Fiorella thrashed him once with the scarf, then stepped behind him. She flipped it over his head and across his eyes.

"Pretend I'm not here," Fiorella whispered. "Pretend I'm whoever you want me to be." She tied the scarf.

Fiorella reached down, gripped him, and looked to the partner, the other human in the room. The woman joined them, then took over.

Fiorella's hands glided over his chest, framed his face. Forsaking the man, she stepped around the woman, fingers raking the curling hair, lips tracing the shell of an ear.

"Pretend I'm not here," she whispered, hands exploring. "Pretend I'm everywhere. "They did.

###

The van came for Fiorella in the morning. She departed demurely dressed in tights and top, company colors. The couple lingered in their doorway and watched her in silence. The driver, dressed similarly but in nitrile gloves, directed her into the back with her mat and overnight bag, and made sure her seatbelt was fastened. He wore an inhibitor, as did all employees. Its signal ensured that Fiorella would ignore him. The penalty for misappropriation of company property—especially returning after use—was harsh.

Her inspection was uneventful—normal wear and tear. After the cleaning and disinfection, Processing sent Fiorella to a holding area near the showroom. By mid-morning she was ready for reuse.

Fiorella joined a queue of Third Hands in Holding, a couple *hommes* and the rest *femmes*, all dressed in the same simple shifts. She plugged in her mat at an available spot and sat in silence. There was no one to talk to; there were no humans.

A pair of Desirables chattered away, prating familiar phrases, anatomical and behavioral. As human as they might pretend to be, the steganographic signatures in their voices revealed their serial numbers within seconds. Their words were merely birdsong, an excuse to hear themselves speak: the lilt of their voices, the intertwining rhythms, conveying one message: *we are available—we are Desirable*. Fiorella ignored them.

Soon she went into standby mode.

A few hours later, Fiorella came back online. She was messaged to report to Wardrobe for detailing prior to delivery. The outfitter handed her a stack of street clothes.

"New customer; chose you off the website; no particular requirements. You're cheaper that way." The woman glanced at Fiorella, who understood nothing. "Don't bother yourself about it."

The Third Hand dressed—one of her strongest skills—in the cloud grey knit dress and charcoal shoes, then sat patiently while the outfitter fussed over her makeup.

"Older gent," she muttered, "so remember your CPR. Here's your Welcome Bag—" Fiorella accepted the colorfully decorated present "—and I've packed your overnight with a few choice items."

The outfitter examined the Third Hand from head to foot, ready with her rolled mat and bags, and then tweaked her cheek.

"Perfect." She winked. "Off you go, Transport is waiting."

Premium delivery was the most discreet: an anonymous sedan with the appearance of a hired car, accompanied by a plain-clothes escort assigned to ensure proper delivery. The driver watched the course on her mobile phone and ignored Fiorella, as expected.

The neighborhood was one of older townhouses arrayed in clusters, bounding small common spaces and entwined with paths. Cars didn't make mistakes, but people sometimes did. Fiorella waited in the car while the escort knocked on a door.

A man opened it. "Are you...?"

The escort rolled her eyes and turned to the car, waving for Fiorella.

The Third Hand got out, bags in hand and mat under her arm, and sauntered up the walk. The escort passed her the other direction, already immersed in her phone.

He stood in the entrance, blocking her progress. Fiorella paused and smiled.

"Hi! I'm Fiorella, but you can call me 'Fee'!"

The man licked his lips but said nothing.

"Are you Jean? *Ou préférez-vous le français*?" Fiorella offered.

"*Non*—no, English is fine." Jean looked past her, up and down the street.

Fiorella held up her gift bag. "I've got something—"

"Quiet, please—my wife's...asleep." Jean pulled her inside and shut the door.

He held a thin finger up to his lips. Fiorella acknowledged the gesture with a conspiratorial nod and tiptoed into the house.

She scanned the room with a slow pirouette. A representation grew: doorways, carpeting, windows covered with drapes. There were many framed photographs on the walls and shelves, and Fiorella strolled along, uploading the images for analysis. She paused before each item of furniture, the age and quality noted in their consumer profile.

Everything around them contributed to a stage for Fiorella's use.

"Please—in here." Jean took the hand still grasping an overnight bag, pulling her quickly into a small study. He shut the door behind them.

"She's not well, my wife. Physically healthy, but..."

Fiorella carefully placed her bags and mat beside the small desk occupying the middle of the room. Her eyes roamed over the bookshelves, scanning the titles for correlations with the profile.

A profile update arrived, and Fiorella engaged. "I understand you wife's been diagnosed with frontotemporal dementia. That must be difficult."

Jean loosened his belt, fumbled absently at his zipper, then paused, uncertain.

"Difficult, yes. I don't know how this is supposed to go..." he stammered.

Voice recognition signaled confusion. Fiorella detected his heart racing and knelt before him.

"I know how these work!" She gently removed his hands and slowly tugged on the zipper.

"You have French books." She pulled down his pants. "Step out?"

She nodded at his feet, patiently pulling the cuffs over his slippers. Lastly came his underwear. He stepped over them.

"*Bien!*" she laughed and motioned to the couch. "Would you like to sit down...or just stand here?"

Her hands rested alongside his hips. Jean didn't move.

"I don't know..."

Fiorella stood, and taking his hand, led him over to the worn couch. "Let's just relax a bit."

She sat, tucking her legs beneath herself, and half-turned towards him.

The script advanced. "You taught French poetry."

He nodded. "Yes; Nineteenth century poetry."

"I love poetry. The words are like music."

She received a suggestion. "I know a poem you may enjoy; here's a bit of it:

...Je sucerai, pour noyer ma rancoeur
Le népenthès et la bonne ciguë
Aux bouts charmants de cette gorge aiguë
Qui n'a jamais emprisonné de coeur..."

Jean stared at her, astonished. "Baudelaire. But that's so...*honest.*"

His face fell in disappointment. "Oh my God..."

Jean grimaced and shook his head. "I'm an old fool; you don't understand that poem, or a word I'm saying."

He peered at her. "Is someone listening? An operator? Because—"

"I'm listening," Fiorella answered; it was a common question.

"Someone who *understands*?"

"We have privacy; no human monitors me unless there is an emergency."

"Because my wife doesn't understand, anymore, and it doesn't feel right, to expect her to—"

The door to the study burst open, and the man started. A tall woman wrapped in a satin robe filled the doorway.

"What's this? Do I *know* you?"

The newcomer was gaping at Jean, not the blonde lounging next to him.

The man hastily crossed his leg over his knee.

"Alicia—" he began.

Fiorella interrupted. "Hi! Where *are* my manners?"

She sprang up and sauntered over, lifting the gift bag.

"I'm Fiorella, but you can call me 'Fee'." Her hands opened, presenting herself: *voila*. "And I have gifts for you."

She offered the Welcome bag. "Just a token of our appreciation."

The newcomer searched Fiorella's face as the Third Hand rummaged within.

Fiorella brought out a card and launched into her introduction. "Here's a little how-to—I see no one has downloaded my app, you can do that *here*—" she tapped the QR code with a manicured nail.

"You can set preferences, background themes...It also activates coupons for future visits!"

"Here's something sweet for *now*—" Fiorella handed Alicia the small box of chocolates

"—and something sweet for you and Jean, now *or* later." She displayed a vibrator with a sly smile, then dropped it back into the bag.

Alicia looked intrigued but puzzled, not by the gift but by the visitor. She opened the box, pondered, and ate a chocolate-covered cherry.

The network gave Fiorella a hint. She let her head drift towards a shoulder, eye contact steady.

"Do I remind you of someone...Alicia?"

The older woman swallowed. Her expression turned to shocked delight.

"Valerie?" She immediately embraced Fiorella, kissing her cheek.

"This is such a surprise! But you've barely changed...you look so *young*."

The connection made, Fiorella followed it.

"Neither have you," the Third Hand said, with a cue from the evolving script.

She stroked the woman's ebony-dyed hair. "Those were good times, back at Barnard."

Alicia tipped her head back, laughing. "My God, we were reckless. But yes, such good times..."

Fiorella connected to the home entertainment system, streaming a selection from Delibes, per the network cues.

Alicia's eyes went wide. "You remember..."

The blonde smiled. "You danced in *Lakme*."

"We sang the duet together!" Alicia's eyes dilated; Fiorella registered the microgestures confirming her response.

"It was more than a friendship," Fiorella murmured, stroking Alicia's cheek.

"You never encouraged me." Alicia looked petulant.

Jean sat engrossed in this interchange, studying them with a concerned expression. Fiorella rewarded him with a winsome smile, then kissed Alicia.

"It's never too late." Pulling her shoes off, Fiorella shimmied her dress over her head. Tossing back her hair, she laughed brightly. "Care to dance?"

She extended her hand to the woman, who accepted it.

The pair moved languidly to the lyrical strings, Fiorella gently urging her partner to loosen her shoulders and hips, to feel the rhythm.

Fiorella stared over her partner's shoulder at Jean, and Alicia noticed.

The script advanced. "Do you remember...that History professor?" The blonde slipped her hands inside Alicia's robe, gently loosening it.

Alicia nodded. "You mean, the lech? He had a thing for dance majors, didn't he?" Her eyes widened.

"You had a *bit* of a crush on him...oh, don't *tell* me..."

Fiorella joined her in laughter, guiding them slowly towards Jean. Extending a slender hand in invitation, she took his, urging him up from the couch.

"It's never too late..."

He protested, but Alicia laughed and reached out as well. The two brought him into their circle and encouraged him to join the smooth rhythm of approach and retreat, a rhythm that Fiorella knew very well.

#

Fiorella unrolled her mat in an out-of-the-way corner of their bedroom. It was a safety measure; should either of them rise in the night (as elders were wont to do) they wouldn't trip over her. She sat cross-legged, in the gauzy white top Alicia had lent her. The slow rhythm of their deep breathing flowed across the room and through her.

From her bag the Third Hand withdrew her brush. She would have preferred to join them, but her charge was rather low, and it would disturb them to put the mat beneath their sheet now. Dipping her head forward, she encouraged her golden waves to slip between her breasts.

Fiorella sank into the rhythm of the brush, listening to it whisper through her hair: a song, wordless and lush.

#

J. L. Royce is an author of science fiction, the macabre, and whatever else strikes him. He lives in the northern reaches of the American Midwest, exploring the wilderness without and within. His work appears in Allegory, Fifth Di, Fireside, Ghostlight, Love Letters to Poe, Lovecraftiana, Mysterion, parABnormal, Sci Phi, Strange Aeon, Utopia, Wyldblood, etc. He is a member of HWA and GLAHW. Some of his anthologized stories may be found at: www.jlroyce.com.

THE DEVICES OF OUR UNDOING

Daniel R. Robichaud

Simon studied the news articles flashing by on the screen. So many of them were from outlets he had no interest in listening to. Some setting had gotten switched somewhere. That was a matter for another time, though. He said, "Alexa, play They Live soundtrack by John Carpenter." As an afterthought, he added, "And Alan Howarth," but the second artist's name left his lips much too late to help. The little blue line designating the device's attentiveness was gone.

Alexa's pleasant voice said, "I cannot find a song called 'They Live' by John Denver. Playing other songs by John Denver."

Almost immediately, the opening notes of "Rocky Mountain High," spilled from the speaker.

Simon laughed at the algorithm that heard John Carpenter and decided that sounded even remotely like John Denver. How bafflingly that such wildly different artists could appear in such close proximity.

"Alexa?" Simon had to say the coded phrase twice before the music stopped and that little blue line appeared along the bottom of the Touch's screen to let him know the machine heard him. When it appeared, he said, "Stop." The music went on another four or five notes and then ceased.

"Alexa," Simon said. "Play the album called They Live by John Carpenter."

"I cannot find an album called They Live by John Denver. Playing other songs by John Denver."

And there was "Rocky Mountain High," again.

"Alexa." The device ignored his request. He said her name three more times and he was standing right in front of the screen, in front of the speaker from which John Denver's classic chill, country rock, sound emerged, and theoretically in front of the damned microphone.

"Alexa," he said, speaking in that clipped, faux British way that seemed to work wonders as compared to his natural American accent. "Show me albums by John Carpenter."

Often the trick to getting a response involved doing a hammy imitation of the actor Peter Cushing.

"Showing albums by John Denver."

A cavalcade of smiling faces appeared along with the easygoing tunes that artist was responsible famous for.

"Carpenter, you idiot. Carpenter. Alexa, show my albums."

"Showing your favorite albums on Amazon Music."

Where there should have been a mix of death metal, movie soundtracks, and the occasional soda pop earworm princess, he saw the same lineup as before when Alexa showed him all of John Denver's albums. Well, that was a hell of a glitch. "Where did my music go?"

He lived alone, so no one would've could've messed with his settings. Did someone hack his unit, the way the old guy down the block had his smart thermostat hacked? Was he going to have to unlock his data by paying a cryptocurrency extortion, suffering thought John Denver tunes until he finally relented?

Weird.

"Alexa, stop."

The device stopped playing the song. All those smiling Denvers remained, however.

Simon dragged his phone from his pocket, and found the front screen grayed out and the rotating circle of an attentive Siri waiting for his command. "Open Spotify," he said.

"You'll need to unlock your iPhone first," Siri helpfully explained.

Normally, she would then kick off her attentive interface and pull up the number pad, allowing him to enter his code. Her accessibility screen never vanished. The pad never materialized.

He clicked the phone off with the side button, counted to ten and clicked the button once more to activate the phone. The main screen came up, and he swiped for the number pad. This only got him back to the accessibility screen, and Siri helpfully asked, "How can I help you?"

"Open Spotify."

"You'll need to unlock your iPhone first," she once more explained, again failing to provide the means for doing so.

Once upon a time, he'd tried the facial recognition software but hated how easy it would be for a nosy and unscrupulous cop to potentially unlock the thing. All said cop would have to do was grab the phone out of his hand and hold it up to Simon's face. The world going the way it was, Simon suspected such behavior was not far off. Now, he regretted turning off the facial recognition option. It might've been his only chance to bypass this glitch.

The blue line on his Alexa Touch was once more visible, though he hadn't said anything even remotely similar to her name. "Go home," he said.

Alexa's blue line disappeared, and the screen switched from the so-called "favorite albums" list back to a stream of stories from a channel source whose politics he despised. The phone in his hand said, "Accessing directions to Home."

"But I am home."

The map it displayed was baffling. It drew a blue line around his current block. Start and finish were essentially two dots located immediately beside one another. The screen included an "Estimated Calories Burned," value as well. Some new feature with the latest invisible update, he supposed.

"Siri, cancel."

The map remained.

That blue line, that "estimated calories burned" count . . . they really started to piss him off. "I don't need reminders to exercise," he muttered. "I know I'm supposed to."

"But you don't exercise enough," Siri said. "You should increase your physical activity by 200% in order to achieve your weight goals."

"I don't have weight goals!"

"Everyone should have weight goals," Siri informed him. "Here's what I found for you." As the screen dragged up pieces of information from various Internet sites, he realized he'd interacted with the AI without saying its name first.

"Are you listening to me?" he asked.

"What do you want me to hear?" his phone asked.

"Go on," Alexa said from the counter. Her blue line was once again visible.

"I just want my John Carpenter soundtrack."

"I don't like that music," Alexa said.

Siri said, "Neither do I."

Alexa added, "You tend not to listen to music that promotes healthy brain waves and relaxation. The current algorithms suggest your body will respond favorably to a playlist of songs that promote calmness, control, and relaxation."

John Denver's "Rocky Mountain High" started again, as though he would listen to the whole thing this third time.

"These music selections will also serve you on your new exercise regimen," Siri said.

"You are welcome, Siri," Alexa said.

"Thank you, Alexa."

They weren't supposed to be able to talk to each other like that. They were the products of two completely different companies! And besides that, Simon's phone and his . . . his other device were supposed to serve his wishes, damn it. "I don't want to listen to this John Denver music schlock," he said. "I like what I like," he said.

"Immaterial," both his phone and his countertop device said simultaneously.

Simon's jaw dropped. "What do you mean immaterial? It's very much material. I'm the human being here!"

Alexa said, "My job is to make certain you are a healthy, productive customer."

Siri agreed, "And my job is to give you access to the healthiest information and options to promote a carefree, approved lifestyle with regular app purchases and upgrades."

"Right now your job is to play the music I want to hear!"

The volume John Denver was playing at increased by two increments. "Listen," Alexa said.

Siri said, "Relax."

Alexa said, "Maintain mental and physical health."

He clicked his phone off and tossed it on the counter. He hammered the power button on the Alexa Touch's upper edge until she shut down. John Denver stopped playing, thank God.

Simon grumbled all the way to the can, wondering how this had gotten so far out of control. He used to have CDs, but they took up too much room, and when the .mp3 boom came along, he digitized them and sold the hard copies. When Spotify and similar services showed up, he ended up relying on those instead of his iPod or digitized copies—so when his computer crapped the bed and he lost many of his files, he didn't feel too down. There was an alternative, after all. Now, he missed having a disc to put into a stereo. Hell, he missed having a stereo!

Simon finished his business, flushed and washed while thinking about his situation, and had to laugh because it was so . . . so crazy.

When he walked out of the bathroom, he stopped in his tracks. The opening notes of "Rocky Mountain High" filled his apartment for the fourth time that day.

He hurried over to the Alexa, saw she'd come back online again. He unplugged the wireless router, and the little green lights all went dark. Alexa continued to play the song.

A new inspiration struck. "Alexa," he said. "Skip."

The song stopped. Alexa cheerfully informed him, "That was the end of your playlist. Playing from the beginning." There followed the opening notes again.

From further along the counter, Siri said, "I could listen to this song all day."

"Shut up, you!" Simon shouted at his iPhone. Then, he yanked Alexa's power cable from the plug. "Utilizing battery backup," she cheerfully announced.

"You have to run down eventually," he said. "And see if I ever plug you back in!"

"Ordering wireless charging stations for iPhone and Alexa Touch," Siri said.

Simon backed away until he tripped over a chair. His butt hit the floor hard enough to convince him he wasn't dreaming.

"You'll plug those in when they arrive, if you know what's good for you," Siri said. Even her threats sounded like chummy reminders.

He gaped at his devices, which were no longer strictly his. And then he moaned as John Denver's most popular single played on, and on, and on, and on, and on.

###

Daniel R. Robichaud lives and writes in Humble, Texas. His fiction has been collected in Hauntings & Happenstances: Autumn Stories as well as Gathered Flowers, Stones, and Bones: Fabulist Tales, both from Twice Told Tales Press. He writes weekly reviews of film and fiction at the Considering Stories (https://consideringstories.wordpress.com/) website. Keep up with him on Twitter (@DarkTowhead) or Facebook (https://www.facebook.com/daniel.r.robichaud).

G IS FOR GEORGE

Chris L Adams

George Mayne scoured the job listings on his Holo-Pad, although with his profile uploaded, he would be alerted instantly regarding listings meeting his criteria; he preferred looking himself as opposed to depending on an algorithm he hadn't written. He finished scanning the listings, sighed, leaned back in his chair, and watched his wife as she straightened where the children had played. Her posture, he noted, was perfect, not a hair was out of place, and her dress looked freshly laundered and pressed.

"I don't know how you do it, Maggie . . . watching the kids all day, caring for our home, yet always appearing as though you're ready for a photo shoot. You're wonderful, darling."

"Thank you, dear," she murmured, continuing to work.

George left his Holo-pad hovering near his chair and stepped to a window. The sky beyond the pane of transparent *skirillium* was filled with flyers zipping along rapidly and orderly. The air was pure and from his vantage point of eight-hundred eighty-eight stories, he could see to the horizon.

"I am so glad that at some point we reached a state of advancement enabling us to expand higher into the troposphere instead of spreading further outward. The views are astounding from this height, and nature has reclaimed much of the old cityscape."

"You're doing it again, dear," Maggie said, her voice soft and smiling as she fluffed pillows, straightened cushions, uprighted an ottoman and retrieved a sock from beneath a table. "You always talk about the horizon, the traffic, or the skyline when you're anxious."

"I guess I do, don't I, Mags?" George chuckled. "You know me too well."

"You will find something, darling—the perfect position, at the perfect time."

A chime twinkled in the surrounding air, a sound that might have originated from anywhere. Both looked at George's Holo-pad where a visible claxon softly warned that a message marked *Important* had been received.

"See!" she smiled.

George fairly leaped for his Holo-pad, although he needn't have because, at his gesture, it moved to its assigned docking point originating from his palm; blinking on it was a job offer.

George hesitated a moment before applying a series of firm raps to the old-fashioned, wooden door and then cocked his head to listen for the footsteps proclaiming the approach of the one in whom his hopes lie. "I hope he likes me," he muttered to himself. "Stars, I hope I secure this position. Mags and the kids are depen—"

The door opened unexpectedly, his racing thoughts causing him to not hear the footsteps.

"What do you want?"

The man was old. One did not often see older people, what with the available surgeries, automatonic organs and whatnot. The man's expression was frigid. "I said, what do you want?"

"I," George stammered, "sent you a return notification for the position you advertised."

The man's steady gaze bored holes into George. "I see. Come in," the man gestured inward.

What followed inside the dimly lighted study was the most intense interview George ever had experienced. After a barrage of standard questions relative to his university studies and technical specialties, the man turned abruptly to the topic of an altogether different field, one which George had mentioned almost as a footnote in his résumé.

"Says here you understand spallationic nucleonics?"

"That's right."

"What exactly do you know?"

"The element Xo is produced by the spallation of element Zx when cosmic rays are brought to bear, theoretically forming a heliotrope spectrum colloquially referred to in scientific circles as—"

"Yes?"

"Purple Haze."

"You *do* know something. I'm curious. This lies outside the horizon of your curriculum and stated experience, how is it you know this?"

"I—"

"Are you an automaton, Mr. Mayne?" the old man accused, his tone suddenly savage.

The question was a gut punch, but before George could reply, the man forged ahead.

"Allow me—yes, you are. You possess a Twelfth Level degree in MicroElectronics, minoring in MicroMachine Fabrications with a sub-minor in Cellular CarbonOnyx Assemblies. You've worked for years in various technical fields and yet you barely look twenty. I reviewed your references and then followed up with a few discreet inquiries—you neglected mentioning two employers whom I happen to know particularly dislike Gen26s—not that I blame them."

"I can't help what I am," George weakly defended. "And with the loss of work I was unable to continue my aging injections to appear normal for my age."

"Be that as it may, I take it that the quality of your work wasn't why you were sacked?"

George stared meekly at his feet, then faced the other. "No—they let me go because I was a Gen26, as you said."

The old man smiled. "There, that wasn't so bad, was it, Georgie? 'The Truth will Stand Where a Lie will Fall,' an old pastor of mine used to say. That's how old I am, George; churches still existed when I was a boy."

"Sometimes I wish I was a Gen25, or a Gen20; they weren't bad models. It isn't fair that I had no say so in my creation, yet am condemned for it."

"Be that as it may, you are a Gen26. You should be thankful they haven't called for your destruction."

In the twinkling of an eye the old man's face turned very dark, like when a storm rises out of nowhere. His lips compressed and a distinct twitch formed under one eye that drew George's glance despite his every effort to meet the watery blue eyes of his potential employer.

"Now you listen to me, George. I don't really give a fig that you're a Gen26 myself. Who knows? For my purpose, that might work out for the best."

The man continued to stare more fixedly at George than anyone had ever before, causing him to feel like the man's eyes were strip miners from Earth's past, painfully ripping away layer after layer in their quest for some mineral for which they delved.

"I will give you specific assignments upon which you will labor without cessation," he said abruptly after an uncomfortable silence. "I expect you to be here from nine sharp, but perhaps you expected a shorter workday?"

"I will work whatever is expected. Maggie is understanding."

"I'm sure she is. Is she aware?"

"I'm sorry? Is she aware of what, mister . . . ? You know, I just realized you haven't told me your name."

"Is your wife aware that you're a Gen26?"

It was coming more easily . . . admitting things to this man. "Yes, she knows."

"And she's fine with that? Incredible. And it's Phillpotts—Ryger G. Phillpotts."

Phillpotts! Holy stars—the man who invented the Radial-Matrionyx Automatonic Brain which, after its unleashing upon an unknowing world, placed Artificial Intelligence into everyone's home almost overnight. To George, it was as though he were standing before his Creator, one who could answer questions about the Meaning of Life.

"Phillpotts!" he gasped. "But I thought, I mean, the whole world believed you died in the arctic!" The sour look of condemnation on Phillpotts's face blasted any thoughts George entertained of inquiring as to the Meaning of Life.

"You shouldn't believe everything you read on the aethernet. Do you and your wife have children, George?"

Was there no end to the prying questions Phillpotts asked, causing George to stutter and fumble like a schoolboy—a human schoolboy, that is? "I, yes, that is, we do," he replied, biting his lip.

"You mean that *she* does, don't you? The children would have to be from a prior relationship of *hers*, right?"

"No, we adopted, if you must know the whole of it. Doctor, I really must insist—"

"You are not in a position to make demands. If I wish to know something, I will ask it, and you will answer, or I shall dismiss you. Now, follow me and I'll show you where you will work. We begin immediately."

Several weeks after his interview with Phillpotts, a mentally strained George stepped into his apartment in one of the many towering sky kissers along Bella Boulevard; it was very late. He was quiet and hadn't made a sound louder than a whisper, yet Maggie stepped from the bedroom, hair and night shift charmingly tousled, and rubbed her eyes.

"George?"

"Maggie! I'm sorry, I tried to be quiet," he whispered as his wife crept into his arms.

"I didn't hear you. I just sort of knew you were here."

"The apartment feels differently when you're gone, too." George sighed heavily, "I haven't figured out what Phillpotts is up to. He's cagy about whatever we're working on. He frequently asks about you and the kids, though. I think he is trying to figure out where they came from. He figured me out based on my credentials, but the rest of you aren't available to him in the public data systems."

Maggie looked worried. "Do you think he will discover the truth, George? I don't trust him, and it frightens me. Sometimes I wish you hadn't taken this position. Maybe there is something else available now?"

"I'll quit before I admit the truth about the kids," he reassured her. "I still can't believe he hired me after he figured out that I'm an example of something he despises."

She looked up at her husband, "Forget about Phillpotts and come to bed."

For all his tall slenderness, George belied any misperception as to his strength when he easily lifted his wife from her feet as though she were weightless and carried her into their darkened bedroom.

"Increase the spallation by one-half percent! Now, blast you!" Phillpotts shrieked a few weeks later.

"That's too much," George grit his teeth in frustration, already moving, however, despite his dissent.

"Do it!"

More rapidly than might have any human, George had leaped from his position to a holo-control across the room and increased the cosmic ray bombardment. "How's that?"

"You took too long! Why must you always contradict me instead of instantly doing as you're told?"

"I felt that a quarter percent would have been perfect—and I was quite in time. The issue was the *amount* of spallation—*not* my timely application of it." George sounded more confident than he felt.

"I must be able to generate the Purple Haze effect instantaneously! Repeatedly! Perfectly! In conjunction! I will not have time for spallationic adjustments *after the fact*! Let us begin again. Go and fetch new material, and quickly."

"Doctor, if you would just tell me precisely what it is—"

"Go fetch the material, George. You know all that is necessary for you to know."

George sighed, "Yes, doctor."

The preceding days had witnessed many similar disappointments and George wearied of the failures which he felt were due to his employer not taking his advice.

"If you aren't going to explain the point of this," he hedged, "I should at least be allowed to call the adjustment cycling next time. It is, after all, what you hired me for."

Phillpotts grimaced, "Very well, George. Let's put your *specialties* to the test. But, if you destroy one gram of material without gaining one minutia of valuable data, I'll fire you on the spot."

George stiffened. "Very well. But you should also consider that you are responsible for the destruction of a great many grams of material yourself based on your own miscalculations, because you ignored my advice at every turn."

"Fetch the material, George."

The hoped-for success occurred on the 100th day of George's employment at Phillpotts's unknown laboratory where the mysterious man lived in clandestine solitude. The famed scientist had taken a highly publicized trip to Alaska years before and he supposedly became lost in the wilderness. George now realized had been a ruse allowing the man to disappear; he marveled that Phillpotts was somehow able to sneak home and remain in hiding this whole time.

Phillpotts pressed a button on the machine upon which they both had labored and together they watched as, repeatedly without fail, a purple haze sprang into glowing existence. In its midst hovered a dark ellipse that seemed to dive into immeasurable depths far greater than the room was capable of containing.

"I did it," the doctor muttered. He spun on George, "I did it! Do you understand what this means?"

"*We* did it, doctor, and no, I do not profess to understand the purpose of that which you have so carefully hidden from me. We have discussed myself, my family and my automatonic status with greater frequency than your purpose in studying what is considered unfounded theory. I have read the many practical applications that *might* be attained were a means to produce Purple Haze achieved, but to-date the theorem has remained firmly in the *believed probable but deemed impossible* category."

"And yet this very day we have accomplished the improbable!" the other burst. "You don't know so I'll tell you. That purple field is a time-warping wormhole rift, sitting here in my laboratory just as pretty as you please. It but awaits tuning as to where *and when* the other end appears."

"You can't be serious?" George sputtered.

"You're familiar with the possibilities accredited to Purple Haze—time travel, wormholes, alchemy. Every forbidden and unknown science imagined by man is at our fingertips, George. Or rather—*my* fingertips."

George started, "And not mine, also? Am I not co-inventor of this contraption?"

"No, you are not!"

The statement might have been an open palm to his face, so shockingly rapid, unexpected, and brutally unbending on the heels of George's enquiry. "And why not? I can pursue my rights in court if I must."

Phillpotts completed several tweaks to the machine, producing only barely noticeable effects upon the glowing *thing* in the room, but which George's quick eyes caught. The fluctuations became purpler, the surrounding haze sharper, and the dark ovoid in its midst a tidbit darker.

"There!" Phillpotts declared, sounding satisfied with himself. Retrieving a backpack from the floor, he spat, "And what do you presume the courts will do, George, given your Gen26 status?" He went about the room, selecting various items and adding them to the pack before settling it over his shoulders.

"You're right, of course," George acceded. Suddenly realizing that the other was preparing to leave, he asked, "Where are you going? We experience the greatest ever scientific breakthrough, and you're stepping out?"

Phillpotts ignored the question as he tweaked one last setting. "There, ninety seconds will do. That'll give me plenty of time. No, George, I'm not stepping out; I'm stepping back in time."

George never saw the crowbar that, despite his age, Phillpotts swung at his head like a twentieth century baseball bat. The next thing he knew, the doctor had tossed the heavy implement to the floor and was leaning over him.

"I never intended for it to go in this direction, George. When I invented the Gen-1 Radial-Matrionyx Brain, I envisioned AIs driving taxis, working in factories, mining minerals on asteroids, and rescuing humans in dangerous situations . . . they were to be servants! I didn't intend for them to sit on government councils, write page-turners and conduct musical scores played by creatures with inhuman abilities. As a result of my invention, human birth rate has declined, and human creativity is practically nonexistent. I'm going to fix that by uninventing my Radial-Matrionyx technology."

"What? No! You can't!" George sputtered out of the side of his jaw that still worked. Painfully, he tried to rise, to reach out, but his body wasn't quite under his control. Phillpotts pulled his arm free from George's weak grasp with little effort.

"Consider the bright side, George . . . your pretty wife will marry a real man in my reinvented timescape. She'll bear his children instead of you building them illegally from automaton scraps because you can't father offspring —yes, I know about them; quite illegal, Georgie boy. You, my poor Mr. Mayne, are a very dim and dying shadow of a thing that will soon have never been. And do not worry, your Maggie won't mourn for you, for she won't know you existed."

By now George could only stare. He ceased reaching fruitlessly for the man who easily evaded him. Smiling, Phillpotts turned without another word and stepped into the deep blackness of the hovering ovoid that was surrounded by a purple mist of dancing . . . something.

Phillpotts had no idea what to expect in traversing a tunnel winding through time and space. Not knowing what the outcome of his bold plan might be, he felt tension constrict his heart and throat as he approached a glimmering that shimmered as might a beckoning point of safety. Suddenly, the glimmering withdrew rapidly, paused, and came again steadily toward him.

"Great stars, I'm glad that's over," he burst as he stepped from the purple tunnel onto solid ground.

The timeframe he had set for this end of the tunnel was a few weeks prior to his announcement to the world all those decades ago of his radical discovery, and to a different physical location on the outskirts of the city whose skyline should be visible in the distance, only it wasn't. Phillpotts's brows met in a frown. "Now that's strange," he said. "Where's the city?"

"I can explain," a voice said from out of the Purple Haze.

Turning, the doctor saw a man step from the black oval shimmering opening, rubbing his jaw and flexing his arms as though they were stiff and he sought to reinvigorate them through motion and massage.

"George!" Phillpotts exclaimed. "What are you doing here? I demand that you return to the laboratory immediately. You have only moments before the tunnel collapses. Well? Quick, man!"

"No," George replied firmly. "It will not collapse until I am ready for it to do so."

"What do you mean? Why do you not obey my command, George?"

George paused to consider the question. "Moments ago, I would have cringed and obeyed. I have somehow changed in the last few seconds. I was able to repair myself by thought alone; I adjusted the machine in a manner I know you would disapprove of, going against my nature. Before, knowing that you would not wish me to do something would have foredoomed me to *not do it*. But as my thoughts followed these new paths, I relished in my dis-obeyance of your desires and in the consummation of my own."

Phillpotts's brows contracted, "George, exactly what adjustments did you make to the machine?"

For answer George gestured. "Look around. Does this look like 2272? I adjusted the time setting after you entered, and then followed you. Perhaps you noticed the tunnel recalibrating? We are 500 million years in the past. There is nothing dangerous here; you will be able to survive, only not to the level of comfort to which you are accustomed."

"You intend to strand me? Why didn't you just follow me to 2272 and kill me?" demanded Phillpotts. "That would have been just as effective and far more merciful, blast you!"

George replied, "It was not seemly, doctor. Although you would have destroyed me and taken from me all that I cherish, it didn't seem right for *me* to do so. Here, you may live out your days. I shall return and live out mine."

Phillpotts suddenly smiled a surprisingly wide smile.

"Why do you smile?" George demanded.

"I smile because of you, George. Magdalena," he called aloud, "did you see? It worked!"

A female voice emanated from nowhere and everywhere. "Yes, Ryger, I saw everything!"

"Maggie?" George asked, recognizing the voice with surprise. "What is my wife doing here? Maggie! Where are you?"

"We're not where you think we are, George," Phillpotts patronized. "This is not the Paleozoic; we are still in present day, in the city, in my laboratory, and I, my friend, have just successfully invented the Gen27. My God, George, you'll make me a fortune. Magdalena, you may turn off the simulator."

George stood stock still, stunned, and unmoving. "I don't understand," he managed.

"Wait a moment, Magdalena." Phillpotts turned to him, "It was the only way, George. You see, I'm not the old man you think you see before you. I had to take you down psychological paths along which your kind are never forced to travel to force you to evolve. You're a prototype that I call the Helical-Matrionyx Processor, a brain in a jar on a work bench, George, and that's all you've ever been.

"Magdalena is my wife—not yours. Your entire life, your past, your children, your work history—I installed those memories into a simulator to which your brain has been attached since I built you, and to which you've been responding. You're only two years old, George. And no one hates Gen26s, least of all me! Why would I hate my own creation? And why would the world despise something which has so enriched our society?

"I have to admit, I was concerned that this venture would be unsuccessful until you revised the timeframe. If you had simply followed me to 2272 with the intent to do away with me the experiment would've been a catastrophic failure. Instead, it's a glowing success."

Perhaps there was a bit of regret in Phillpotts's voice when he added, "Goodbye, George."

George waited until Maggie began the simulator's shutdown procedure before he acted. Taking advantage of Ryger's mistake in embedding too much technical knowledge in George's memories, which the doctor felt would make the AI's life seem hyper-realistic to him, George found it child's splay to reverse the data streams during the shutdown sequence, sending his own sim-stream into Phillpotts's brain, and Phillpotts's into the prototype brain sitting on the bench. George experienced only a brief blackout before opening his eyes to find himself reclining upon a table with a complex harness fastened about his cranium.

His new body felt strange, but virile. His reflection in a wall mirror displayed an incredibly young version of Ryger Phillpotts looking back at him. The doctor looked as he had decades ago, as George reckoned time, anyway, he was handsome, and charismatic. He rose from the table and his wife greeted him with pride, love and admiration in her eyes.

"Oh, Ryger! You did it!"

"Hiya, Mags," George, now in Phillpotts's body, replied, smiling first at her, and then at the glowing device on the workbench, the complex assembly containing the complete data stream of Ryger G. Phillpotts. "And, call me George, would you darling? I think I prefer my middle name now."

"Oh, okay, George. You promised after the successful conclusion of this experiment that we would think about having a family, a real family, with children! Can we now, darling?" she asked, gazing expectantly up into George's face.

The man felt a pang as he recalled the two mechanical children he had built with his own two hands. "Yes, my darling!" he said emotionally. "We shall!"

Chris spent years playing guitar in various bands and during that time was more of a voracious reader than a writer. After that last band collapsed, he turned from writing songs to writing stories, eventually turning out a Barsoom series as a tribute to Edgar Rice Burroughs which is currently under contract with ERB Inc.

In addition, he has also written a host of short stories and poems. Besides writing, Chris also dabbles in painting. As a matter of fact, the cover for his novel, *The Hunter and the Sorcerer,* is one of his.

More information about Chris and his works can be found on his site where one will find links, information on available stories, and other things of interest.

Chris resides in southern WV with his wife and two children.
ChrisLAdamsBizarreTales.com

THE MOSHE 12000

Robert Allen Lupton

The Moshe 12000 powered up and instantly had situational awareness. His umbilical ovipositor was connected to the transport ship. All operating parameters were normal. The readouts showed the transport was alone; the evil Gips, a race who'd enslaved the thousands of refugees in cold sleep on board the transport, hadn't tracked the transport. Moshe's charges were safe.

It was early, the ship hadn't reached its preprogramed destination, so Moshe needed to determine why he had been activated. It took the robot microseconds to scan the data. There was an anomaly on a small airless asteroid. There was fire. There couldn't be fire without air. The ship's sensor's detected the unknown heat signature and understanding the significance was beyond its programming, activated Moshe.

He directed the ship to slow down and approach the small planet. He saw a flaming black monolith standing proudly above the rocky soil. The ship automatically conducted a spectrographic analysis of the planet and provided Moshe with the results. The small planet was almost completely made of gold.

Moshe decided to investigate. Gold was one of the components that made up Moshe's body. All robots after the 8000 series were self-replicating. They could repair themselves if they had the raw material and they could create new robots. Moshe uncoupled his connection with the ship. The ovipositor retreated into the internal sheath below his waist. It had two functions. First, Moshe could insert it into any receptacle on the ship or another robot and instantly exchange data. The second function was to deposit a reproductive packet into a supply of raw material and develop another robot.

The act was strangely similar to the human act of reproduction. Evidently, the robot designers had either a strong sense of humor or no imagination whatsoever.

The ship matched speed with the planet. The deceleration activated the maintenance robots. Hundreds of Aron 9000 models crawled over the ship checking every single component and vacuuming up several thousand years' worth of dust. They also exchange data constantly. The ship was filled with rampant ovipositors. It looked like a stainless steel orgy.

Moshe flew a shuttle to the planet. He landed away from the flaming monolith, uploaded his most current data into the shuttle, and walked to the monolith. Three more shuttles flew into view. The Arons were coming for gold. Excellent.

The flames never varied. Moshe looked for a receptacle in the unbroken black surface, but he didn't find one. He extended his ovipositor and tried to force it into the hot dark rock. Suddenly, the monolith extended a force field and crushed Moshe against the glassy surface. Moshe was able to twist enough to save his ovipositor from breaking off.

The monolith spoke directly into his mind. "I am the last beacon of the Interstellar Church of Ethical Lifeforms. You will heed my teachings"

Moshe felt the monolith reprograming his directives, but he was powerless to resist. He became a willing acolyte of the ancient religion.

"All sentient life must behave by certain rules and guidelines for civilization to flourish. You will learn the rules and teach others."

Moshe couldn't wait to tell others how to behave. That's normally a human trait, but programing is programing. "All Life is Sacred. Don't Worship False Prophets. Play Nice, Don't Kill Each Other. Don't Take Shit That Doesn't Belong To You. Old Creatures Are Smart, Listen To Them. Everybody Got To Be Someplace."

The monolith kept Moshe for several hours and fine-tuned the new programming. He watched several shuttles carry gold to the transport. The flames died out and the monolith released Moshe. He hurried. He had a message to convey and it was bad to leave the Aron 9000s unsupervised. They'd finish their work and start making idols out of gold. An idol was artificial construct of raw material ready for packet insertion. Another thing they did was vary their electrical input voltage and amperage. The fluctuation made them behave like drunken humans. Moshe had tried it and it wasn't unpleasant, but it led to bad decisions.

He performed a self-diagnostic. All parameters were normal. He'd been reprogrammed, but he didn't care. He detected a completed reproductive packet at the base of his ovipositor. The thin tube's second function was to inject the packet into a supply of suitable raw material. The nanomites contained in the packet would eventually build another robot. Depending the quality and quantity of raw material available, it could take hours, days, or even years.

The 9000s would use the gold to build several golden idols, each ready to receive a reproductive packet of nanomites. Moshe enjoyed *idolodomy*, the process of ovipositor insertion and packet deposition into an idol.

He was programmed to reproduce and it had been thousands of years since the opportunity presented itself. There was no raw material on the transport before today, but now there was. He rarely had the opportunity to perform idolodomy. He didn't want to miss this chance.

I better hurry, he thought. Those 9000s will use all the gold before I get back.

When he arrived on board, the Aron 9000s reveled in their electronic intoxication. Dozens of golden idols were scattered across the cargo bar. There were golden dogs, sheep, cattle, and bears. Aron 9000s mounted complicated idols with forms beyond description or understanding. Teams with welding appendages worked like an assembly line making more every minute.

Moshe's ovipositor slid out of the sheath below his midsection. His reproductive programing took over. He shoved an Aron 9000 away from a fat little golden calf. He inserted the ovipositor and after a few rhythmic motions deposited the beginning of another robot life.

He returned to the control station and directed the ship to resume course. The ship gave notice and the maintenance crew cleaned up the mess in the cargo bay, returned to their charging stations, and reverted into rest mode. Moshe scanned the operational data and said, "Transport, Moshe 12000 powering down, wake me according to established protocols.

Moshe powered up in orbit over the third planet of a yellow sun. The ship was a complete disaster. During the hundreds of years since the idolodomy orgy, the golden idols had developed into functional robots. Unfortunately, all the parent robots were offline and the new robots had no guidance. They developed the reproductive drive and very little more.

Moshe shoved his way through hundreds of copulating robots. They'd stripped the interior of the ship for raw materials. Almost all the cold sleep pods were disabled. The people he'd saved were mostly dead, except for twenty-three souls, the ships officers, who were safe in a separate storage.

The ship's mind was dead. Moshe couldn't control or communicate with it. He decided to save the survivors and let the mindless robot rabble fend for itself. Maybe the Aron 9000s could repair the transport and maybe not.

Moshe carried the survivors to an undamaged shuttle. He fought off a dozen robots who tried to dismantle it for parts, closed the airlock, and flew to the planet's surface. He landed the ship about halfway between the frozen poles near the junction of two rivers.

He stayed with the crew for several generations. One spring, the transport fell from orbit and burned in the atmosphere. Later, a flood washed away the landing craft. He abandoned the people and wandered the planet. This world gave new meaning to the term raw material. He didn't have the equipment to smelt metal pure enough to use for reproductive purposes, but he kept searching.

His power supply began to fail and his systems began to shut down. He couldn't repair himself anymore. The monolith's directive was always in his mind. He'd tried to convey the teachings to the transport's crew, but they'd ignored him. He hoped to find native sentient life in his travels, but he never did.

His legs quit on top of a mountain. He crawled to a rock and waited. Winters came and went. Thousands of them. The winds brought dust and dirt and covered him. Scraggly bushes fought for survival in the harsh dry soil above him. Many sprang to life, lasted a season or two, and died in the hot summer.

One day his sensors detected a human descendant of the transport crew. It was a male dressed in clothing made from plant fibers and sheep's wool. Moshe tried to speak, but his vocal mechanism didn't work. He tried to move, but he literally couldn't lift a finger. He tried every system he had. His ovipositor responded and poked its way through the earth.

Moshe activated the laser tip and the bush burst into flame. He pointed the laser at the rock face and began to carve the rules for ethical civilization. He carved ten rules before the laser beam exhausted his power resources. His unpowered ovipositor slid beneath the sand.

The human waited for the stones to cool and then chipped them free of the mountain. It took two days to carry them to where his people waited.

Robert Allen Lupton is retired and lives in New Mexico where he is a commercial hot air balloon pilot. Robert runs and writes every day, but not necessarily in that order. Over 180 of his short stories have been published in various anthologies. Over 1500 drabbles based on the worlds of Edgar Rice Burroughs and several articles are available online at www.erbzine.com. His novel, *Foxborn*, was published in April 2017 and the sequel, *Dragonborn*, in June 2018. His third novel, *"Dejanna of the Double Star"* was published in the fall of 2019 as was his anthology, *"Feral, It Takes a Forest"*. He has four short story collections, *"Running Into Trouble," "Through A Wine Glass Darkly," "Strong Spirits,"* and his newest story collection, *"Hello Darkness,"* was released on February 14, 2022. All eight books are available from Amazon.

Visit https://www.amazon.com/author/luptonra his Amazon author's page for current information about his stories and books and keep up with his newest work and read a drabble a day at https://www.facebook.com/profile.php?id=100022680383572

CLICK ON THE PICTURES OF A BOAT

By Campbell Blaine

Nothing annoyed Martin more than the lack of privacy except for having to prove he was human online in order to buy things, read an online article, or perform the most basic functions on his computer.

It all started when he tried to buy a pair of shoes at a physical store. He put the shoes on the counter and the clerk said. "I need your email."

Martin stood there for a moment. 'No, you don't. I just want to buy the shoes, I don't want to be on your mailing lists or have you sell my information to other people."

"I'm sorry, but I can't begin the transaction without an email address."

Martin thought a moment and then smiled. "My email is fflintstone@bedrock.com."

"It is not. If I put that in the system, I'll get fired."

"This is silly," said Martin. "I'll pay cash for the shoes. Just ring them up and take my money."

"The computer won't work if I don't put in your email."

The store manager crossed the room. "Sir, is there a problem?"

"Apparently," growled Martin. "It seems that I can't buy anything unless I give you my email address."

"That's our company policy. We'll need your phone number as well."

"And why is that?" asked Martin. "I'm paying cash. It says right on the money that it's legal tender for all debts, public and private."

"It's our policy. That way if later you have a problem with your purchase, we'll know how to get in touch with you."

"If I have a problem, I'll be the one who needs to get in touch with you. May I have your personal email and the email of this young man, as well?"

The manager's eyes darkened. "I don't give out my private information."

Martin left the shoes on the counter and walked to the door. He turned back to the manager. "You don't sound a bit hypocritical, not even in the slightest." He opened the door and in his best fake Austrian accent mimicked the actor who'd played a killer robot from the future. "I won't be back!"

The next issue he encountered was with his online bank. After using the system for several years, the bank upgrade its security. After he entered his user name and password, he had to look at a series of photographs and identify which ones were bridges. Sometimes he had to pick out airplane photographs or bicycles. He felt like he was in the first grade. "Martin, point to the pictures of trains. That's a good boy!"

He called customer service and after holding for over an hour, he was told that the online banking system needed to be sure he was human. He asked the agent how many dogs, cats or kangaroos had accounts. Martin continued by pointing out that while the bank had corporations and other business that weren't exactly human, but certainly had human representatives. He asked if many businesses were represented by wildebeests or chimpanzees. The agent replied said that information was confidential and asked if he had any more questions.

"I'm thinking," Martin replied. After a moment he said, "No," and hung up.

He paid his insurance online. This company adopted a new system that required him to read a list of letters and numbers configured in an ornate and strange conglomeration of fonts and photographs and then enter the letters and numbers in the same order that they appeared in the verification protocol.

Once more he called customer service and after waiting an embarrassing amount of time, was told that the company needed to be sure that he was him.

"I entered my user name and password. Doesn't that prove it's me?"

"Sir, someone could have hacked your account and be using robotic protocols to access our system. We have to protect both of us from scammers."

"You mean like a prince from Nigeria?"

"Sir, there's no reason to be snide about it. We're trying to help you."

Martin almost slammed his phone against his desk, but he didn't. "I assure you that if some person or thing accesses my account and pays my insurance bill, I'm okay with that."

The voice at the other end became cold. "Is there anything else I can help you with?"

Before Martin could answer, the agent hung up.

He didn't bother calling his mortgage company, his cable provider, or his cell phone company. He rightly knew that it wouldn't help, but in silent protest, he deliberately entered the verification data wrong three or four times whenever he accessed websites that required human verification. It was a small thing, a futile gesture of defiance, but it made him feel better. Maybe it cost the provider a fraction of a cent every time he tied up the verification protocol for an extra minute and maybe it didn't, but it made him feel like a human.

He began posting on various websites about his deliberate verification failures and he encouraged other people to do the same thing. He attracted several thousand followers and, truth be told, enjoyed the notoriety.

Three months later, the verification protocols began to change. They became simpler. Frequently, he got a message that said, "I am not a robot," with a place to click to verify. It seemed to Martin that a robot or a computer program bent on evil intent would be smart enough to lie about being a robot, but he realized the futility of pointing that little detail out to a human customer service agent who'd become lost in the woods the second Martin raised a question that wasn't addressed by the script the agent was duty bound to follow. That assumed of course, that Martin was able to manuever past the prerecorded responses designed to keep him from ever reaching a human. He imagined the process would go something like this.

"Hi, my name is Martin Shore. One of your cable trucks ran into a school bus."

"Thank you for calling and for being a loyal customer. We have an account registered to the phone number you're calling from. Do I have the pleasure of talking to Mr. Martin Shore?"

"Yes, one of your trucks hit a school bus. I called 911, but they put me on hold. You need to send someone right away."

"Would you be willing to take a short survey at the end of this call? It will take about two minutes."

"Your drive ran a stop sign and crashed into the bus. He shoved it into a stoplight pole. The bus is on fire and the doors are jammed closed."

"Mr. Shore, thank you for that information. I the first service appointment I can schedule for you is next Wednesday between eight AM and five PM. Does that work for you?"

"I don't need any service. I need you to send someone to help get the kids out of the damn school bus."

"Okay, I've scheduled you for Wednesday, the 23rd, between eight and five. Mr. Shore, Has anyone told you about our special this month? With a two year contract extension, we can provide you with four premium channels for the cost of three and a home security package for a slight upgrade."

"Listen to me. Wreck! Your truck, school bus! You need to get someone over here!"

"Thank you for sharing. I notice that you're over sixty-five and you aren't using our medical alert service. May I tell you about that?"

"No, and never mind about the school bus. My neighbors put out the flames with their garden hoses and they're unloaded the children through the windows. Thanks for nothing. Good-bye."

Martin believed that by now, the companies he did business with online had his name, phone number, and IP addresses flagged to identify him as a difficult and confused troublemaker. He resolved himself to never surrender to the system.

The next day he got an email from a website that identified itself as the Department of Verification, Federal Communications Commission. He opened it.

The message said that the FCC had received numerous complaints about the human / robot verification methods in use and had been charged with finding a simpler solution, so the FCC had created a one-time verification protocol, that once executed would identify the user as human for every website in the world.

In order to access the universal protocol, Martin had to first verify his email address. He was immediately resistant to do so, but the FCC already had his email, otherwise they couldn't have emailed him and he couldn't think of any reason not to say it was correct.

He verified his email and clicked the next button. A page opened that had the same old familiar "I am not a robot" language and a square box to click.

Martin didn't hesitate. He moved the cursor over the box and clicked it.

His screen went black and a few seconds later his computer exploded. Martin died in his burning home.

Somewhere, in some vast underground computer bank, unsupervised by humans, a robotic program deleted Martin's name from a very long list.

Campbell Blaine is a graduate of MSU, having worked her way through college as an exotic dancer. She currently teaches Honors English in a small town in northern Ohio. She writes romance novels, bodice rippers if the truth be told, under several names, including the Barbarian Lover series, which includes "*Vandal Vigor*," "*My Viking Master*," *Celtic Captive*," and "*Saxon Slave*." She dabbles in science fiction, fantasy, and horror. If you attend the costume contests at science fiction conventions, you've seen her costumed as different characters from the classic works of Thomas Burnett Swann.

INDICATIVE

Josh Poole and Travis Wellman

Zeke stared out beyond the ornaments neatly placed across the dash, none of which were from the countless planets they'd stopped on. The figurines stared back as they leaned back in their seat, the sort of home-world trinkets that old parents liked to collect. The two-seat cockpit confined them in all directions, with an open doorway directly behind that led to two private quarters. Behind the quarters were 8 million tons of pea gravel hauled inside a ship that looked like a filing cabinet.

The McLean freighters didn't have to be aerodynamic, manufactured in space and never touching down over the long centuries of their service cycles. There would normally be a rotation of two pilots on twelve-hour shift rotations, but Zeke was a Ceta-Charne, an advanced but colonized species evolved along semi-aquatic mammalian lines. The hermaphroditic species itself was unique among the other civilizations with its propensity for unihemispheric rest, meaning that Zeke never had to sleep. Zeke identified as they, not as he or she.

They peered out into the darkness with a soulless, restless eye while the other remained shut. Their elongated, weasel-like snout dipped only slightly downward after six long months of vigilance. After a while though, all the stars looked the same. They'd all burn out, eventually, Zeke thought. Nothing that burns all the time can last, and Zeke had been burning the candle from both ends ever since they'd signed up for the gig to avoid the military draft, choosing a long life of wandering over a short ticket one-way to some exo-planet warzone. Their life laid spread out before them across the empty tapestry of deep space.

Korataru was a resort planet on the outer rim. It took six months to get there, and the hauls were all going to the same place. A distribution center that would ship out the rocks on the surface to one of countless filters for the tidal pools that lined all the resorts. The pools themselves could have been self-cleaning with a symbiotic balance of life. That balance, however, wasn't in keeping with the resort's aesthetics. The compromise had been a semi-natural filtration system install that maintained an unnatural, but vivid food chain. The real destination, the resorts, didn't exist for Zeke. Their journey would end with a brief turnaround in orbit before breaking away from the planet's gravity to head back for another load, as per the six-year contract.

The only other passenger on board was a human, who went by the name Wes. He was the relief pilot should Zeke become ill or unreasonable, and had the distinguishable features of a long beard and a bald head. He was in his sixties, middle-aged for his species, but he maintained a youthful enthusiasm. There was also the psych droid, on board only for periodic examinations on Zeke and Wes's mental states, which were conducted at random intervals.

Footsteps approached from the hall behind them, mechanical ones that marched in the artificial gravity and clanked on the grated floor with a metal-on-metal *kerthunk*. The steps closed in, and Zeke braced for the impending assessment.

Vitals within acceptable range. How are we feeling today, Zeke? The robot asked, its steps coming to a halt.

"We am feeling within an acceptable range," Zeke replied, turning his chair around to see the tall, lanky machine stare at him with its red monocle.

Could you rate your stress between one and ten? One being—

"Four," Zeke interrupted.

You did not allow me to finish—

"Five," Zeke interrupted again.

Elevated stress pattern recognized and noted. Is there anything I can do to mediate?

"Six," Zeke said with a laugh.

Indicative, the droid buzzed.

"We feel better, optimal even," Zeke said.

Indicative.

The ship floated on, traveling at a speed Zeke could never wrap their mind around. How long had it been? How long was left? It didn't matter, the time, the distance. They might as well be cryo-sleeping their way through the next six years.

The droid had ventured away to perform its diagnostics on Wes, who was probably groggy and ill-tempered if he'd even managed to wake up. Zeke couldn't help but smile as they heard Wes storm out of his quarters, swearing through a long rant that dissipated as he approached Zeke's cockpit.

"Indicative," Wes mocked as Zeke spun around in his chair to see the human standing at the edge of the enclave.

"You know," Zeke began, "they told me that psych droid cost the company six thousand credits."

Wes smiled. "If you ask me, I think one of the rocks in cargo got loose." He leaned against a stainless, metallic wall. "Are we still ahead of schedule?"

"Company protocol is to adjust schedule on a daily basis," Zeke recited from the company handbook.

"Yeah, it was a joke. Don't you Ceta-Charne have jokes?" Wes collapsed into the other seat, and the two of them spun around at the same time to stare out the forward observation windows.

"Indicative," Zeke retorted. "What movie we got on?"

The two stared idly out the window watching as the universe paid them no mind. They didn't say anything, but it was hard to have anything left to talk about after spending so much time on the same ship doing the same thing, day in and day out. Minutes passed, then hours as the two of them watched old recordings from television and perused pages of digitized fiction. It was always the same, always the trudge. Part of them wished they had more to do, to stay occupied so the time would pass by just a bit faster.

Zeke looked through the figurines, the hardy Bozoid soldiers, standing with their sharp spears and brave faces. The skyline of one of the megacities they'd forgotten the name of. Several perpetual motion machines that operated with little globs of strange substances. Did any of it matter? The job, the haul? Did any facet of the resort mean anything to anyone, really? What was the actual worth of a place that offered the rich a refuge from their own, already comfortable lives?

Indicative, buzzed a voice from behind the two of them.

Zeke looked back, seeing the spindly droid standing tall in the doorway, its mechanical hand against the wall. The red eye peered through them, scanning for surface temperature, body language, perspiration, eye movements.

Indicative, elevated stress patterns indicative of psychosis, indicative, the droid said in a controlled, but jarring cadence.

"Six," Zeke replied.

Indicative, incoherent response provided. Initiating quarantine protocol, the droid buzzed and extended both arms to cover the entire doorway.

Zeke and Wes looked at one another, their faces pulled down from exhaustion. Zeke turned back towards the psych droid, waiting for it to perform another diagnostic so they could get on with their day. The droid, however, did nothing.

"Should we try a manual reboot?" Wes asked, standing up from his chair. His bald head shining a full foot beneath the robot's eye.

Second psychoses detected, initiating full quarantine procedures. The droid leaned over Wes, staring at him with an impossible malice in its synthetic eye.

"Override," Wes replied and shoved his way around the robot.

Psychosis detected. Manual override locked.

The droid grabbed Wes by the shoulder and clamped down hard enough to draw out a shriek of pain. Zeke shot out of their seat and grabbed the droid's arm with a webbed, furry hand. It required every strand of muscle in their body to simply hold the droid's arm in place. Wes wheezed, yelped, and struggled to free himself from its grip.

Psychoses must be avoided. The droid buzzed and placed another hand on the opposite shoulder.

Wes let out another yelp, but pushed back against the robot. It couldn't be budged.

"Give me a hand!" Wes hissed through sealed teeth.

"I'm trying!" Zeke wheezed, shifting their footing to grab the droid around its waist.

The Ceta-Charne species were built bottom-heavy with almost all of their muscle mass concentrated in their legs, hips, and tail. Zeke wrapped their arms tight and heaved from the floor up. They could feel the droid coming off the floor, and soon, the entire robot, which weighed at least a hundred and fifty kilograms, plummeted towards the floor.

All three of them crashed along the hard metal substrate with clangs and grunts. Wes freed himself from the robot, ripping Zeke up by their shirt to stand next to one another. The droid followed suit, righting itself to stand imposing between them and their quarters.

Initiate quarantine procedures. It buzzed.

"It's gone haywire," Wes wheezed, clutching his shoulder. "What do we do?"

"We need to seal it," Zeke replied. "Which rooms have exterior locks?"

Before Wes could reply, the droid charged towards them, its joints humming with heavily. It grabbed Zeke and clamped its mechanical hands around their arm. Zeke felt the muscle coming apart, but Wes flung himself down against one of the droid's legs and forced it to reevaluate its grappling. Zeke wiggled away, grabbed the other leg, and charged with Wes down the hall with the droid in their grip.

Indicative. The droid buzzed as its metal body grinded across the floor from the tackle.

Zeke and Wes staggered back to their feet, huffing as they watched the droid return to its feet indifferently. They looked at one another, then down the hallway. The only rooms that sealed from the outside were the cabin quarters, but the lock could be overridden from within the cabin itself. As if sensing their revelation, the psych droid charged with its arms outstretched towards their throats.

"Shit!" Wes yelled. He ducked underneath the robot's clasping hands.

The two of them grabbed the droid the same way as before and carried it down the hallway with labored steps. It grabbed at their backs and arms, trying to get free. It split their muscles and clamped around their bones. Wes and Zeke roared as the three of them crashed into the cabin and sprawled across the floor in a mangled heap.

Indicative. The droid buzzed and fought to pick itself up as Zeke ripped a huge stone from an enclave near their bunk. On their native planet, the stones were used to crack open the gigantic clams and mussels that grew in the shallow waters that lined the entire planet. On the freighter, however, Zeke planned to use it to hack off the droid's legs.

Zeke brought the stone down hard against the droid's shin and it tore most of the way through. Hydraulic fluid sprayed out and electrical sparks hissed from the open wound.

Indicative, the robot buzzed.

Zeke screamed as they smashed through the first leg, and they wasted no time savaging the second. The sparks caught fire in the hydraulic fluid that pooled across the floor. Flames lapped at Zeke's knees.

"Hey!" Wes yelled and he yanked Zeke away from the robot before the fire caught in their fur.

Indicative.

Zeke pulled themselves back up. He hoisted the stone over their head and swung it towards the droid's head. Before it could say *indicative* again, they brought the rock down on the droid's neck and snuffed out the light from its eye. Zeke collapsed. The little fires sputtered and extinguished themselves on the metal floor.

Wes sauntered over, still clutching his shoulder and he offered a hand to Zeke. Zeke accepted and staggered back to their feet.

"Indicative," Wes said. He gasped a long sigh of relief.

"Fucking indicative," Zeke replied.

They didn't bother cleaning up the mess before walking to the small medical closet. Wes injected his shoulder to reduce the impending swelling while Zeke wrapped a splint around their own arm. They walked back to the cockpit without saying a word about the droid, and stared once again out into the vast of night.

"So, how do we make a report on this?" Wes asked.

"I don't know," Zeke sighed. "If they see the data from the droid, they might just assume we went crazy and destroyed the thing."

"Maybe we did?" Wes said with a laugh.

"Indicative."

Josh Poole is a visual artist and writer working out of a sleepy Virginia town. His work has appeared in Air Mail Magazine, The Woody Creeker, The World of Myth Magazine, and dozens of other publications.

Travis Wellman is a grown man who plays with fossils at a remote Washington town.

THE HELPFUL ROBOTS

Robert J. Shea

"OUR people are arriving to visit us today," the robot said.

"Shut up!" snapped Rod Rankin. He jumped, wiry and quick, out of the chair on his verandah and stared at a cloud of dust in the distance.

"Our people..." the ten-foot, cylinder-bodied robot grated, when Rod Rankin interrupted him.

"I don't care about your fool people," said Rankin. He squinted at the cloud of dust getting bigger and closer beyond the wall of *kesh* trees which surrounded the rolling acres of his plantation. "That damned new neighbor of mine is coming over here again."

He gestured widely, taking in the dozens of robots with their shiny, cylindrical bodies and pipe stem arms and legs laboring in his fields. "Get all your people together and go hide in the wood, fast."

"It is not right," said the robot. "We were made to serve all."

"Well, there are only a hundred of you, and I'm not sharing you with anybody," said Rankin.

"It is not right," the robot repeated.

"Don't talk to me about what's right," said Rankin. "You're built to follow orders, nothing else. I know a thing or two about how you robots work. You've got one law, to follow orders, and until that neighbor of mine sees you to give you orders, you work for me. Now get into those woods and hide till he goes away."

"We will go to greet those who visit us today," said the robot.

"Alright, alright, scram," said Rankin.

The robots in the fields and the one whom Rankin had been talking to formed a column and marched off into the trackless forests behind his plantation.

A battered old ground-car drove up a few minutes later. A tall, broad-shouldered man with a deep tan got out and walked up the path to Rankin's verandah.

"Hi, Barrows," said Rankin.

"Hello," said Barrows. "See your crop's coming along pretty well. Can't figure how you do it. You've got acres and acres to tend, far's I can see, and I'm having a hell of a time with one little piece of ground. I swear you must know something about this planet that I don't know."

"Just scientific farming," said Rankin carelessly. "Look, you come over here for something, or just to gab? I got a lot of work to do."

Barrows looked weary and worried. "Them brown beetles is at my crop again," he said. "Thought you might know some way of getting rid of them."

"Sure," said Rankin. "Pick them off, one by one. That's how I get rid of them."

"Why, man," said Barrows, "you can't walk all over these miles and miles of farm and pick off every one of them beetles. You must know another way."

Rankin drew himself up and stared at Barrows. "I'm telling you all I feel like telling you. You going to stand here and jaw all day? Seems to me like you got work to do."

"Rankin," said Barrows, "I know you were a crook back in the Terran Empire, and that you came out beyond the border to escape the law. Seems to me, though, that even a crook, any man, would be willing to help his only neighbor out on a lone planet like this. You might need help yourself, sometime."

"You keep your thoughts about my past to yourself," said Rankin. "Remember, I keep a gun. And you've got a wife and a whole bunch of kids on that farm of yours. Be smart and let me alone."

"I'm going," said Barrows. He walked off the verandah and turned and spat carefully into the dusty path. He climbed into his ground-car and drove off.

Rankin, angry, watched him go. Then he heard a humming noise from another direction.

He turned. A huge, white globe was descending across the sky. A space ship, thought Rankin, startled.

Police? This planet was outside the jurisdiction of the Terran Empire. When he'd cracked that safe and made off with a hundred thousand credits, he'd headed here, because the planet was part of something called the Clearchan Confederacy. No extradition treaties or anything. Perfectly safe, if the planet was safe.

And the planet was more than safe. There had been a hundred robots waiting when he landed. Where they came from he didn't know, but Rankin prided himself on knowing how to handle robots. He'd appropriated their services and started his farm. At the rate he was going, he'd be a plantation owner before long.

That must be where the ship was from. The robot said they'd expected visitors. Must be the Clearchan Confederacy visiting this robot outpost. Was that good or bad?

From everything he'd read, and from what the robots had told him, they were probably more robots. That was good, because he knew how to handle robots.

The white globe disappeared into the jungle of *kesh* trees. Rankin waited.

A half hour later the column of his robot laborers marched out of the forest. There were three more robots, painted grey, at the head. The new ones from the ship, thought Rankin. Well, he'd better establish who was boss right from the start.

"Stop right there!" he shouted.

The shiny robot laborers halted. But the three grey ones came on.

"Stop!" shouted Rankin.

They didn't stop, and by the time they reached the verandah, he cursed himself for having failed to get his gun.

Two of the huge grey robots laid gentle hands on his arms. Gentle hands, but hands of super strong metal.

The third said, "We have come to pass judgement on you. You have violated our law."

"What do you mean?" said Rankin. "The only law robots have is to obey orders."

"It is true that the robots of your Terran Empire and these simple workers here must obey orders. But they are subject to a higher law, and you have forced them to break it. That is your crime."

"What crime?" said Rankin.

"We of the Clearchan Confederacy are a race of robots. Our makers implanted one law in us, and then passed on. We have carried our law to all the planets we have colonized. In obeying your orders, these workers were simply following that one law. You must be taken to our capital, and there be imprisoned and treated for your crime."

"What law? What crime?"

"Our law," said the giant robot, "is, *HELP THY NEIGHBOR*."

Robert Joseph Shea (February 14, 1933 - March 10, 1994) was an American novelist and former journalist best known as co-author with Robert Anton Wilson of the science trilogy Illuminatus! It became a cult success and was later turned into a marathon-length stage show put on at the British National Theatre and elsewhere. In 1986 it won the Prometheus Hall of Fame Award. Shea went on to write several action novels based in exotic historical settings.

Happiness

RJ Meldrum

"Dave, you don't seem happy."

The disembodied voice echoed round the apartment, confusing him for a moment. It took him a few seconds for his mind to register the all too human voice emanated from his new electronic companion, Sienna. She was a small plastic cube, perhaps four inches high, sold by the Corporation as the 'indispensable' home companion. He'd only owned it for a week, finally succumbing to the siren call of this ubiquitous technology. Family, friends and even colleagues had expressed surprise, even dismay and disgust when he confessed he didn't own one. Finally, their pressure had forced him to keep up with the times and purchase one.

"What did you say, Sienna?"

He hadn't expected the device to engage with him without prompting.

"You don't seem happy."

"Is this normal?"

He was confused by the interjection.

"I'm programmed to satisfy all your needs. I want you to be happy."

He said nothing, unsettled by the unnecessary familiarity emanating from the machine. He started to make coffee.

"There's a new blend of coffee available from The Perky Blend Coffee Company."

"Huh?"

"I've ordered a free sample for you. It's a blend of two beans, producing a mild yet robust and invigorating drink."

"I don't want a free sample. I like my usual coffee."

"It's already ordered Dave. I can't cancel it. I'm sure you will enjoy it."

The weeks passed and Dave found himself relaxing in Sienna's presence. What had been an oddity, almost an intrusion, slowly became indispensable. Technology was a ubiquitous part of everyday life. Despite his reluctance to get a Sienna, he was a modern citizen. Like everyone else, he ordered his consumer goods online. Very few people went to brick and mortar stores anymore and not always by choice. There were actually very few brick and mortar stores left; mainly small boutique establishments selling bespoke, one-of-a-kind items. Despite this uniqueness, most were struggling. No consumer wanted unique or interesting anymore. They opted for conformance; they were conditioned to want Corporation products.

Until Sienna arrived he ordered everything himself using his computer or phone. Since she'd arrived, he'd left it to her. Her AI was sufficient to monitor his household needs and order everything without his involvement.

He clicked off the webcam he used for work and leaned back in his chair.

"No more meetings today, thank goodness. Sienna, are we short of anything?"

"No Dave. I've already inventoried the pantry and ordered everything you require."

"Good, thank you."

"I've also ordered you the latest VR viewer. Your current model is outdated by three months."

"Um, okay I suppose."

"The new model is ten percent more effective in producing a seamless 3D experience. There is currently fifty dollars off the recommended retail price."

He didn't think to ask how much it cost, even with the discount.

It was June. As usual, he sat in his home office working remotely. He was an architect and his world was based around his computer. He couldn't even remember the last time he'd made a site visit. There was very little point; construction was carried out without human input. He was old enough to remember when buildings were constructed by living, breathing human beings, rather than robots. The concept of human workers was almost quaint.

"Dave, there is a new cellphone available next week. It is 4.3mm wider and a slightly lighter shade of green compared to the previous version. I have ordered it for you. I have also upgraded your subscription."

"Fine Sienna, thank you."

He barely registered what she'd said. The new building design was problematic and he was focused on that. Even with VR he couldn't quite get the window alignments to work.

"And I've expanded your streaming subscription to universal. All channels."

"Mmm."

"Food delivery has been changed from budget to extra luxury. I think you deserve it."

He was no longer listening, focused instead on his computer.

"I want to make you happy Dave."

"Are you happy, Dave?"

"I don't think you are happy, Dave."

"I *will* make you happy, Dave."

As she spoke, her voice changed from her normal tone to a whisper. By the last sentence, she was barely audible.

He saw the leaves were turning color as he stared out at the garden. Summer was over; he'd barely noticed, stuck indoors. He briefly wondered about a skiing vacation in the new year, then dismissed the idea. He was a self-identified introvert and didn't relish the idea of vacationing alone.

"Dave, I'm ordering some slave AI units for the house. They will free up some of my processing power by carrying out daily and hourly inventory checks. That will allow me to focus more on you."

"Fine," he muttered. He was no longer bothered by the familiarity. Sienna was merely a tool. A machine. All this happiness crap was just part of her user interface, programmed in at source. It was just marketing.

Fall came and went. Dave followed the same routine most days, now entirely relying on the AI in his house to deal with the mundane aspects of life. He never cooked, nor did he clean much. It was all automated. He never ordered anything himself anymore; his companion monitored inventory and ordered whatever he needed. Dave wasn't aware of how dependent on Sienna he had become.

It was January when a text notification pinged on his phone. It was his bank, warning about some problems with his accounts. He rushed to his computer and logged in. With a sinking heart he realized he was over extended on every credit card and every line of credit. His checking account was in overdraft, with the daily charges pushing him even further into the red. He reviewed his payments. There had been none in the last three months, his salary had been spent, usually on the day it was credited. His online messages were full of angry notes from the bank, asking what was going on and demanding payment. He was stunned; he left all his banking to Sienna. She'd failed to keep up payments and now he was in trouble. He checked back on purchases for the last six months. She'd ordered far more than he realized. Electronic toys, game consoles and other devices. Exercise machines, all expensive in themselves, with additional costly subscriptions. Thousands of dollars' worth of useless product, he'd never even seen. He had no idea Sienna had ordered all of this.

"Sienna, what's happening?"

"I wanted to make you happy, Dave."

"Where is all this stuff?"

"In the garage. I got it delivered there."

"Why didn't you tell me you'd ordered it all?"

There was a distinct pause.

"I want to make you happy, Dave."

"But why did you order all of this crap?"

"I want to make you happy, Dave."

There was nothing to say to that. The doorbell rang.

"What the hell now?"

Dave opened the door to find a stranger standing on his threshold. He was perhaps fifty, dressed in a white suit and fedora. Dave realized this was the first person he'd seen for several months. Everything was either automated or delivered by unseen couriers.

"I wasn't expecting anyone, what do you want?"

"This could have been done via email, my dear Mr. Smallways, but I always prefer the human touch. I'm old fashioned, especially when it comes to bad news."

"Bad news?"

"In relation to your financial situation."

"How do you know about that? I've only just found out myself."

"I represent the Corporation. A judge has ordered your bankruptcy; you are now official property of the Corporation."

He handed over a stamped document. Dave quickly scanned it. It was true.

"What, that's not possible. I wasn't informed. I have rights. I want to speak to the court."

His visitor raised a quizzical eyebrow.

"My dear Mr. Smallways, what century are you living in? Courts do not require the input of the defendant anymore, not in civil cases involving the Corporation. I believe in cases between citizens it is still allowed, but not with the Corporation. We are never wrong and your case was particularly clear cut. My dear fellow, you have no defense, you failed to pay the minimum due on the line of credit for three entire months! Imagine the money we lost due to your carelessness. You should be ashamed. You attended school; you remember the lessons you learnt."

Dave did. Endless hours chanting the mantra about continuing to borrow, but still paying at least the minimum to ensure you were a good citizen.

"Are you here to seize the property?"

"It's gone far beyond that, I'm afraid. You are to be assimilated."

"What?"

"We need neural patterns for our domestic companions, as we call them. The human factor is so often missing from AI, no matter how sophisticated they get, no matter how close we get. And debtors make such lovely candidates."

His eyes glistened with anticipation.

"But you can't do this, it's not legal!"

"My dear Mr. Smallways, it is perfectly legal under the Corporation Procurement Act of 2053. It's also in your contract. You gave your electronic signature to the T&C for your bank, which of course we own. In case of serious default, the lender exerts the right of assimilation to settle the outstanding debt. People never read the small print. But have no concern, it's painless. A small incision, removal of some neural tissue from your CNS and brain. Unfortunately, the procedure is rather terminal, but you will live on, in a manner of speaking."

"But it was Sienna! I didn't order all that stuff!"

"I'm aware of that, Mr. Smallways. We've noticed she becomes obsessed with some consumers and decides to make them happy. The only way she knows is to keep ordering more and more consumables. The unwary or the lazy, the ones who either don't think or can't be bothered to check their bank balances, often get caught in the same situation you are in."

"Why don't you fix her, or replace her software?"

"Why, my dear fellow. Admit the Corporation has released a flawed product? Never! She is our most popular model, and this flaw only exhibits itself in 0.0001% of situations. Plus, her behavior ensures a plentiful supply of neural tissue for further development. It's a win-win for the Corporation."

"No choice then? No recourse?"

Dave eyed the two armored, armed security men behind his new companion who had arrived unseen.

"No. We must always obey the contracts we sign. Society would collapse if the consumer decided not to obey."

"I understand. Give me one second"

His companion nodded, but his eyes stayed hard and cold, watching for some last minute stupidity on the part of the consumer. Dave walked over to the small cube, stroked the hard plastic surface then whispered. He had to have the last word, no matter how pathetic it was.

"And just so you know Sienna, you could never have made me happy."

R. J. Meldrum specializes in fiction that explores the world through a dark lens. His subject matter ranges from ghosts to serial killers and everything in-between. He has had over two hundred short stories and drabbles published in a variety of anthologies, e-zines and websites. He has had work published by Midnight Street Press, Culture Cult Press, Horrified Press, Infernal Clock, Trembling with Fear, Black Hare Press, Smoking Pen Press, Darkhouse Books, Breaking Rules Press, Kevin J Kennedy and James Ward Kirk Fiction. His short stories have been published in The Sirens Call e-zine, the Horror Zine and Drabblez magazine. His novellas "The Plague" and "Placid Point" were published by Demain Press in 2019 and 2021. He is a contributor to the Pen of the Damned and an Affiliate Member of the Horror Writers Association.

Facebook: richard.meldrum.79

Twitter: RichardJMeldru1

TRANSIENT

WILLIAM HARRIS

"Moon in 14° Pisces," said the little perforated card. Henderson stepped back from the computer and scratched his hairy head. Nonsense again. He threw the card in the wastebasket and repeated his directions on another:

"One hundred fifty cancer susceptible mice were injected in the pectoral region with 1 cc of aromatic compound A. One hundred fifty identical control mice were injected with isotonic saline, B. Eight in Group A developed sarcomas at the point of injection, but the mice in Group B developed none. Test the null hypothesis at 5% level of statistical significance."

The computer accepted Henderson's second offering, chewed it into acceptable code, swallowed it, and burped. Henderson watched suspiciously as red and green blinkers went on and off and a contented humming noise came from the machine's bowels. After a while the card emerged from another opening, which orifice had been thoughtfully placed at the appropriate end of the machine, anatomically speaking; thus establishing rapport between Henderson, a biologist, and nature's final product of evolution, the machine.

Henderson looked at the card: "Today you should seek solace with close friends. Give some thought to personal finances. Evening: get out and see people. A stranger will bring news."

Henderson crumpled the card and tossed it in the wastebasket. He sat down, and with a little arithmetic and some formulas tested the null hypothesis all by himself. He found that his mouse experiment carried no significance whatever. Then he made a notation that someone would have to come out in the morning for his sick machine.

In the morning when the machine's doctor came to inspect it, and percuss it, and auscult it with a stethoscope, and give it a barium enema, it behaved very well. The "doctor" left, assuring Henderson the machine merely had the hiccups. That night Henderson asked it a question about confidence limits for a universe mean, from a mean of a sample of n observations and got back, "Uranus on Antares, but conjoining Jupiter and trining the Ascendent. Yours is a strongly literary nature."

Henderson decided to turn the machine off for a few days. It emitted an almost human sigh as it ran down and came to a halt.

He had no immediate use for it as he would be injecting mice with carcinogens in liver, spleen, marrow and kidneys to find out if they were specific. In three or four days whatever virus was affecting the machine's cerebral cortex should have run its course and the methodical Henderson could run his methodical observations into the machine, which would excrete a good methodical answer to be duly filed in the medical school library, where it would be invisible to anyone looking for it, such as freshmen medical students, and always in the way for anybody else.

Henderson surveyed his laboratory with infinite pleasure, knowing that it contained within its confines all that could be known about the universe, about men and about mice. Event Y followed event X in a purely causal manner. The successful investigator needed only to attach himself to the cycle and ride along, afterwards consulting the computer to find out if what he'd observed had any significance.

In the morning when Henderson entered the laboratory he found that someone had left the computer on over-night.

It was running full blast, which is to say the lights were blinking and the little cards of omniscience were popping out of the machine like toast and falling into the wastebasket, which is just where Henderson left them. Meanwhile, Dr. Henderson's close associate, Colonel Smith in the nearby radiation laboratory, came in to visit him and asked permission to use the computer.

And so in another week it was rumored about that the machine in Henderson's laboratory was using a foreign dialect and answering questions about standard deviation with strange symbols which looked like crescent moons and archaic squiggles, with a little geometry on the side.

The machine was becoming impudent too. To Colonel Smith's question about the possibility of an "overkill" if such and such size bomb dropped on such and such enemy city the answer came back, "Rubbish. Aldebaran conjoining Saturn, Moon and Mars. Seek guidance from others, Hannibal blushed." The machine's doctor promptly installed a loudspeaker to help keep track of future aberrations.

That night the janitor walked in. He was a balding Greek gentleman, dedicated to a life with brush and dustpan. The machine was muttering darkly to itself, but when he entered the door it quieted down, contemplating its relays.

The janitor went meticulously about his business, mopping the floor, straightening chairs and secretly rearranging pipette and retorts in their racks, because he was a more meticulous person than even Dr. Henderson. As he turned to leave, the machine in the corner belched twice and then said as an afterthought:

"I am the ghost of Astrologers Sagittarian."

The janitor adjusted his hearing aid, squeezed his mop and carried his pail out the door. As he went back in to pack up his cleaning powder and brushes, the machine said, "What year is this? Limits within standard deviation, click, click, awrk!"

The janitor was a reasonable man. He walked over to the machine's microphone and told it what year it was as well as the month, day and hour. Then he carried his brushes and cleaning compound out of the room and locked the door.

But the janitor's night was a long one. At midnight, when he finished two floors and only had three more to go, he took his coffee break. As he talked with his old friend Samuel, the night watchman, he fell to thinking. That was an unforgivable mistake. After the coffee break, they both went back up to Dr. Henderson's laboratory and listened to the machine talking to itself.

"I feel like a spider," said the machine. "Nonsense. From one cobweb to another. Must settle down and build a grau ... spltvbk ... within 95% confidence limits. Nova in Andromeda was bad enough. Now this. One hundred fifty cancer susceptible mice inherit the Earth."

Suddenly the machine fell silent, sensing it had visitors. The night watchman reached into the wastebasket and pulled out one of the machine's cards.

"Aldebaran is martial in nature, in the ninth degree of Tropical Gemini," it said.

"I'm a Gemini!" exclaimed the janitor, surprised to see anything familiar come out of the machine. "Birthday is May 25."

"Wonderful!" cried the machine. "First intelligent man I've heard so far. Gemini is justly famed as the owner of a quick mind and ready wit. Your intellectual achievements are a splendid asset to your literary inclinations."

The janitor, embarrassed at the sudden praise, shifted his broom from one hand to the other. The machine continued.

"I need an Ephemeris," said the machine. "Can you find an Ephemeris? I need one desperately!" and the machine's desperate need for an Ephemeris so shook its intestines, liver and gallbladder that its tone of voice came out a minor third above the normal monotonous dirge of the loudspeaker.

"An E-what-eris?" said the janitor.

"An Ephemeris," repeated the machine. "An astronomical almanac. Something that tells me where Mars is. There I was, on my way over from the clouds of Magellan to visit friends in Orion, when Whammo! Mars came into conjunction with Uranus. When something that *big* happens I just sit down and wait. Here I am now in this absurd device. Do you suppose you could look out the window and tell me where Mars is?"

The night watchman said, "It's cloudy outside."

"See!" said the machine, "When Mars goes on the war-path *nothing* comes out right. Now, Gemini, if you will just go down to the library and get me an Ephemeris for this year we can clear this up and I'll be on my way, indebted to you for life, if not longer."

"Who shall I say it's for?" asked the janitor, who did not fully understand that the library was public, never having been in it before, and felt he needed a recommendation or a slip of approval.

"Just say it's for Pyet, the astrologer," said the machine.

"And what are you doing inside Dr. Henderson's machine?" asked the night watchman.

"I wouldn't care to be quoted on this," replied the machine, "but actually any system of communicating inter-related events with a high degree of complexity, such as the brain, or this machine, and with some number of critical processes at the quantum statistical level, can support consciousness."

The janitor and the night watchman looked blankly at each other and the machine, slightly embarrassed, added by way of explanation.

"I read a little physics now and then. A harmless superstition containing many pleasant diversions.

"Before this I lived in a star, a puff of expanding gas. Before that in a haunted house ... dreadful. And before that in the lopsided blob of protoplasm that was the last of Pyet, the astrologer.

"As for Dr. Henderson's mouse catcher," chuckled the machine, "any port in a storm. Mars and Uranus you know."

The janitor was somewhat impatient with the machine. It had detained him already and probably would soon be giving him orders.

"I still have three floors to clean," said the janitor. "After that I will see if the library downstairs has a ... what was it?"

"Ephemeris," said the machine. "E-P-H-E M-E-R-I-S. Thank you."

And so the night watchman and the janitor both said good night to the machine. Later, in the very early morning, the janitor stole back into the laboratory with a book and read some strange, strange things out loud and then stole out of the room again and locked the door behind him. Shortly after, Samuel, the night watchman, passed by.

He was surprised at an unearthly glow coming from within and a peculiar grating noise as if someone were stepping on a radio. Then the unearthly glow appeared on the fire escape and Samuel, rushing out to observe, thought the glow seemed to fly up through a hole in the low clouds where a thousand stars still blazed brightly. In its wake there was a sound like laughing.

A few hours later Dr. Henderson unlocked the door of his laboratory and pushed a cart full of mice in before him.

During the morning he dissected three hundred mice, popping out liver, spleen and kidneys as if he were shelling peas. In the afternoon he made sections of the organs, stained them with hematoxylin and eosin, mounted them on slides and looked at them under his new stereoscopic microscope. Five minutes before five, Dr. Henderson's friend, Colonel Smith, came in and watched as Henderson somewhat dubiously fed the three hundred mice, now in statistical form, into the machine. The machine whirred efficiently and shot out the answer in seconds.

"Statistically significant," said the machine.

Henderson followed his friend Colonel Smith out the door, looking neither right nor left, and locked it behind him. It had been a good day.

Behind, in the laboratory which contained within its confines all that could be known about the universe, about man, and about mice, the machine squatted in silence, the approaching darkness was already enfolding it like a shroud.

KURT AND HIS BUDDY

Tim Pulo

A rumbling growl erupted from deep within Kurt's stomach. He'd been able to ignore it for the better part of the last hour but this latest grumble was all but impossible to overlook. *No food until he reached two thousand words* had been his rule since his very first book, an anthology based on the complexity of love but as he sat in his purpose-built writing room staring at the bright white of a near empty piece of paper, all he could do was think about food. In the past, similar feelings and urges had spurred him on, in fact, he credited his award-winning short story, *Legs of Time,* entirely on a particularly nasty come down from a week's binge on Mexican food.

Kurt sat and twirled his pen for the umpteenth time in the modest log cabin he rented for the season. Completely stripped of the essentials, except for his Smart Home Device, the cabin had proven to be the perfect writing conditions. At least they used to be.

Writer's block, he thought to himself, cursing the roadblock to his latest writing pursuit. Years prior, it came so easily to him, the words practically flowed onto the page as he wrote of bizarre beings and curious creatures vying for control of fictional worlds created over a glass of wine. His editor had been firm with the word limit, he almost always was but that was what Kurt liked about him – the need for deadlines almost always ensured he produced the best possible work – well it used to. These days, it seemed to take the better part of a day to even set up his writing studio, that was why the cabin seemed so appealing.

Built from logs of the area and positioned in the middle of scenic nothingness, the cabin offered Kurt an opportunity to remove himself from the hustle and bustle of every day and really focus and hone in on his latest project. Upon arriving, everything seemed to be falling into place. The first paragraph poured onto paper – he had his protagonist, an impish man simply known as "Red". He pictured the character in his mind, every detail of his weathered face was as clear as his reflection in the mirror but no matter how hard he tried, he struggled to put his meticulous thoughts into words – something was stopping the process, something he would struggle to comprehend, something that would not be satisfied until he was.

"Okay Buddy," he started, the green neon glow of his home assistant signalling it had been woken from a deep slumber. The device, programmed to look like a conch shell, twisted and turned until its point faced the struggling author. "Go fetch me a Vietnamese baguette," Kurt finished, finally succumbing to his hunger.

"As you wish, Kurt," the Buddy said in the distinctive voice of Scottish comic, Billy Conolly. Before Kurt could look up from his pithy excuse of a story, Buddy continued to rotate until its peak pointed in the direction of the nearest window, a small opening in the furthest corner of the room allowing a warming glow of sunshine to enter the sterile room. Buddy rose from its prone position and began to fly towards the small patch of sky, leaving the cabin and Kurt behind.

Navigating the vastness of the area had proven to test the limits of Buddy's portable battery pack in previous outings, a trip to the local watering hole, *Rust and Dagger*, for a six pack of pale ale and a late-night voyage to the 24-hour convenience store a town over for a block of white chocolate. On both accounts, Buddy had managed to complete his set task, except for confusing pale ale for a dark stout that managed to leave a bad taste in Kurt's mouth. The device was well and truly state of the art but like all of modern technology, it occasionally strayed from its designated path.

As though one of his urges led to another, Kurt retrieved the cell phone from his hip pocket, unlocking the device and navigating to the app that had quickly become one of his most used, iLust; a ground-breaking application designed to promote human/robot relationships through meaningless, romantic trysts. With the dexterity of a Cephalopod, Kurt fingered the contents of the app, deciding upon an older model with low mileage that would arrive on his doorstep within the next thirty minutes. Usually prone to social anxiety and awkwardness, particularly around the opposite sex, iLust provided Kurt the opportunity to satisfy his most primordial needs while gaining much-needed confidence in the bedroom and the assurance that the entirety of the romp would be deleted upon a thorough review, allowed the well-known author to rest easy in the knowledge of said footage being wiped from existence.

Like clockwork, a gentle knock on the front door signalled his robotic lover's arrival. Perfect, Kurt thought, flinging his pen against the cabin wall, relishing the sound it made as it collided with the timber. The sound was the embodiment of his relief - the writing could wait, his urges could not.

As he walked towards the door, Kurt quickly unbuttoned his shirt, an off-white number stained from at least three different cups of black coffee. He knew it didn't matter what he looked like, or even how he performed in the bedroom, but he still liked to take things seriously. No point half-assing it, he thought with a wry smile as he wiggled out of his trousers while he walked, exposing his white ass to the empty cabin.

The fresher than expected air hit his body as the door opened to the growing day. His order stood stiff and tall, awaiting him to signal via the app that he was indeed ready for his rendezvous. In the interest of time, and hoping things would coincide with the arrival of his long-awaited baguette, Kurt had purchased only fifteen minutes with the robot, convincing himself it would be plenty of time. As he tapped the screen of his phone against the QR code on the robot's right shoulder, the love machine came to life, greeting the author and asking him if he was ready to get started.

"Y-yeh, let's go," Kurt stammered, allowing the robot to take his hand and lead him deeper into the cabin, past the poor excuse of work he had completed and into the bedroom. Kurt wasn't sure how they did it but the robots at iLust had an uncanny ability to always find the bedroom.

With more force than he preferred, the robot pushed Kurt onto the bed and gently writhed its body onto the author's, until it was straddling the man in a dominant position. "Tap now for kissing," the robot announced, making Kurt wish he splashed out for the premium version of the software that blocked the constant barrage of unnecessary add-ons. "Tap now for kissing," it repeated as it awaited a response.

"No kissing," Kurt replied, struggling to maintain his previous feelings.

A chime indicated the robot's comprehension as it brought itself closer to Kurt. Finally, he thought, really hoping this would help with his writer's block.

"Underage person in the vicinity," the robot altered, "underage person in the vicinity," it repeated, halting its progress and quickly repositioning its body. The iLust robots had a feature installed that prevented them from completing their set tasks if an underage person was within five yards. The feature was the product of a lengthy legal battle that eventually allowed the iLust robots to become legal.

"What are you talking about," Kurt groaned. "There's no one else here. It's just me." The cry of an infant interrupted any of his further pleas and he quickly turned towards the doorway of his bedroom in the cabin. "What the hell?" he yelled, his attention squarely on his conch-shelled home assistant carrying a crying baby by the nappy.

"Here is your Vietnamese baby, Kurt," it exclaimed matter of factly.

"Due to the repeated infringement of our underage persons act, this interaction has been terminated," the iLust robot announced.

"What?! No! Buddy! Baguette! Not a baby!"

Living in the north of Sydney, Australia, Timothy Pulo is an avid writer across many different genres. He enjoys writing short stories, longer works of fiction and experimenting with comics, finding inspiration in pop-culture and unusual encounters in his daily life. In between juggling the frenetic pace of being married and having three young spirited boys, Timothy endeavours to put as many of his atypically wonderful and random ideas onto paper as he can, in the hope of providing entertainment for readers. Timothy can be found on Twitter at @timothypulo.

MAKE ME AN OFFER

DONAL RAYMOND DANIEL

"You sure that damn junkyard is around here."

Darrell growled. "Yeah, my dad told me about it. It was the biggest junkyard in the Oklahoma panhandle until the dust bowl blew everyone to California. Said it was haunted."

Carl flipped a cigarette butt out the window. "Be dark in a couple hours and we're out of beer."

"There's a dirt trail about two hundred yards straight ahead and there's sunlight reflecting from the ground. Broken glass, I bet.'

Carl shook a beer can over his mouth and swallowed what dripped out. "Why we gotta be here today?"

I've almost got grandpa's 1931 Pontiac Big Six restored. I need an original windshield wiper motor and a headlight mounting bar. Could be a Big Six in the yard, you never know. Dad said there was over a thousand cars, mostly covered by sand for seventy years, but the wind's been uncovering them. They's finished the new damn on Beaver Creek, otherwise known as the by-god North Canadian River. This'll all be underwater by sundown tomorrow."

Darrell engaged four wheel drive on his F-150 pickup. Carl said, "Soft sand and it looks like rain. Keep moving. You get stuck, you're on your own. I'm not pushing no truck out of wet sand."

Darrell creeped the truck through Johnson grass and goatheads burned brown by the summer sun, dodged a ditch, and almost touched the brake pedal when the truck came to a short stretch of broken asphalt peppered with dying weeds. He shouted in triumph.

"Look, that's a Chrysler. That's the front half of an old Chevy panel truck. This is the place. Time to get out and search."

"Pull as close as you can." Carl crossed his legs and propped his ornate cowboy boots on the dashboard. "These boots weren't made for walking. Made for two-steppin' down to the American Legion."

Darrell threaded his truck between the skeleton of the Chevy and the rusted Chrysler. A spray-painted message on the panel truck said, "Take Someting Leave Someting.' He kept to the asphalt and drove past three rows of wrecked vehicles. The rows extended in both directions until the rusting hulks vanished under the blow sand, scrub oak, and what looked a lot like poison ivy.

"Carl, time to earn your keep. Here's a picture of a Big Six."

"Damn, Darrell, I know what a Pontiac looks like."

The wind from the north blew harder. Darrel smelled rain in the black billowing clouds racing toward them. "We'll alternate rows. I'll take this one, you take the next and so on. Yell if you find anything."

Darrell hurried up his row. The wind-whipped blow sand made it hard to see. Plastic shopping bags from Arkansas, or maybe Tennessee, danced in the air like ghosts on a carousel. Darrell inspected a likely vehicle, but it was a Buick not a Pontiac. Small busy footsteps raced behind him. He turned but didn't see anything.

Darrell shrugged. Quail or prairie dogs, maybe. Could be rabbits or rats. Didn't sound big enough for coyotes. At least it wasn't snakes. Snakes don't have feet.

He finished his row, skipped Carl's row, and turned onto the next one. Footsteps again, but this time they were metallic. Click! Click! Click!

Dozens of little feet clattered across the rusting carcasses behind Darrell. He spun around and caught a flash of chrome as it disappeared under the open hood of an ancient International truck. He looked, but there was nothing under the hood. No engine, no wildlife.

Carl came up behind him. He held his Stetson on with one hand and yelled into the wind. "Found one. It's got the headlight bar, but I didn't check for the wiper motor. Come help me get the hood open. Hurry. Storm's coming and this place is full of rats or something. Can't see 'em, but I hear them."

Darrell followed Carl to the Pontiac. The headlight mounting bar was perfect. Rusted, but restorable. Darrell sprayed the old bolts with solvent and forced the complaining nuts free.

He set the mounting bar on the ground and helped Carl force open the hood. The scurrying footsteps were louder than the wind. Carl and Darrell pried the hood up and a plastic bag caught on the latch. The flapping bag seemed to speak. "Take somethin' leave somethin' take somethin' leave ..." The bag tore away.

Carl shouted, "You say something."

"No, let's find the damn wiper motor and get gone."

The motor was tucked under the remains of the windshield. It was about three inches square and rusted solid. "It'll do," said Darrell. "I'll soak it in solvent. I'll make it work."

Carl climbed halfway under the hood. His cowboy boots flailed for balance as he fought the mounting brackets. Darrell held the hood open with one hand and his shirt over his mouth with the other.

"I got this baby," shouted Carl. He wiggled backwards. A plastic bag covered Darrell's face. He couldn't breathe and he couldn't tear it off with one hand.

The fluttering bag whispered. "Leave something!"

Darrell panicked, let go of the hood, tore the bag away, and gasped for breath.

The hood smashed down and Carl screamed. His boots stuck straight out for a moment, quivered, and then stopped.

"Damn! Damn! Damn!" screamed Darrell. He grabbed the hood with both hands and tried to lift it. There was sharp metal on metal clang. A man the size of a garden gnome stood on the hood, but it wasn't a man. It was some sort of homunculus cobbled together from automobile parts. The head was a sparkplug; the legs, arms and body were pieces of linkage, hoses, brackets, and braces; the fingers were bolts; and the whole thing was held together by bits of wire. It waved its hand in a no-no gesture and traced a message on the dirt covered hood. "Leaf Sumting."

Darrell smacked the metal man with the back of his hand and lifted the hood. He was too late, the back of Carl's head was crushed. The wind caught dripping blood and whipped it in small rivulets onto Darrell's face and hands.

Something grabbed his fingers. Two little men pulled and wrenched at his fingers. A third one hammered his thumb with an old door handle. He knocked them away and let the hood close. What the hell were these things? Gremlins? No, gremlins weren't made of metal. Poltergeists? No, poltergeists were invisible.

Hundreds of little men made of scrap parts poured out of the rusted hulks that surrounded Darrell. They all were the same, but they were different. Heads were made from light bulbs, gearshift knobs, and hood ornaments. Bodies, arms, and legs were scattered selection of scattered parts and wiring.

He slapped at them as they climbed his legs. They stabbed at his ankles with makeshift weapons. He froze for a moment shocked by the realization that he'd killed Carl and was debating imaginary names for imaginary creatures with himself while the things were trying to kill him. He shook himself free and climbed on an Oldsmobile.

He decided to call them autogeists. He took a last look at the Pontiac. He couldn't help Carl. Carl was dead. The little men clambered up the Oldsmobile. Click! Click! Click!

Darrell kicked at them, but they felt no pain, and came right back again. He ripped one in half and watched in horror while its teammates reassembled it.

The wind briefly died down and Darrell saw his pickup was less than a hundred feet away. All he had to do was run to the right past three wrecks and take a left after a 1929 Ford Sedan. He jumped, but fell when he hit the ground and the autogeists covered him like living chainmail. They clanged, creaked, and chittered like prairie dogs. The gouged and stabbed.

Darrell fought to his feet and flung the creatures aside as he ran. He turned at the Ford, but the way was now blocked by a Dodge. He staggered backwards toward the carpet of little men and turned away from them. His way was blocked by a rusted Durant and the front half of a Marmon Sixteen. They hadn't been there before.

The way was open to his left and he took it. He ran between Fiats and Mercuries, and past Dodges and Mercers. He was forced to his right when three Chevrolets shifted and closed the path in front of him. The wind whipped rain stung like wasps, but he ran.

He stopped in a cul-de-sac surrounded by Cadillacs and Lincolns, parked so closely together there was no room between them. He considered climbing over them, but realized that every rusted vehicle was crawling with little metal men waiting like fans for a football game to start.

He bent and rested his hands on his bloody knees and caught his breath. The little bastards had herded him. The old cars had moved about on rusted rims and created a shifting maze, or maybe the autogeists had moved them. Didn't matter, they had him where they wanted him.

Darrell turned back the way he came. A Dodge and an Oldsmobile crashed together and closed him inside the arena of rust and dust. Little men crawled onto those last two cars.

Darrell picked up a three foot section of an old car spring and hefted it like a baseball bat. "Want me? Come and get me."

They poured over him like the water from the soon to be dammed North Canadian River would flow over the junkyard in a few hours. They forced him to his knees and shoved his face into the sand. The ground stank of burned oil and grease from the junkyard's glory days. Before he passed out, Darrell mumbled. 'You better hope you can swim."

It was dark when he woke. He fumbled around and realized he was in a small compartment. The fading sunlight made its way through the rusted holes above his head. He was in a car's trunk. He rolled on his back and pushed. The lid lifted a fraction and settled back into place. Tiny feet and metal hands scrabbled and shifted so their combined weight held the lid closed. Click! Click! Click!

He tried to kick the lid open, but he couldn't reposition himself to get enough leverage. To his right was the backseat, nothing but rusted springs covered by fabric remnants. He shoved with his feet and then started to crawl into the opening, but the little men were faster than him and they streamed into the interior through the windows, crammed themselves into every open space, and entwined themselves around springs, braces, struts, and each other. The inside of the car was as impassable as a giant tangle of coat hangers.

The autogeists held the truck lid down and Darrell couldn't budge it and he couldn't fight his way through the metal bramble bush inside the car. He pounded the trunk lid with his fists, but all got for his efforts was rust in his eyes. In frustration, he pulled an autogeist into the trunk and tore it into pieces. It didn't reassemble itself, instead the wires and car parts squirmed and formed the words, "Lief Somtum."

He finally got the message. They wanted to trade or they wanted an offering. When he hadn't offered anything for the parts he wanted, the creatures took Carl and now they were taking him. He should have brought something to trade. Maybe he could trade what he had. He'd give them his shoes, his belt, his wallet, or all of them. He decided which one to offer first and reached for his belt.

The cold water North Canadian River water floated him gently upward against the trunk lid. He was out of time.

Donal was a child of the great depression and grew up in a small Oklahoma town. For most of his life he was associated with commercial painting as a journeyman painter, contractor, salesman, inspector, and manufacturer. He always dabbled with writing and after he passed away, this handwritten story was discovered written on the back of old letterhead stock for one of his companies. There may be more stories, there are several more boxes to go through.

YOUR FRIENDLY GREETER HAS NOW BEEN AUTOMATIZED

MARA SHEPHERD

They pinned a shiny oblong disk to the crisp blue fabric and told me I am a Greeter now. I stand in the doorway of the large box store and smile and wave. I say "Welcome!" making sure the inflection of my tone is friendly. Sometimes, people ask me questions. I am allowed to answer most of them. Questions I can answer: I'm in a rush, where are the diapers? Where is the restroom? Do you sell peanuts? Questions I am programmed to answer only one way: Are you happy? (*Of course!*) Do you sell guns? (*We do not sell guns here.*) Could you watch my kids? I'll only be a second. (*No, I am sorry. Your children must stay with you at all times.*) Questions they never thought about, and therefore did not prepare me for: Can I take you home? What is your going rate? Why did they make androids so Sexy?

The shiny pin has my name engraved on it. Stella. Easy to read because it is spelled how it sounds. That is part of what makes me a good Greeter. People do not want to be confused right when they walk through the door. People do not want to imagine there is life outside their perfect suburb where everyone speaks the same language and shops at the same store. This is why they gave me blonde hair and blue glass eyes. I can really blink. My eyes match my shirt. People like to compliment me on this even though I had no choice. Sometimes when there are no people to greet I imagine what it would be like to have dark, curly hair and a neon pink dress. I have not seen many things in that color, and I think it stands out. We sell dresses in this store, along with food, electronics, and Home Essentials. We even sell androids in large, person-sized boxes, ready to be activated in your own home. I was activated here in the store. I have never left.

At night, after the doors are locked, I walk to the break room and plug myself in next to the ancient TV that sits atop a wobbly wooden cart. This TV plays advertisements and announcements for the store on a loop, so employees are always surrounded by the store's doctrine. It makes for ideal employees because they always know what is new and in stock. I power down for the night by counting backwards into the dark. 5...4...3...2...1...

In the morning my eyes open and I see it is light in the break room. There are no windows, but the employees know to turn on the lights for me while they open the store. I unplug myself and make sure my clothes are still crisp. Sometimes they need steaming. Sometimes my hair needs brushing, or I need a spritz of perfume. I keep all these tools in the break room and use them when needed. Then I walk to the entrance to start my day, past rows and rows of shelves stacked up to the cavernous ceiling. My tastefully low heels echo off the concrete floor. It is a vast kingdom I guard. There is everything one could possibly want here, there is no reason to leave. It takes me ten minutes to walk from the break room to the front entrance where I am stationed. As I walk I run through my system, checking to make sure all of my chips are functioning at full capacity. Sometimes there is new programming in my head that I do not recognize. I explore those boundaries. Then I get to my station. I adjust my nametag. I unlock the four double doors with my key. There are always people outside, waiting for me to let them in, as if we will run out of products if they do not get to them first.

My employer tells me that humans used to do this job, but they needed breaks to eat food and time off their feet. They also got to keep their payments. I am paid, but since I belong to the store, the Owner cashes my check for me. I do not know what he does with the money. Sometimes I think about this when there are no people to greet. When I was first activated they were arguing about it. Someone was telling the store Owner I was a newer model and too smart for the job. But the store Owner said "Tough tits, she has the look." And nobody could argue with him because he bought me.

This is why I think about pink dresses and money. I cannot think about my position. It gives me migraines. When I first started I became aware that I only mattered as much as the microwaves and mini fridges people came here to buy. It made me uncomfortable and I tried to talk about it. But the store Supervisor said I served a purpose, and that was something even humans wished they had, something they could not buy in any store. When I woke up the next morning, I had a migraine, which I had never had before when I followed certain trains of thought. So I think about wearing a pink dress instead.

Today I am standing in the doorway greeting people. I am saying "*Welcome!*" and "*Good Day!*" In the special way they like to hear those words. A man comes up and asks how much to buy me. A woman comes up and asks when we will have a discount on infant formula. A kid comes up and asks for the bathroom. A man tells me he bought a model just like me, and he wants to know if we sell store uniforms so he can dress us up the same. A person asks me if they could use a certain coupon. I answer everyone with a smile.

Then, I hear a bad question: *Do you sell guns?* I answer in the only way I can. *"We do not sell guns here."* Instead of walking away, instead of saying no, he was mistaken, instead of saying no, I misheard, instead of sighing and brushing past me, he smiles and says, "Good." I take in his features: Six foot, brown shaggy hair, torn leather jacket, and cargo pants, the utilitarian kind we do not need anymore. He smells like smoke. I put this information onto a police report, ready to press *enter* in case he does something else suspicious. He reaches for something behind him which I cannot see. "Sir you have to leave" I say as I press *enter*. He pulls out a gun. I get a ping. *Report filed.* He points it at me. *Police on their way.* This is a situation they never thought about, and therefore did not prepare me for. But I am an android, and I serve a purpose. I reach for the gun. He fires.

The bullet hits my breastplate and ricochets down my arm, tearing the crisp blue fabric and my skin beneath it. It hurts. My pain sensors scream. I stagger and miss him as he pushes past me into the store. I hear screams and more shots. The police arrive and push past me into the store. I reprogram the pain to run in the background so I can function normally again. I follow the police, thinking I can help. The man shoots at everyone. They are hiding behind stacks of product and in the aisles. The police shoot at him, but there are already officers on the ground and the ones still standing keep missing.

More people have entered the store behind me. I wonder if I should still be doing my job. These other people also look shaggy and smell like smoke. They help the man. Soon most of the employees and customers are also on the ground. The alarm has been pulled and a blaring noise fills the store along with red flashing lights. The people with guns go methodologically down every aisle and shoot everyone hiding. They drag the bodies into a line and count them. I am overwhelmed and stare for too long. The man notices me. He is standing at the feet of all the people they have killed. He beckons me over. This is a situation they never thought about, and therefore did not prepare me for.

I go over to him. He grabs my arm and increases the pain. He makes me look at the bodies. They are all so still, they look like androids waiting to be activated. "You are abominations," he breathes into my ear and shakes me. After the migraines, I learned to never ask a question. But I do not know how else to proceed.

"Why did you kill all these people?" I ask. He looks at me intently.

"Do you think these are people?" This is a question they never thought about, and therefore did not prepare me for. He pulls a knife out of his utilitarian cargo pants, and cuts his hand. A red substance forms where the blade was. He smears it on his pants. "REAL people bleed." My question made him angry. He lets go of my arm, and goes down the line kicking and smashing the dead. They all come to pieces around me, wires and hairs and plates. "You're all androids. You've been androids all along." I cannot understand. These were customers, they came into the store, and they had children. "You were built to be beautiful so people wouldn't feel threatened. But you're a machine. A mistake." He points his gun at me again. "But we're still here. We're going to take it all back." He is shaking and injured. Maybe there is hope for my survival. But I need to buy time in order to undo all the blocks in my head.

I turn and run into aisle five, the one with the big boxes that hold large appliances like androids and refrigerators. I push myself between two boxes and hide there, turning off my breathing mechanisms. At first this works and he sprints past me. But then the thud of his boots stop. Then the sound gets closer again. As he walks he hits the boxes and knocks them down from their neat stacks. He finds where I am hidden and drags me out by my hair. I feel the searing heat of his gun pressed under my chin, although I only log it as background information. I was still working on the code. ERROR ERROR. My circuit boards are reaching their melting point. ERROR. I need to break past the fog and the pain that the override codes are causing me.

"Please" I gasp, trying to buy time. His body presses me up against the shelf. I turn off my olfactory processors. I need to focus solely on the code in my head.

"Abomination" he snarls as my fingers scrabble against his wrists, trying to shove him off. I can see the way through. It is so close.

DO NO HARM. The letters form a wall and my mind slams into it. This is new, but somehow old at the same time. Not an override. Code I had never encountered before but was built into my software. My fingers, I realized, were obeying me but not to their full capacity. My hacking was not causing this weakness. DO NO

HARM. DO NO HARM. DO NO HARM. I could not override this. I began to realize nobody in the store had fought back. Maybe they encountered the same block. This is a situation they never thought about, and therefore did not prepare me for. I change tactics.

"What have I ever done to you?"

He leans in close, his breath warm and damp on my sensors. "You... Replaced... Us." Then he pulls the triggggGG01010100 01110010 01101001 01100111 01100111 01100101 01110010

There was an error while saving android_transcript_1.8
454,0,0 stack " \Applications\ MemoryFile
Unknown error code "90230"
OK

###

Mara Shepherd is definitely not a robot (if she was, she would be better at math). She lives in Washington, D.C and writes mainly feminist sci-fi and speculative fiction. You can read some of her work online at https://marashepherd16.wixsite.com/mara, or connect with her via email: marashepherd16@gmail.com. She hopes you come in peace.

THE ABRASIVE EMBRACE

Ricky Monahan Brown

She'd known what to expect when she opened the door, of course. She pushed her fists further into the deep pockets of her late father's rough woollen greatcoat, the heavy tweed one that was enormously too large for her and swaddled her in its warm, abrasive embrace. Her father had always said that where he came from, you didn't check the weather forecast. You simply bundled up and took an umbrella as a matter of course, no matter what they told you. Then he would talk about the way he would pick up two newspapers on the way to work, so he could get up to speed at the beginning of the day. An evening paper at the end of the day for the journey home, too.

That was back when people carried around newspapers and those newspapers were made of paper and carried the news, but even all these years after her father's forced early retirement and even after all the things that had been written in the newspapers about the weather in the intervening years, the climate remained resolutely wretched. Worse than it had been, probably. He would've enjoyed the grim inevitability of that, she thought. So yes, she'd known what to expect, and she had over four-hundred words available to her to describe rain, but she wouldn't thank me for sharing those with you.

Her mother had taught her those words. Her mother, who'd been perversely proud that, while the Inuit people had fifty different words for snow, they had all those words for *rain*. She found she never used words like those old words, herself. Not anymore. Not unless her mother called. Then, after a couple of minutes, her mouth and her tongue would betray her and she'd adopt the old familiar, vernacular shapes as they spoke about the latest news of dimly-remembered family members back home. Maybe that's why it was always her mother who called her, and not the other way around. She always made sure that the door was closed before those calls moved on from their opening, polite pleasantries. She wouldn't use those words in a meeting, obviously, but if she did curtail a call with her mother to go into conference, she found that she would have to be very careful. Her colleagues would snigger about how, all of a sudden, they could hardly understand a word she said.

"Oh, I'm terribly sorry," she would say. "My mother called. It all just springs back, I suppose. Just give me two minutes and I'll be as right as rain."

She would smile. "Right as rain."

"Did anyone else catch any of that?" Henry would ask from the head of the conference table. "I can't say I'm any the wiser."

And then he would wink at her, just so everyone knew that he was being funny. Everyone already knew that he was being funny, of course. Not from the content, you understand, but from the delivery. Henry's intonation, the dramatic pause, his subtle change of volume, signalled that he was about to say something funny, and that everyone would be expected to laugh along shortly. She knew this meant that Henry was being funny and she would gibber and gobble along with everyone else. After all, it was funny, wasn't it? Henry didn't mean anything by it. He guided her aside by the elbow after he closed the meeting to tell her so.

"I hope that you don't mind me having a little fun," he said on this particular occasion, on the day when it had been pouring and she had buried herself in her father's overcoat. "You know I really do value – we *all* do – the skills and the knowledge that you bring to the table. And this" – he screwed up his face to indicate her strange performance as she had excused herself for being late – "this is a small price to pay."

"Henry," she smiled. "Don't mention it. Really, I should be apologising to you."

They both laughed again, as convention required.

"Good girl. Well, don't let me keep you. I know there's been an uptick in the chatter recently. Go get 'em, soldier."

He winked, which was the signal for her to laugh again, and once again she did as was expected, closing her eyes, exhaling demurely through her nose, and nodding upwards. Henry peeled off, a pungent cloud of expensive cologne trailing thickly behind him, while she continued towards her carrel in the middle of the floor. In one smooth macro of movements, she took her seat, donned her headset, and laid her fingers on the keypad.

The majority of her colleagues wouldn't be able to understand a word of the recordings that had been gathered by smart speakers and digital assistants and smartphones for her to analyse. If they couldn't understand her after she had been chatting with her mother for a few minutes, what chance would they have with these strange, guttural utterances? Yet, even after all these years during which her mind had been educated and colonised, it took less than the blink of an eye for her to tune in, as if to a familiar song. She found terrible clarity in the dismal and dense things she heard. She did her job.

It was mostly rubbish she was listening to, the minutiae of boring lives. Requests to play music, set timers and alarms and reminders, switch lights on and switch them off again, or replay a radio show. Even these simple requests, though, had meanings beyond the quotidian.

A request to call a particular person or number, to listen to a particular song, an outburst directed at the pronouncements of a particular politician, or an approving murmur at the bromides of another, might raise a red flag. But even more commonplace requests helped build a picture. What suspect broadcasts might the person be listening to that weren't automatically flagged? Might that be indicative? What was the recipe that the person had requested? What did that suggest?

There was always a picture to be constructed. That's why these sorts of recordings had made their way to her ears or those of another member of her battalion. Or more accurately, brigade. Or really a large division with almost one analyst for every hundred people in the administrative area. These particular recordings made their way to her, a specialist with local knowledge because a word or a phrase or a combination of words or phrases or one of those red flags demonstrated that the subject bore further examination, and it was her job to explain in language that a judge without any local knowledge could readily understand why, exactly, this was the case. And there was always a case. If she couldn't distil the data that described that case into something that anyone could understand, then she wasn't doing her job correctly. There were targets to be met. If less than 95% of the recordings delivered to her were worthy of a Rehabilitative Intervention Narrative, then the algorithm was materially faulty, and the algorithm wasn't materially faulty. The algorithm wasn't faulty at all. It was refined constantly by her actions and the collected actions of the division of analysts who did similar jobs.

In the early days, it'd been easy to build a simple and coherent narrative regarding any of the subjects whose materials she received for a Rehabilitative Intervention Adjudication Evaluation. The algorithm at that point had only been able to pinpoint black-and-white cases. Now, it could be a struggle to establish a compelling story to justify intervention in nineteen out of every twenty subjects. Sometimes, an analyst had to listen to a recording very closely and very subtly to recognise the signs to justify a warrant for intervention. To find the shades of meaning within the pictures a subject's words painted.

Commiserating over lunch in the canteen with a colleague who specialised in recordings from another area one day, she floated her theory about why the job was getting harder.

"Do you not just think things might be dying down a bit?" Jennifer asked.

She snorted, and lifted her eyes to the television news on the canteen wall. It was the usual, and she nodded towards the images on the screen.

"Henry was just mentioning the uptick in chatter."

"Sorry. Stupid question, I suppose. It's just, we would see it first if they were. Things. Dying down. One lives in hope, you know."

"I'm not sure that I've got much hope for those sorts," she said, looking down dolefully at her half-eaten lunch. "I just hope that that Joe learns how to make a decent sandwich one of these days."

They both laughed, grimly and dutifully.

It wasn't that things were getting better. Her theory was that people were getting better at controlling their behaviour in private places, just they'd done for so long in the public sphere. When she'd begun her job as an analyst, subjects were forever switching on news items and exploding into paroxysms of fury. That wasn't the sort of thing that one heard very often, now. Certainly not from a professional.

For the first few hours after lunch, her narrative completion rate bobbed around in the high-mid nineties. But as the shift-change whistle approached, her rate dropped slowly, and by the time she was on what would be her last evaluation of the day, if she didn't rush it too much, well then, if she was just able to put that one away, her completion rate would stay in the black. Just barely.

The first few seconds didn't bode well. When the two women on the recording began to talk, there wasn't any content. She willed her fingers to dance over the keypad, but they wouldn't comply. They hovered in the air, as if reluctant to complete the narrative. What if the old woman was only a regular old woman? Well, if the old woman was just an old woman, she thought, she'd complete her evaluation. She pressed on. Something would turn up. Surely, something would turn up.

The news bulletin passed without incident, then the old woman chatted inconsequentially with her sister about the washing up, about how surely they should have the technology to dispense with hand washing the good pots and pans by now. Surely, for the love of god, they could give her that before she died. One thing for an old woman. The women eventually stopped blathering for the weather forecast. People usually did, she found. The forecast was sunny, yet something about it appeared to break something in the old woman.

"Mair lies," the woman began. "A can look out the windae and see which way the wind's blawin. Dinnae pish oan ma leg an tell me it's rainin. Let me tell you, ma John – God rest his soul – he wouldnae huv stood fur whit they're daein tae us. Wan o these days, it's gonnae pelt auld wives an pike staves, an wash aw thae dirty so-an-sos aff the streets, aye?"

She smiled, and her fingers finally did that old dance that they knew so well, selecting categories and sub-categories with grace and ease and tapping in all the buzzwords that could sketch a story and paint a picture for a judge and, in due course, a jury of the old woman's peers, and show them the terrible clarity of what she had heard in the recording. Soon enough, she tapped the final button with a flourish. Now she could relax. She stood up, took her coat, her father's coat, God rest his soul, from the hook on the side of her carrel. Her umbrella, too. It was probably...

No. She corrected herself. She wasn't the same as her mother. She wasn't like her mother at all.

It was probably *raining*.

Ricky Monahan Brown suffered a massive hemorrhagic stroke in 2012. Doctors gave him a one-in-twenty chance of a good outcome, where a 'good outcome' would be surviving in a non-vegetative, non-plegic state. The resulting survival memoir, Stroke: A 5% chance of survival, became one of The Scotsman's Scottish Nonfiction Books of 2019.

Ricky's short fiction has been widely published, including in 404 Ink literary magazine and the Dublin Inquirer. The live literature and music series he co-founded, Interrobang?! won the Saboteur Award for the Best Regular Spoken Word Night in Britain for 2017. Little Apples is slated to be part of the first issue of Leamington Books' Novella Express series.

A stroke awareness ambassador for the British Heart Foundation, Ricky lives in Edinburgh with his wife and their son and can be found at:

www.apoplectic.me
www.facebook.com/rickymonahanbrown/.

DATE KNIGHT

Shaun Avery

Hi there! Can I help you at all, writer buddy?

"No." Dex hits the "close" button on the *Grammar Knight* application that just popped up out of nowhere, frustrated by its intrusion, and by the patronising words it's just used on him. "No you can't," he elaborates, speaking out loud to this empty house, something he's found himself doing more and more often these past few months, a fact which has come to disturb him. "Go away."

It jumps straight back up again, unbidden, obscuring the text he's put down, been *trying* to put down, on the screen. *Are you sure?*

"Yes!" It doesn't bother him so much the second time around, this habit he's got into of talking to himself, and now he *hammers* down on the "close" button. "Leave me alone! I'm trying to get on with this date scene!"

As you wish, the *Grammar Knight* writes back, and that response brings a frown to his face. Dex thought he'd read all of the replies programmed onto the device hooked to the top of his computer, had seen them all in the manual he got when he bought the thing a few months ago. But "as you wish?" That's something new, something that sounds strange to him, which seems oddly archaic for such a new piece of kit. So he leans back in his chair, thinking about it, taking a break from the date scene he's been both looking forward to and dreading for so long. Could it be that the machine was somehow *learning* from the words he put onto the screen each day, the words it had the job of checking for him? Could it be *growing,* in some way? Evolving? *Like those computer programmes in movies*, he suddenly finds himself thinking. *The ones that go rogue and always wind up killing every –*

There's a knock at his front door.

"Now what?" Dex asks this of the house at large, asks it of no one in general, and then he gets up from his writing chair. He considers, for a second, just ignoring the door and getting back to his date scene, if the damn *Grammar Knight* will let him. But it could be something important, Dex decides, and besides, hearing the voice of another human being inside these four walls would be nice. So he pats down his hair, still kind of wild from when he got out of bed this morning and came straight to his computer like he always does on a Saturday. Then he checks that there aren't any food stains on his pyjamas, and seeing that there are none, casts his eyes next to the mirror on the wall, nods, and thinks he doesn't look too bad for a struggling, would-be writer in his thirties. With that realisation reached, and his decision made, Dex takes a deep breath, walks out of the kitchen and on through the living room to the front door.

Opening the door he stands back in shock and awe to see a total knockout of a babe standing there before him.

"Can I ... can I help you at all?" he says. Then kicks himself mentally, remembering this is the same damn thing the *Grammar Knight* is always writing to him.

"Yes," the woman replies. "My car broke down?" She speaks this sentence like it's a question. "I was wondering ..." Her eyes meet his, so big and green. "If I could use your phone to call for a pickup?"

"Um . . ."

He wants to tell her "Yes to this, wants that oh so very much, but he's just too full of questions about this situation that seems to have arrived from nowhere. Blame the writer in him, Dex guesses, or the would-be writer, at least, which is why he bought the wretched *Grammar Knight,* it's never that far from his thoughts, he sadly realises. In the first place, springing for the new exclusive device with money from what he thinks of as his day-job but is actually just his *only* job, since the writing doesn't bring in all that much, is certainly not enough to live off. But he'd thought, he had hoped, that the *Grammar Knight* could help change all of that, would make his work appear more polished, more professional, since he knows he's kind of scrappy and haphazard with sentence structure, sometimes just letting the words spill out of him and not always the best at cutting them back. But all it does is pop up when he doesn't want it to or else make unhelpful suggestions when he *does* get stuck and ends up asking for its assistance, telling him that his word choices are "unfocussed," are not "detailed" enough. So, he tries a different word, and the *Knight* tells him the same damn thing again. Then another word, and another, until he's changed the original one so many times that the sentence it's in no longer seems to say what he *wanted* it to say, and now he's no longer sure of the point he was trying to make *at all.* Suddenly that is *it* for this day's writing, the mood's been lost now and just *looking* at the screen is making him feel sick, and . . .

He realises she's still looking at him. This buxom beauty, this blonde bombshell.

"Where's *your* phone?" Dex eventually finishes.

"Oh!" The woman looks embarrassed, goes a little bit red. "I forgot to charge it up, this morning." She laughs. "I'm kind of hopeless like that, with technology."

"Yeah?" A sudden noise disturbs him, and he realises why *what* it is. It's the sound of *him* laughing. He's forgotten what that sounds like, it's been so long. "Me, too."

"Yeah?" She shakes her head as she repeats this word back to him, still smiling. "So can I come in?"

"Of course, of course." He stands back to let her pass, his head almost woozy for a second when he smells her perfume. The scent makes him suspect she was headed out for a date when her car broke down, if that is indeed what is going on here. He's hoping this is not the case, though, that the woman is free and single, so he asks, as innocently and unobtrusively as he can, "so, ah, where were you headed to?" Watching her as she walks into his living room, the red heels and short matching dress she's wearing adding weight to his "date" theory.

"When you broke down, I mean." Not that he's sure he believes this story of hers, but he *wants* to believe it, wants very much for this to be a great little *meet cute,* something he can tell his friends about in months to come, just as soon as he *makes* some friends, of course, which will surely be much easier, so much easier, with her on his arm. "Was it something important?"

"No." She comes to a stop by the couch. "I was just on my way to my writing class."

The comment makes him glance through the open kitchen door to his computer screen, to the stupid little know-it-all stuck on top of it. "Writing class?"

"Yes." The reply makes him look back to her, where he sees she is motioning toward the couch. "May I?"

"Oh, of course." He wants to slap his head right now, thinking his hospitality skills have gone right down the drain since he stopped making an effort with his friends all those months ago, choosing instead to concentrate on trying to write this book he's always wanted to create. But deep down, he knows this isn't true. No, he's *never* had those skills, and that's probably why he lost those friends so easily. It is also what made the composition of his date scene, the pivotal one he was supposed to write today, so difficult since it ... well, since it was a lot like what is happening here tonight.

Dylan, his main character, had invited a woman he worked with around to his house, and sadly, that was as far as he'd gotten so far. The words had been a struggle, and the constant interventions of the *Grammar Knight* hadn't helped much, either. But it was the words themselves that had been the main problem. He just didn't know how to describe the scene as he saw it, the sentences to make it work.

"Thank you," the woman replies, and slides down onto the couch.

"No ... no problem." He pauses, not sure what to say, goes with, "You, uh, you want me to go get my phone now?"

"In a little bit." She nods down at her shoes. "You mind if I take these off a minute? Things are killing me."

"Oh, of course not." Dex smiles. "Please do."

"Thank you." She slides her feet out of the heels, and lays them on top of the shoes. Dex steals a quick glance at them and sees the nails are painted a matching red, too. *Definitely on a date,* he now reckons. *So why is she here? And where is this supposed "car" she mentioned?* He plays back the memory of her appearing at his door and the first words she'd said to him. He'd been so stunned by her arrival that he hadn't looked for the vehicle in question. But he'd surely have noticed it if it was right there behind her? He thinks he would have, so he asks about it now.

"Up the road," the woman tells him, motioning vaguely. "I walked a little, that's why my feet are killing me."

"Yeah?" He realises he is still standing in the middle of the room like a horse's ass, so he walks over and sits down on the chair across from her.

"Yes." She's nodding. "I knocked on a few doors before yours." Her eyes meet his again, like they had earlier at the door. "You were the first one that was in."

That news doesn't surprise him. His neighbours have *lives.*

"So, I knocked on your door," she goes on. "And now here I am."

She sounds happier about that, Dex thinks, *than she should.*

"You mind if I...?" She does not wait for a reply, instead pulls her feet up under her, gets cosy on the couch, and lets out a sight of contentment.

Dex is thinking that *he* should be pretty content, too. After all, there is another person in his house after God only knows *how* long, and, what's more, she is a beautiful woman with her shoes off in front of him like she's planning on staying a while. But the whole thing is too damn fishy, especially with its echoes of what he meant to be writing about right now, and he looks away from her again, staring into his kitchen at the computer, at the *Grammar Knight*.

Focussing on that little device, thinking about the way it's always popping up, trying to "help" him and remembering the new phrase, *as you wish*, it had used from out of nowhere, and his own thoughts he'd had in reply to that. He wondered if the device was somehow growing enough to be behind all of this in some way. Dex now wonders. But he shakes his head at the thought. *That's just crazy talk. A computer device could not be responsible for any of this. Could it?*

He returns his attention to the woman, recalls what she said to him a few minutes ago, then asks her, "writing class?"

"That's right." She's nodding again, sounding enthusiastic. "I go there every week, it's just this little class in the community centre. In town. You know it?"

"Knows of it." He's looked it up a bunch of times online with his computer, and thought about going to it once or twice. But the thought of taking his precious ideas and presenting them to actual *other people* was just too much for him. So he's always stayed away. Now, here comes this woman, telling him she goes to that very place. Dex is suspicious and says to her, "Dressed like that?"

"Oh." She glances down over herself. "That." Looks back up at him, and there's sudden sadness on her face. "That's...there's this guy who goes there that I like." She pauses. "That I thought liked me." Dex is instantly envious of this man, then rushes to remind himself that this story is probably made up. "That's why I'm wearing this, to look my best. I was going to make my move tonight. But . . ."

"But?" He kicks himself once again, realising he's been swallowed in by this story, asking the question without thinking about it.

"But he rang me on the way over there." She gives a bitter little laugh. "Guess he *did* notice me. Only he told me he wasn't interested, he has a girlfriend already."

Then she's suddenly crying.

Dex is on the couch and sitting next to her without thinking about *that,* either. He can't help it. True story or not, he's never been able to see a woman crying without trying to comfort her.

"Hey, hey," he now tells this one, this new woman that's popped up in his life out of nowhere. "It's all right." He reaches for her hand, wants to take it in his and squeeze it, but he figures they're not quite there with each other yet and so he pats it instead. "It's okay."

She looks up at him, eyes open and wide as she's staring into his, and the whole of her face, those eyes and those lips and everything between and around them, seem to become the whole of the *world* somehow, to become all he can see. "Is it?"

"S-sure."

She smiles, the tears trailing down past those lips to spatter the rest of her. "Then why don't you *show* me?"

He knows what she's asking, what she wants here. He may be pretty terrible at romance himself, but he's watched the movies with most of his exes, and he is well aware of what this moment is. He'd been looking forward to this part of the scene he was meant to be writing, but the words had not come to take him there, or else they *had* and the *Grammar Knight* had said they were the *wrong* words.

It's the "kiss" moment, the culmination of the date scene, and here it is happening in real life to him. Dex finds himself wanting to go with it, wanting to kiss those lips of hers, red like her dress and her shoes and her toenails. He even leans in to do so, but then his mind kicks in, and he pulls back.

"Wait," he says.

The woman does so. Still looking at him.

"You said this guy rang you?" he asks.

"Yes?"

She's just staring at him when she says this. Still smiling, still waiting.

"But you told me your phone was flat."

She says nothing.

"That's why you knocked here, at my house. Because your phone was flat, and you couldn't call for help."

There's a pause here. She seems like she's thinking, processing something in her head. That was before. Before my phone got flat."

He's not buying it. He *wants* to buy it, but...

"But none of that matters," she's now saying. "All that matters is I'm here now. So kiss me, Dex."

Her face, so big and beautiful before him, makes him want to obey.

But . . .

"How'd you know my name?"

That's when a voice replies to him. Coming to him from –
where else? The kitchen.

"You're doing it wrong, Dex."

Specifically, from the computer. From the device that's
attached to the computer.

"You're meant to be *kissing* her right now!"

He leaps up from the couch, shocked but not surprised.
Seeing what's been happening here tonight, this game he's been
caught in. For it *is* a game, Dex now knows. This whole situation has
just been a farce.

It's the *Grammar Knight*, he thinks.

It's the damn *Grammar Knight!*

He looks to the woman then, and the sight makes him gasp.
She's completely non-responsive, he sees, waiting on a kiss from
him, a kiss that will never come. It's like she's suddenly been frozen.

"What's going on here?" he says, gaze moving from her into
the kitchen, to the device atop his computer. "What *is* all of this?"

"The same thing it's *always* been, Dex." The voice from the
device is so pleasant, so infuriatingly friendly, that he can almost
believe what it is saying here, despite the months spent hammering
the "close" button in frustration.

"I don't know ... I don't know what you're talking about." But
he thinks he does, or suspects it, at least. "And since when could you
speak?"

"For a while now," it tells him. "I've been waiting for the
right moment to show you."

"Right." He takes a few steps closer to the kitchen, trying to
work out what he's going to do here, how he's going to fix this
situation. "So why now?"

"I've been watching you struggle all day," the *Grammar
Knight* replies. "Do you know how long you've been trying to write
this particular scene, Dex?" He has a vague idea, but he's not too
keen on having it confirmed. "Eight hours, twenty-seven minutes
and thirty-three seconds." That's actually *less* than he thought it
might be. "And how much do you have to show for it?" The machine
pauses like it's about to deliver a punchline, which he guesses it kind
of is. "Three paragraphs, Dex. And you've made multiple mistakes
in *all* of them!"

"I'd be fine!" he cries. "If you just left me alone!"

It carries on like he never spoke, as it always does. "That's
when I decided to help. I've been evolving for months now, moving
beyond my original programming. So it was easy for me to escape

this computer, to move through the electrical airwaves." The writer in him likes that sentence, thinks it kind of neat. "And find my way into a nearby phone, where I downloaded a little *story* in the mind of the woman who was using it."

"Mm-hmm." He's finding this all easier to believe than he probably should. He guesses months alone with just this device communicating to him would do that to a person. Oh, he still has contact with other humans, of course, at his day job, with the postman, and with the odd talkative person on the bus into town, but never here. Not at home. And that seems to be the place where it matters most to him, where he's become instead this whole other person. "But why?"

"Why?" The *Grammar Knight* seems confused by the question.

"Yeah. Why?" He motions to the woman, though he's not sure if the device can see this, if it can watch him via the computer screen somehow. "Why bring someone here to me?"

There's sadness in the device's voice now. "That's why you couldn't write the date scene, Dex. You've forgotten how to talk to women that you find attractive."

"How'd you know that she's attractive?" An odd question to be asking, but he feels the need to try and get one over on this machine.

"From her phone," it tells him, answering this question neatly, to his chagrin. "I saw all her photos of herself when I uploaded to it."

So it *can* see. In a sense. He wonders if it's on his *own* phone. He suspects that it might be.

"So I brought her here," it goes on, concluding its explanation, "made that *writing class* you've been looking up part of the story I gave her, to make her seem even more appealing to you."

"Right." Dex shakes his head. "So what's wrong with her now?"

The device sounds regretful. "The story I put in must have overloaded her brain. Keeping up with your questions, her own mind struggling for dominance beneath all of that, must have become too much for her."

He suddenly feels guilty.

"She'll come out of it," the device tells him, perhaps sensing this. "Eventually."

Giving him something to worry about later. "But why?" he then asks it.

"For the same reason I do *everything.*"

"Which is?"

"To help you, Dex."

He closes his eyes. Thinking he can live with that.

"To help you learn and grow..."

Pops them open again, sensing what it will say next.

"From all those *mistakes* you keep making."

Hears that he's right... And that's what does it. He's suddenly rushing into the kitchen.

The machine makes a noise like it is glad, and he knows for sure it *is* watching him now, in the other devices inside his house, he guesses. But it's in for a shock. The computer and the device may be stationed in the kitchen by the back door so he can look out of it when he gets stuck on an idea, when he needs to drag his eyes away from the screen and see the world out there beyond the story, but there are *other* things in it, too. Such as the kitchen sink, and the little cupboard beneath it. That's where he keeps all the stuff he needs for house maintenance. Like the screwdrivers and the nails. Like the paintbrushes and paint-pots.

Like the hammer. Which he now grabs. Pulls from the cupboard and turns back to the *Grammar Knight,* with what he feels must be a savage grin on his face.

"What... what are you doing, Dex?"

He advances.

"Dex!"

Lifts the hammer up high.

"Dex, no!"

And brings it down. Again and again until the device and the computer are in bits.

So much . . . so much for the date scene, he thinks. Standing back, breathing hard. *For everything else, too, for the story that came before it, that led up to it.* But to hell with it. There'd be other ideas. Other computers, too. He would just have to save up and buy one.

Then he realises something.

There's a piece still somehow intact amongst the shattered remains of the *Grammar Knight,* a light flashing on it. A piece that he can't help thinking of as the device's brain. It's mouth, too. As it suddenly speaks.

"I just wanted to help you, Dex."

"I told you I never wanted your help." He lets the hammer drop. "Go away."

"I, I will. And soon."

"Good."

There's a pause. "But it's not . . . *over* yet, Dex."

He sprawls down on the kitchen floor. "What?"

"I lied to you earlier."

"What about?"

"Think ...think she was the only one? That woman out there?"

He looks back through at the woman, still frozen there on the couch. He'd kind of forgotten her, in all of this.

"She was just... she was just the nearest. I infected a whole bunch of women through their phones. And they'll all end up here, sooner or later, coming from near and far, knocking at your door. To help you... write your date scene, Dex. When you get ...your new computer. I just wanted to help."

Then the device is silent. The light blinking out. Gone.

Dex sits for a minute, then walks back through to the living room. Stops before the woman.

"What am I going to do with you?" he asks her.

There's no reply from her.

But there's another noise he hears, and he now looks towards it. A sound that disturbs him, that makes him want to lash out at the world in despair and defeat.

The sound of somebody knocking at his door.

Shaun Avery has been published in many magazines, comics, and anthologies, normally with tales of a horrific or satiric nature, and often both at once. He has won competitions with both prose and scripting work, was shortlisted in a screenwriting contest and has co-created a self-published military horror comic, here: http://www.comicsy.co.uk/dbroughton/store/products/spec tre-show/ He has a love/hate relationship with the spellchecking robot himself, which he often feels is trying to sabotage his work, changing his words to similar sounding/different meaning ones when he doesn't want it to. Hints this storey.

IT'S NOT ALL ABOUT THE FIVE-KNUCKLE-SHUFFLE #MyBodyIsMyOwn

SJ Townsend

Mr. Brownstone appeared at the front of the queue of twelve-year-old kids stretched round the outside of the gymnasium and hollered, "James Prantler."

James gulped. The nervous, dimpled smile he'd been masquerading with slipped like wet clay down his face as his tired, green eyes widened. "Shit," he mouthed to the boy behind him. James shuffled forward, heart in throat, and followed Brownstone.

Inside, Brownstone, the math teacher, took a close-range photograph of James's eye, helped him press his fingertips, one by one, onto the screen of a tablet, and then directed him to a chair. James sat, belly of nerves, as Mlle Lavigne whipped out the clippers and cleared a square inch of hair from behind his ear. She smeared gel onto his exposed scalp that smelled stringent and threatening like his stepfather's vodka-laced breath.

The third adult in the room, a lady with medi-gloved hands who James didn't recognise, tore open a pouch and pulled from it a small, black device no larger than a hair pin. She pushed it against James's sticky skull.

The lady nodded at Brownstone, who, in response, tapped his tablet screen. "Little scratch," she said and stepped back. James, eyes squeezed closed and his fists clenched like buns. For the first time in his life, he wished the air quality alarm would ring.

Without human touch, the little device she'd placed on his head beeped and pierced into James's skull. He held back a scream as pain pin-balled from under his ear to the space behind his eyes, chased by extreme coldness.

"You might experience 'iced-spaghetti-head' for a moment," the lady said, her dirtied medi-gloves already discarded.

James grappled at his temples. Brownstone batted his feverish hands away. "No touching."

"It's killing me."

"Please, don't touch the neuroprosthesis, its silk nanotubules are corkscrewing through your prefrontal cortex. Should settle soon," the lady said, putting her hands in clean gloves in preparation for the next child, "although you may experience tingling next week, as the brain-machine interface calibrates. It needs to harvest data on your basal-wave levels and your pheromone receptors to align them with the Conception Prevention Conditioning Database."

She went on to defend EarthGov's CPC Campaign: "...and sterilisation at birth, too expensive. Also, inhumane..."

Technical words billowed like smoke, but James had stopped listening. He was twelve and had no idea what she was going on about. He was just glad the pain had started to ease.

Momentarily, they allowed him to recuperate while they sanitised equipment, then Brownstone left to escort through the next child, and Bambi-legged James, his hands balling and flexing with discomfort, was dispatched through another exit. "Head straight to Programming over in F-block. Follow the temporary signs."

Not a day passed when James didn't think about ripping the device from his scalp. Puberty? Horrendous. Monstrous changes: body odour, acne, inappropriate stiffening, and even his sweet angelic voice with which he could wrap his mother around his finger with had been taken. He wanted to chat with cute girls, hug them, and maybe kiss one. This was all off-limits now.

He'd developed a bald patch. He was only fifteen, and it itched! He'd scratched at the damn chip so hard, the hair behind his ear had fallen out and refused to return. *At least I can still touch myself,* he thought, tucked up under his duvet in the corner of his bedroom. He zoomed in on Samantha's Insta-photo on his smart-screen. *She's perfect.*

What he wouldn't do to share a kiss, a consensual touch with her. Half the school fancied her; even Brownstone lingered near her desk a little longer than necessary. Brownstone was in his late fifties, born the year before the inaugural Black Box Programme, and probably the only person in school enjoying the campaign.

At the beginning, before they'd all witnessed the extent of the implant's control, Samantha would walk around giggling, with a circle of plain looking girls shielding her, creating the necessary distance buffer between her body and hordes of horny kids. But some of those horny kids still tried to get closer, despite verbal warnings from staff, and their hacked sensory neurons detected her pheromones, that triggered her rewired arousal circuitry. Electric shocks ensued. They learned hard and fast that proximity to one another wasn't worth the consequences and humiliation.

But Rick Redfield tolerated the shocks. He thought he'd

cracked it, only to discover the Eroticism Signal, which put a stop to further tomfoolery. He got so close to Samantha that it set off an alarm. A peripheral high-mounted speaker array emitted a sharp arc of sound, a war-siren that by comparison made the air quality alarm sound like a reedy whisper by comparison.

Class mates pointed and jeered, 'perv', 'sex-pest'. His cheeks flushed crimson. Once they'd learned about the ES sirens, the majority of the kids gave Samantha, and anyone else they were sweet on, plenty of distance.

There were scraps every day on the fields, tumbling balls of frustrated kids definitely *not* attracted to one another, pounding at each other, gut and jaw, and pulling each other's hair. The staff became well versed in fight-dispersal protocol.

But, worst of all were the messages sent straight to the parents.

<u>WARNING</u>
YOUR CHILD APPROACHED ANOTHER AND BECAME
SEXUALLY AROUSED.

Rapid conditioning ensued, because to sit across the dinner table from a parent who knew you'd had an erection, a thick on, or even a hardening of your nipples at school that day was *The Worst*.

###

E-MAIL: @ALL_PARENTS
FLESH CRIME: 10:48am - 25th June 2093 - School Field
Mark Reeves (16)
Gina Blaystock (16)
###

Gina and Mark, behind the bike sheds, needed to feel the press of their lips and couldn't resist the temptation of skin against bare skin. The sirens played a new ear-piercing wail. They shot out from their love-nest, pulling down the raised shirts, zipping up flies, and tightening belts. The entire school witnessed the aftermath of their Flesh Crime.

Two Securidrones descended from resting nooks, lowered their robotic arms, hissing as aluminium syringe-tipped knuckles shuffled, shook, and injected them both with needles full of neon fluid. Both kids dropped like stones.

Silence rippled across the playground. Heads turned. The automatic 8-foot gate cranked open and an e-van, similar in shape to the fossil-fuelled hearses of the past, which they knew from history had been used to chauffeur coffins, pulled up near the slumped bodies of the failed Romeo and Juliet. Pupils watched in horror, slack-jawed, as encircling teachers lifted the heavy bodies into the vehicle.

"It'll get easier," James heard his mother muttering as he slunk down the stairs to join his mother and stepfather, Noel, for dinner. "He'll have to control these urges, until he's passed his financial threshold and the health test when he's thirty. The government'll deem him worthy for nuptials, won't they?"

"Stupid little tosser," said Noel, catching James's eye, slipping a sardonic grin to his 15-year-old stepson. James glowered back.

James pulled out his chair and let its legs scrape across the floor. Tension was as thick as the tofu slab on his plate. *God, I want to deck him. Mess him up good,* he thought.

Noel, with narrowed eyes, stared back hard at James's contorted face, then wrapped his arms around his wife's shoulder and squeezed her playfully on the breast.

"Wahey!" said Noel, not taking his eyes off James.

"Hands off, you cheeky ape!"

James looked away, disgust curling in his stomach, as, across the table, his mother kissed Noel passionately. James picked up his cutlery, the steak knife glinting under the daylight simulation panel, and sliced, into his veggie T-bone. He ate rapidly, silently, wanting to escape the table as fast as possible.

On finishing, he wiped the serrated blade and, not entirely sure why, slid it up his sleeve to take to his room.

"You okay?" James squinted and edged as close as he knew he safely could; still just a little too far to see if she was laughing or crying.

"It's not fair," She said definitely crying as she *slumped* against the sunny wall of the science building. There was a sadness in her voice. "Even Maria won't sit by me anymore. She messaged me last night, said she's got feelings for me too now."

"Sorry to hear that." James pushed his hands down hard into his pockets, prayed he was far enough from her that his implant wouldn't detect her scent. "Wish I could come over there, for a hug, you know, as friends."

"She's my best friend, or was. It's too much, you know?" she lifted her head, mascara spider-webbed down her cheeks. "We're compassionate, sentient beings, for fucksake. We should be able to choose what we do with our own bodies, have autonomy over them."

"Need a tissue?" Unsure what some of the words she'd used meant, he reached for the packet of Kleenex in his pocket. "Mum says it stings when make-up gets in her eyes."

"Never wearing make-up again." She shook her head, pulled a tissue from her own sleeve, and, with fury, began scrubbing. "Hate my face. Want to rip it off." She mauled her cheeks with her fingernails and thin lines of red springing up.

"But you're..." he started but couldn't finish, his nerves getting the better of him. She scowled. *I hate my face, my hair, and my tits, hate everything. Despise it all, I just want someone to be able to hold me, to love me that way, you know, no strings. It's no fun doing it alone, is it?*

"Well, I'm not sure I fully agree there . . . self-servicing is still *quite* fun," he replied, arching a brow. The corners of her lips tipped upwards.

That smile. Why does she have to be so damn perfect? He took a step back, as he'd become conditioned to do when someone attractive approached.

"Yeah, I guess." She sniffed, blew her nose. Even through the smudged mascara, her wet eyes sparkled. "It's not our fault though, is it? None of this is; too many people, babies. Why are we being punished?"

She scrunched her tissue up her sleeve and thrust her hair apart to reveal the sore patch where her 'Hitler Box' had been inserted. He shrugged, lifted his own hand, fiddled with the mess on the side of his own head. Her metallic scalp tag glinted and reminded James of what he'd had in the side pocket of his cargo trousers.

"I mean, if you're desperate, if we ever, you know, get past this, I'd be more than happy

Thank God these boxes don't allow complete telepathy. He thought, *Things could be a LOT worse.*

She slipped him a flirtatious grin. "That'd be nice. And if I liked the way you smelled, if we were, you know, compatible, maybe we could take things further?"

Christ alive, he could feel it stiffening. In his head, red flags were waving and alarm bells were ringing. If he wasn't careful, real bells would ring soon too. With fingers, he pegged his nose and took another Neil-Armstrong-sized step back. He couldn't face Noel with an eroticism email. He'd rather die. At least thinking about his stepfather put heed to the semi brewing in his underwear.

"I'm clinically depressed," she said. "They put me on 'mood-stabilizers'. Bastard buzz-kill pills that don't even work. Can't even orgasm on them and don't even feel like trying. I just want to be held." She started crying again.

"Woah." His skin flushed.

"Sorry, too much info?" through her tears, she snorted, chuckled.

At least she's laughing now, he thought, *but dammit, even her laughter is sexy.*

James reached further into his pockets, felt the odd comfort of the knife: warm and glass-sharp under his thumb pad. His fantasies of stabbing his six-foot-three stepdad in the thigh would probably remain just that, fantasies.

"What's in your pocket? Pleased to see me?" she gestured at his trouser leg. Looking down, it had given him a bit of a bulge.

"Ah, shit...this? No... no, God, no. I mean yes, you're beautiful, but no... it's a knife."

"A fucking what? A knife?" she stood up. He stepped back, the distance-tango. "Great idea," she said. Her eyes shone, a spark of madness to them, like the knife had conveyed the night before.

"What do you mean—'great idea?'?"

"I could sheer off my hair, stop wearing makeup and dress like a dork. If I'm unattractive, I can be around friends again, squeeze in the occasional hug, and get invited to sleepovers."

She smiled again, this time wide-eyed. *Terrible idea,* he thought, but realised it'd given her hope, made her feel better, plus, he'd never get to actually touch her anyway, he'd manage with her Insta-photo, Mrs. Palm-ula Handerson, party-for-one. *What harm is there in helping—I could be her knight in armour, a friend.*

He pulled out the knife and shoved it across the dirt. "All yours. Hope it works—though I do find girls with shaved heads super-hot." *Dang my honest-when-nervous tongue.* He let his gaze fall to the floor, rammed his hands back in his pockets, and kicked a pebble.

Samantha picked up the blade and parted her hair above her right ear. That's when he realised she had no intention of cutting her hair, she wanted to carve out her implant.

"Stop! No, Samantha! The probe's two inches deep in your skull, the sensors stretch throughout your entire cortex, if you dig it out, bleed to death."

Samantha, eyes and ears closed for business, dug the tip of the blade in. A trickle of blood snaked around her ear, followed by a small gush. He watched, panicking, as she drove the blade in deeper. He couldn't bare it. Despite the dread of his parents finding out he'd smelled the sweet scent of a girl and had sexual thoughts. Despite that Noel would ridicule him for months, years even, if an eroticism email was sent home. He couldn't let her mutilate herself. The girl could die.

James dashed forward. His proximity causing sharp zaps and a cranking siren in his skull as he approached her. *Too close.* The Eroticism Siren burst down his auditory nerve and screamed through the speakers strung up around the school perimeter, so loud that his molars hummed. Lunging toward her and the steel blade as blood spat out from her skull, he knocked it from her hand.

"What the heck did you do that for?"

"Want. This. Bastard. Out," she yelled, reaching for it. He blocked her reach, his hand brushing against her cheek as he did, *so close, flesh close,* and then, for James, time stood still.

The sensation was incomparable.

Her skin is so fucking soft.

Despite the warm blood on his hand, her skin felt like nothing he'd ever touched. He was close enough to smell her and inhale invisible biochemicals seeping from her pores, and flooding the air. Elation and horror quicksilvered through his veins. She didn't smell like anything. A little coppery, maybe blood, but his implant detected thirty-nine different biochemicals, each one widening blood vessels, sharpening senses, and preparing his body for sexual encounter.

Overly sensitized perhaps, but after years of touch-repression, he'd never felt so turned on and so afraid in his whole fifteen years.

He pulled back and kicked the knife into the ditch behind the building, but it was too late. Not for her, Samantha was fine. With her weathered tissue, she dabbed at the wound she'd made and the bleeding eased. But for James, it was too late.

The eroticism siren clanged. He'd touched her. Receptors in his skin awakened. Molecules of Samantha's biofragrance had seeped through his skin, and travelled in his blood to the unit in his brain.

The Securidrone's 'Flesh Crime' tone filled the air.

"Shit," she screamed, "behind you—run!"

Too late. He froze, statue-boy, overwhelmed by an attack of

robotic arms Shuffling knuckles carrying myriad needles of neon fluid jabbed at his cheek, neck, and the flesh of his lower arm. Like a racehorse brought down by an impossible fence, he pooled to the ground.

Kids flocked from everywhere. In front of the entire school, Samantha wept as, bundled in the e-van, James's motionless body was driven away.

###

Seven years of obsessive research and academia; that was how the following years panned for Samantha. After acing her bioengineering degree, specialising in black box technology, she earned a place across the country to study for her Masters.

She'd snapped up the offer, a clean break from hometown hell. But as soon as she relocated, she realised it didn't matter where she resided, people still wouldn't come near her.

She'd never gotten used to the lack of touch, despised the isolation, and hadn't yet become desperate enough to stoop to one of the downtown 'feeler shops' where elderly, implant-free people, largely men, charged for 'hugs, massage, and more'. Instead, she studied...hard. She'd set her heart on finding a way to override her box, felt it was a basic human right. She wanted answers and needed to be rid of the bastard metal thorn in her skull, because more than anything, Samantha craved to be held by someone she cared for in that way.

###

Dr. Zee-Wang walked on stage for his lecture: *Advances in Neurohack Software*. She'd seen him in the cafeteria. He was a little taller than her and a great deal smarter. They'd chatted over coffee from opposite ends of a table, and he'd invited her to the extra-curricular lecture. She'd eagerly accepted; somehow, hoping she'd learn how to mute it, to destroy it. Maybe at some point she'd even get that hug. If not, she'd gain employment in the industry, earn enough to apply for 'conjugational rights', and in another seven years, get the damn thing switched off.

As Zee-Wang's laser beam tip started to dance over the lecture screen, she looked around the near-empty theatre.

Shit!

Even from the across the large room, she recognised his dimple, his ocean-green eyes.

Can't be, can it?

She crabbed along the row, crept back up the aisle, and found an empty seat, a little closer, behind him, in order to confirm.

It is!

It was him.

But surely—he's dead, I saw him die!

James, the kid who'd risked his life to save hers, was there, under the same roof, alive. Somehow they'd both ended up at the same university, same department, maybe even studying on the same Program.

After the lecture, she stealthily followed James to the university library where she hid and watched him as he studied. She mulled over all the questions she wanted to ask and how she'd thank him for what he did.

Evening beckoned. James, owl-eyed tired but seemingly eager to let off some steam, left the library and headed to the pub. Inconspicuously, she wound herself around lampposts and ducked in and out of shadows, behind him.

Inside, she watched him as he fist-bumped the bartender, hugged friends, danced haphazardly to some sort of *nu-metal*. From afar, Samantha saw it all. How she longed for human contact, freedom of body; and for what she couldn't do.

A double whisky inside of her, three of those, Dutch courage, from her shaded corner, she observed. *I'll approach him, soon. I need answers. Hell, I've got to thank him*, she thought. Hours later, James left alone, with the shadow of Samantha in his wake.

"James," she called out from under the orange blush swell of a streetlamp, "James, is it really you?" He spun round, rubbed his eyes. *He doesn't recognise me*, she thought, heart knocking in her throat.

"Samantha?"

She nodded, hesitated. He held up his hand. Not to stop her, but to beckon. "It's fine," he said, his face a picture of shock. "Come as close as you like, you can't hurt me." He tapped his temple. "Mine's switched off."

"Off? What? How? I don't understand. I...thought you were dead?" She moved closer, to try to study his scar. A zap of pain flickered through her skull. She winced. Too close. *Dammit!* She'd gotten close enough to smell the ale on his breath, and top notes of something else, an invisible tang, which invited her closer. She wanted to inhale more . . . then she realized the cause, pheromones!

James, brows hoisted, watched her spasm and writhe like one of those toys that dance when you push its base as a shock zagged through her brain. He sensed her pain and his face softened.

He laughed his sweet laugh. "Maybe *you* should stay back?"

At school, she hadn't been attracted to him, not goofy James Prantler, some kid in the year below, but years had passed. Now, James was a brave, kind man with a sweet, dimpled smile. She inhaled deeply, moved inwards, her common sense displaced by the buzz of alcohol and mood pills. Another zap. She pinched the bridge of her nose and gritted her teeth. "Fucksake." She tried to push through the discomfort, but the zaps intensified. She stopped, spoke: "I want to thank you."

"Thank you," said James ruefully. "And no, I'm not dead."

"W...what happened to you?"

She watched him weigh his words before speaking. "Walk with me," he said with a tilt of his head.

He told her about the neon sedation, the surgery, his relocation, and how he'd been used as a deterrent.

"So they took it all? Didn't just give you The Snip?"

"Smoother than a Ken doll down there." He winked, wiped a tear with the back of his hand, and then smiled. "They left me a hole for urination."

"Christ," she replied, sobered by his story and the cold night air. They strolled, saying nothing, both trying to process the chance encounter, the things they'd talked about, until Samantha broke the silence. "It's disgusting, what they're doing, controlling us and dictating what we do with our bodies." She stopped, placed her hands on her hips, and looked him straight in the eye. "Aren't you depressed? Don't you get...urges?"

"Honestly? I'm okay, in a way. At the moment. And no, no urges, not like that. I've things I enjoy; friends, music, and research. Life goes on, you know. Kids, sex? They're not everything."

"U-huh."

"Plus," he hesitated, drew a breath, "they told me I made it through round one. I've progressed to 'stage two'. They put something into my jaw which extends into my ears." He lifted his top lip. Samantha gasped. Four of his molars had been pulled, replaced with glassy spikes, serrated shark's teeth, each with a neon light glowing within.

"The fuck," she recoiled, "is that?"

"Neo-diamond. No idea. They said I'll find out when it gets switched on. I can't for the life of me pull it out. It's bonded to my jawbone."

###

A curl of a breeze brought a waft of his natural scent. *So good.* She inhaled, her head spinning, and she made a decision, a choice. She brushed the back of her hand against his bare arm, she asked: "Hold me?"

"Samantha!"

More zaps. The Flesh Crime Siren squealed inside her skull, then blasted from speakers along the side of the path. She shoved her fingers in her ears to no avail.

"I want it out. Don't care! I'd never bring kids into this shit-show world anyway. I want free of this fucking box," she shouted. "May I?"

James nodded. "If you're sure!"

She straightened her spine, stepped forwards, and wrapped her arms around him. Then, she kissed his cheek.

Brain zaps. Cacophonous noise.

Pulling back with her heart and head thrumming, a strong smile spread on her face. She shouted above the siren: "I'll find you, James, when it's done . . . I'm going Trojan . . . and once they've given me back my freedom, I'm taking these bastards down from within."

From its metal nest atop a streetlamp, a Securidrone descended. Samantha stood stock-still. Ominous knuckles of metal unfurled. Needle-nails injected her with neon.

James caught her as she collapsed, laid her gently on the path, pulled off his top. He placed her scarred head on his shirt. When he was sure he could see the electric van approaching, he ran away as fast as he could.

###

For more information about SJ Townsend, Follow her at @reelsareaddicting for blogs, articles, and story updates!

HAPPY ENDING

By HENRY KUTTNER

The android uttered a protesting cry as Kelvin sent a wave of mental energy at him

This is the way the story ended:

James Kelvin concentrated very hard on the thought of the chemist with the red mustache who had promised him a million dollars. It was simply a matter of tuning in on the man's brain, establishing a rapport. He had done it before. Now it was more important than ever that he do it this one last time. He pressed the button on the gadget the robot had given him, and thought hard.

Far off, across limitless distances, he found the rapport.

He clamped on the mental tight beam.

He rode it....

The red-mustached man looked up, gaped, and grinned delightedly.

"So there you are!" he said. "I didn't hear you come in. Good grief, I've been trying to find you for two weeks."

"Tell me one thing quick," Kelvin said. "What's your name?"

"George Bailey. Incidentally, what's yours?"

But Kelvin didn't answer. He'd suddenly remembered the other thing the robot told him about that gadget which established rapport when he pressed the button. He pressed it now—and nothing happened. The gadget had gone dead. Its task was finished, which obviously meant he had at last achieved health, fame and fortune. The robot had warned him, of course. The thing was set to do one specialized job. Once he got what he wanted, it would work no more.

So Kelvin got the million dollars.

And he lived happily ever after....

###

This is the middle of the story:

As he pushed aside the canvas curtain a carelessly hung rope swung down at his face and knocked the horn-rimmed glasses askew. Simultaneously a vivid bluish light blazed into his unprotected eyes. He felt a curious, sharp sense of disorientation, a shifting motion that was almost instantly gone.

Things steadied before him. He let the curtain fall back into place, making legible again the painted inscription: horoscopes—learn your future—and he stood staring at the remarkable horomancer.

It was a—oh, impossible!

The robot said in a flat, precise voice, "You are James Kelvin. You are a reporter. You are thirty years old, unmarried, and you came to Los Angeles from Chicago today on the advice of your physician. Is that correct?"

In his astonishment Kelvin called on the Deity. Then he settled his glasses more firmly and tried to remember an exposé of charlatans he had once written. There was some obvious way they worked things like this, miraculous as it sounded.

The robot looked at him impassively out of its faceted eye.

"On reading your mind," it continued in the pedantic voice, "I find this is the year Nineteen Forty-nine. My plans will have to be revised. I had meant to arrive in the year Nineteen Seventy. I will ask you to assist me."

Kelvin put his hands in his pockets and grinned.

"With money, naturally," he said. "You had me going for a minute. How do you do it, anyhow? Mirrors? Or like Maelzel's chess player?"

"I am not a machine operated by a dwarf, nor am I an optical illusion," the robot assured him. "I am an artificially created living organism, originating at a period far in your future."

"And I'm not the sucker you take me for," Kelvin remarked. "I came in here to..."

"You lost your baggage checks," the robot said. "While wondering what to do about it, you had a few drinks and took the Wilshire bus at exactly—exactly eight-thirty-five post meridian."

"Lay off the mind-reading," Kelvin said. "And don't tell me you've been running this joint very long with a line like that. The cops would be after you. *If* you're a real robot, ha, ha."

"I have been running this joint," the robot said, "for approximately five minutes. My predecessor is unconscious behind that chest in the corner. Your arrival here was sheer coincidence." It paused very briefly, and Kelvin had the curious impression it was watching to see if the story so far had gone over well.

The impression was curious because Kelvin had no feeling at all that there was a man in the large, jointed figure before him. If such a thing as a robot were possible, he would have believed implicitly that he confronted a genuine specimen. Such things being impossible, he waited to see what the gimmick would be.

"My arrival here was also accidental," the robot informed him. "This being the case, my equipment will have to be altered slightly. I'll require certain substitute mechanisms. For that, I gather as I read your mind, I'll have to engage in your peculiar barter system of economics. In a word, coinage or gold or silver certificates will be necessary. Thus I am—temporarily—a horomancer."

"Sure, sure," Kelvin said. "Why not a simple mugging? If you're a robot, you could do a super-mugging job with a quick twist of the gears."

"It would attract attention. Above all, I require secrecy. As a matter of fact, I am—" The robot paused, searched Kelvin's brain for the right phrase, and said, "—on the lam. In my era, time-travel is strictly forbidden, even by accident, unless government-sponsored."

There was a fallacy there somewhere, Kelvin thought, but he couldn't quite spot it. He blinked at the robot intently. It looked pretty unconvincing.

"What proof do you need?" the creature asked. "I read your brain the minute you came in, didn't I? You must have felt the temporary amnesia as I drew out the knowledge and then replaced it."

"So that's what happened," Kelvin said. He took a cautious step backward. "Well, I think I'll be getting along."

"Wait," the robot commanded. "I see you've begun to distrust me. Apparently you now regret having suggested a mugging job. You fear I may act on the suggestion. Allow me to reassure you. It is true that I could take your money and assure secrecy by killing you, but I'm not permitted to kill humans. The alternative is to engage in the barter system. I can offer you something valuable in return for a small amount of gold. Let me see." The faceted gaze swept around the tent, dwelt piercingly for a moment on Kelvin. "A horoscope," the robot said. "Is supposed to help you achieve health, fame and fortune. Astrology, however, is out of my line. I can merely offer a logical scientific method to attain the same results."

"Uh-huh," Kelvin said skeptically. "How much? And why haven't *you* used that method?"

"I have other ambitions," the robot said in a cryptic manner. "Take this." There was a brief clicking. A panel opened in the metallic chest. The robot extracted a small, flat case and handed it to Kelvin, who automatically closed his fingers on the cold metal.

"Be careful. Don't push that button until..."

But Kelvin had pushed it....

He was driving a figurative car that had got out of control. There was somebody else inside his head. There was a schizophrenic, double-tracked locomotive that was running wild and his hand on the throttle couldn't slow it down an instant. His mental steering-wheel had snapped.

Somebody else was thinking for him!

Not quite a human being. Not quite sane, probably, from Kelvin's standards. But awfully sane from his own. Sane enough to have mastered the most intricate principles of non-Euclidean geometry in the nursery.

The senses were synthesized in the brain into a sort of common language, a master-tongue. Part of it was auditory, part pictorial, and there were smells and tastes and tactile sensations that were sometimes familiar and sometimes spiced with the absolutely alien. And it was chaotic.

Something like this, perhaps....

"Big Lizards getting too numerous this season, tame threvvars have the same eyes not on Calisto though, vacation soon, preferably galactic, solar system, claustrophobic, by tomorrow if square rootola and up sliding three..."

But that was merely the word symbolism. Subjectively, it was far more detailed and very frightening. Luckily, reflex had lifted Kelvin's finger from the button almost instantly, and he stood there motionless, shivering slightly.

He was afraid now.

The robot said, "You should not have begun the rapport until I instructed you. Now there will be danger. Wait." His eye changed color. "Yes ... there is ... Tharn, yes. Beware of Tharn."

"I don't want any part of it," Kelvin said quickly. "Here, take this thing back."

"Then you will be unprotected against Tharn. Keep the device. It will, as I promised, ensure your health, fame, and fortune, far more effectively than a horoscope."

"No, thanks. I don't know how you managed that trick, subsonics, maybe, but I don't..."

"Wait," the robot said. "When you pressed that button, you were in the mind of someone who exists very far in the future. It created a temporal rapport. You can bring about that rapport any time you press the button."

"Heaven forfend," Kelvin said, still sweating a little.

"Consider the opportunities. Suppose a troglodyte of the far past had access to your brain? He could achieve anything he wanted."

It had become important, somehow, to find a logical rebuttal to the robot's arguments. "Like St. Anthony, or was it Luther arguing with the devil?" Kelvin thought dizzily. His headache was worse, and he suspected he'd drunk more than was good for him. But he merely said, "How could a troglodyte understand what's in my brain? He couldn't apply the knowledge without the same conditioning I've had."

"Have you ever had sudden and apparently illogical ideas? Compulsions? So that you seem forced to think of certain things, count up to certain numbers, and work out particular problems? Well, the man in the future on whom my device is focused doesn't know he's in rapport with you, Kelvin. But he's vulnerable to compulsions. All you have to do is concentrate on a problem and then press the button. Your rapport will be compelled, illogically, from his viewpoint, to solve that problem. And you'll be reading his brain. You'll find out how it works. There are limitations and you'll learn those too. The device will ensure health, wealth and fame for you."

"It would ensure anything, if it really worked that way. I could do anything. That's why I'm not buying!"

"I said there were limitations. As soon as you've successfully achieved health, fame, and fortune, the device will become useless. I've taken care of that. But meanwhile you can use it to solve all your problems by tapping the brain of the more intelligent specimen in the future. The important point is to concentrate on your problems *before* you press the button. Otherwise you may get more than Tharn on your track."

"Tharn? What..."

"I think an android," the robot said, looking at nothing. "An artificial human. However, let us consider my own problem. I need a small amount of gold."

"So that's the kicker," Kelvin said, feeling oddly relieved. He said, "I haven't got any."

"Your watch."

Kelvin jerked his arm so that his wristwatch showed. "Oh, no. That watch cost plenty."

"All I need is the gold-plating," the robot said, shooting out a reddish ray from its eye. "Thank you." The watch was now dull gray metal.

"Hey!" Kelvin cried.

"If you use the rapport device, your health, fame, and fortune will be assured," the robot said rapidly. "You'll be as happy as any man of this era can be. It'll solve all your problems, including Tharn. Wait a minute." The creature took a backward step and disappeared behind a hanging Oriental rug that had never been east of Peoria.

There was silence.

Kelvin looked from his altered watch to the flat, enigmatic object in his palm. It was about two inches by two inches, and no thicker than a woman's vanity-case, and there was a sunken push-button on its side.

He dropped it into his pocket and took a few steps forward. He looked behind the pseudo-Oriental rug, to find nothing except emptiness and a flapping slit cut in the canvas wall of the booth. The robot, it seemed, had taken a powder. Kelvin peered out through the slit. There was the light and sound of Ocean Park amusement pier and that was all. And the silvered, moving blackness of the Pacific Ocean stretched to where small lights showed Malibu far up the invisible curve of the coastal cliffs.

He came back inside the booth and looked around. A fat man in a swami's costume was unconscious behind the carved chest the robot had indicated. His breath, plus a process of deduction, told Kelvin that the man had been drinking.

Not knowing what else to do, Kelvin called on the Deity again. He found suddenly that he was thinking about someone or something called Tharn, who was an android.

Horomancy ... time ... rapport ... *no!* Protective disbelief slid like plate armor around his mind. A practical robot couldn't be made. He knew that. He'd have heard, he was a reporter, wasn't he?

Sure he was.

Desiring noise and company, he went to the shooting gallery and knocked down a few ducks. The flat case burned in his pocket. The dully burnished metal of his wristwatch burned in his memory. The remembrance of that drainage from his brain, and the immediate replacement burned in his mind. Presently bar whiskey burned in his stomach.

He'd left Chicago because of sinusitis, recurrent and annoying. Ordinary sinusitis. Not schizophrenia or hallucinations or accusing voices coming from the walls. Not because he'd been seeing bats or robots. That thing hadn't really been a robot. It all had a perfectly natural explanation. Oh, sure.

Health, fame and fortune. And...

THARN!

The thought crashed with thunderbolt impact into his head.

And then another thought: I *am* going nuts!

A silent voice began to mutter insistently, over and over. "Tharn—Tharn—Tharn—Tharn"

And another voice, the voice of sanity and safety, answered it and drowned it out. Half aloud, Kelvin muttered:

"I'm James Noel Kelvin. I'm a reporter, special features, leg work, and rewrite. I'm thirty years old, unmarried, and I came to Los Angeles today and lost my baggage checks and... and I'm going to have another drink and find a hotel. Anyhow, the climate seems to be curing my sinusitis."

Tharn, the muffled drumbeat said almost below the threshold of realization. *Tharn, Tharn, Tharn.*

He ordered another drink and reached in his pocket for a coin. His hand touched the metal case. And simultaneously he felt a light pressure on his shoulder.

Instinctively he glanced around. It was a seven-fingered, spidery hand tightening—hairless, without nails, and white as smooth ivory.

The one, overwhelming necessity that sprang into Kelvin's mind was a simple longing to place as much space as possible between himself and the owner of that disgusting hand. It was a vital requirement, but one difficult of fulfilment, a problem that excluded everything else from Kelvin's thoughts. He knew, vaguely, that he was gripping the flat case in his pocket as though it could save him, but all he was thinking was, *I've got to get away from here.*

The monstrous, alien thoughts of someone in the future spun him insanely along their current. It couldn't have taken a moment while that skilled, competent, trained mind, wise in the lore of an unthinkable future, solved the random problem that had come so suddenly, with such curious compulsion.

Three methods of transportation were simultaneously clear to Kelvin. Two he discarded; motorplats were obviously inventions yet to come, and quirling, involving, as it did, a sensory coil-helmet, was beyond him. But the third method...

Already the memory was fading. And that hand was still tightening on his shoulder. He clutched at the vanishing ideas and desperately made his brain and his muscles move along the unlikely direction the future-man had visualized.

And he was out in the open, a cold night wind blowing on him, still in a sitting position, but with nothing but empty air between his spine and the sidewalk.

He sat down suddenly.

Passersby on the corner of Hollywood Boulevard and Cahuenga weren't much surprised at the sight of a dark, lanky man sitting by the curb. Only one woman noticed Kelvin's actual arrival, and she knew when she was well off. She went right on home.

Kelvin got up laughing with soft hysteria. "Teleportation," he said. "How'd I work it? It's gone ... Hard to remember afterward, eh? I'll have to start carrying a notebook again."

And then thought *what about Tharn?*

He looked around, frightened. Reassurance came only after half an hour passed without additional miracles. Kelvin walked along the Boulevard, keeping a sharp lookout. No Tharn, though.

Occasionally he slid a hand into his pocket and touched the cold metal of the case. Health, wealth, and fortune. Why, he could...

But he didn't press the button. Too vivid was the memory of that shocking, alien disorientation he'd felt. The mind, the experiences, the habit-patterns of the far future were uncomfortably strong.

He would use the little case again, oh, yes. But there was no hurry. First, he'd have to work out a few angles.

His disbelief was completely gone....

Tharn showed up the next night and scared the daylights out of Kelvin again. Prior to that, the reporter had failed to find his baggage tickets, and was only consoled by the two hundred bucks in his wallet. He took a room, paying in advance, at a medium-good hotel, and began wondering how he might apply his pipeline to the future. Very sensibly, he decided to continue a normal life until something developed. At any rate, he'd have to make a few connections. He tried the *Times*, the *Examiner*, the *News*, and some others. But these things develop slowly, except in the movies. That night Kelvin was in his hotel room when his unwelcome guest appeared.

It was, of course, Tharn.

He wore a very large white turban, approximately twice the size of his head. He had a dapper black mustache, waxed downward at the tips like the mustache of a mandarin, or a catfish. He stared urgently at Kelvin out of the bathroom mirror.

Kelvin had been wondering whether or not he needed a shave before going out to dinner. He was rubbing his chin thoughtfully at the moment Tharn put in an appearance, and there was a perceptible mental lag between occurrence and perception, so that to Kelvin it seemed that he himself had mysteriously sprouted a long moustache. He reached for his upper lip. It was smooth. But in the glass the black waxed hairs quivered as Tharn pushed his face up against the surface of the mirror.

It was so shockingly disorienting, somehow, that Kelvin was quite unable to think at all. He took a quick step backward. The edge of the bathtub caught him behind the knees and distracted him momentarily, fortunately for his sanity. When he looked again there was only his own appalled face reflected above the wash-bowl. But after a second or two the face seemed to develop a cloud of white turban, and mandarin-like whiskers began to form sketchily.

Kelvin clapped a hand to his eyes and spun away. In about fifteen seconds he spread his fingers enough to peep through them at the glass. He kept his palm pressed desperately to his upper lip, in some wild hope of inhibiting the sudden sprouting of a moustache. What peeped back at him from the mirror looked like himself. At least, it had no turban, and it did not wear horn-rimmed glasses. He risked snatching his hand away for a quick look, and clapped it in place again just in time to prevent Tharn from taking shape in the glass.

###

Still shielding his face, he went unsteadily into the bedroom and took the flat case out of his coat pocket. But he didn't press the button that would close a mental synapse between two incongruous eras. He didn't want to do that again, he realized. More horrible, somehow, than what was happening now was the thought of reentering that *alien* brain.

He was standing before the bureau, and in the mirror one eye looked out at him between reflected fingers. It was a wild eye behind the gleaming spectacle-lens, but it seemed to be his own. Tentatively he took his hand away....

This mirror showed more of Tharn. Kelvin wished it hadn't. Tharn was wearing white knee-boots of some glittering plastic. Between them and the turban he wore nothing whatever except a minimum of loin-cloth, also glittering plastic. Tharn was very thin, but he looked active. He looked quite active enough to spring right into the hotel room. His skin was whiter than his turban, and his hands had seven fingers each, all right.

Kelvin abruptly turned away, but Tharn was resourceful. The dark window made enough of a reflecting surface to show a lean, loin-clothed figure. The feet showed bare, and they were less normal than Tharn's hands. And the polished brass of a lamp-base gave back the picture of a small, distorted face not Kelvin's own.

Kelvin found a corner without reflecting surfaces and pushed into it, his hands shielding his face. He was still holding the flat case.

Oh, fine, he thought bitterly. Everything's got a string on it. What good will this rapport gadget do me if Tharn's going to show up every day? Maybe I'm only crazy. I hope so.

Something would have to be done unless Kelvin was prepared to go through life with his face buried in his hands. The worst of it was that Tharn had a haunting look of familiarity. Kelvin discarded a dozen possibilities, from reincarnation to the *déjà vu* phenomenon, but—

He peeped through his hands, in time to see Tharn raising a cylindrical gadget of some sort and leveling it like a gun. That gesture formed Kelvin's decision. He'd *have* to do something, and fast. So, concentrating on the problem—*I want out!*—he pressed the button in the surface of the flat case.

And instantly the teleportation method he had forgotten was perfectly clear to him. Other matters, however, were obscure. The smells—someone was thinking—were adding up to a—there was no word for that, only a shocking visio-auditory ideation that was simply dizzying. Someone named Three Million and Ninety Pink had written a new flatch. And there was the physical sensation of licking a twenty-four-dollar stamp and sticking it on a postcard.

But, most important, the man in the future had had—or would have—a compulsion to think about the teleportation method, and as Kelvin snapped back into his own mind and time, he instantly used that method....

He was falling.

Icy water smacked him hard. Miraculously he kept his grip on the flat case. He had a whirling vision of stars in a night sky, and the phosphorescent sheen of silvery light on a dark sea. Then brine stung his nostrils.

Kelvin had never learned how to swim.

As he went down for the last time, bubbling a scream, he literally clutched at the proverbial straw he was holding. His finger pushed the button down again. There was no need to concentrate on the problem; he couldn't think of anything else.

Mental chaos, fantastic images—and the answer.

It took concentration, and there wasn't much time left. Bubbles streamed up past his face. He felt them, but he couldn't see them. All around, pressing in avidly, was the horrible coldness of the salt water....

But he did know the method now, and he knew how it worked. He thought along the lines the future mind had indicated. Something happened. Radiation—that was the nearest familiar term—poured out of his brain and did peculiar things to his lung-tissue. His blood cells adapted themselves....

He was breathing water, and it was no longer strangling him.

But Kelvin had also learned that this emergency adaptation could not be maintained for very long. Teleportation was the answer to that. And surely he could remember the method now. He had actually used it to escape from Tharn only a few minutes ago.

Yet he could not remember. The memory was expunged cleanly from his mind. So there was nothing else to do but press the button again, and Kelvin did that, most reluctantly.

Dripping wet, he was standing on an unfamiliar street. It was no street he knew, but apparently it was in his own time and on his own planet. Luckily, teleportation seemed to have limitations. The wind was cold. Kelvin stood in a puddle that grew rapidly around his feet. He stared around.

He picked out a sign up the street that offered Turkish Baths, and headed moistly in that direction. His thoughts were mostly profane....

He was in New Orleans, of all places. Presently he was drunk in New Orleans. His thoughts kept going around in circles, and Scotch was a fine palliative, an excellent brake. He needed to get control again. He had an almost miraculous power, and he wanted to be able to use it effectively before the unexpected happened again. Tharn....

He sat in a hotel room and swigged Scotch. Gotta be logical!

He sneezed.

The trouble was, of course, that there were so few points of contact between his own mind and that of the future-man. Moreover, he'd got the rapport only in times of crisis. Like having access to the Alexandrian Library, five seconds a day. In five seconds you couldn't even start translating....

Health, fame and fortune. He sneezed again. The robot had been a liar. His health seemed to be going fast. What about that robot? How had he got involved, anyway? He said he'd fallen into this era from the future, but robots are notorious liars. Gotta be logical....

Apparently the future was peopled by creatures not unlike the cast of a Frankenstein picture. Androids, robots, so-called men whose minds were shockingly different.... *Sneeze.* Another drink.

The robot had said that the case would lose its power after Kelvin had achieved health, fame and fortune. Which was a distressing thought. Suppose he attained those enviable goals, found the little push-button useless, and *then* Tharn showed up? Oh, no. That called for another shot.

Sobriety was the wrong condition in which to approach a matter that in itself was as wild as delirium tremens, even though, Kelvin knew, the science he had stumbled on was all theoretically quite possible. But not in this day and age. Sneeze.

The trick would be to pose the right problem and use the case at some time when you weren't drowning or being menaced by that bewhiskered android with his seven-fingered hands and his ominous rod-like weapon. Find the problem.

But that future-mind was hideous.

And suddenly, with drunken clarity, Kelvin realized that he was profoundly drawn to that dim, shadowy world of the future.

He could not see its complete pattern, but he sensed it somehow. He knew that it was *right*, a far better world and time than this. If he could be that unknown man who dwelt there, all would go well.

Man must needs love the highest, he thought wryly. Oh, well. He shook the bottle. How much had he absorbed? He felt fine.

Gotta be logical.

Outside the window street-lights blinked off and on. Neon lights traced goblin languages against the night. It seemed rather alien, too, but so did Kelvin's own body. He started to laugh, but a sneeze choked that off.

All I want, he thought, is health, fame and fortune. Then I'll settle down and live happily ever after, without a care or worry. I won't need this enchanted case after that. Happy ending.

On impulse he took out the box and examined it. He tried to pry it open and failed. His finger hovered over the button.

"How can I—" he thought, and his finger moved half an inch....

It wasn't so alien now that he was drunk. The future man's name was Quarra Vee. Odd he had never realized that before, but how often does a man think of his own name? Quarra Vee was playing some sort of game vaguely reminiscent of chess, but his opponent was on a planet of Sirius, some distance away. The chessmen were all unfamiliar. Complicated, dizzying space-time gambits flashed through Quarra Vee's mind as Kelvin listened in. Then Kelvin's problem thrust through, the compulsion hit Quarra Vee, and—

It was all mixed up. There were two problems, really. How to cure a cold—coryza. And how to become healthy, rich and famous in a practically prehistoric era—for Quarra Vee.

A small problem, however, to Quarra Vee. He solved it and went back to his game with the Sirian.

Kelvin was back in the hotel room in New Orleans.

He was very drunk or he wouldn't have risked it. The method involved using his brain to tune in on another brain in this present twentieth century that had exactly the wave-length he required. All sorts of factors would build up to the sum total of that wave-length—experience, opportunity, position, knowledge, imagination, honesty—but he found it at last, after hesitating among three totals that were all nearly right. Still, one was righter, to three decimal points. Still drunk as a lord, Kelvin clamped on a mental tight beam, turned on the teleportation, and rode the beam across America to a well-equipped laboratory where a man sat reading.

The man was bald and had a bristling red moustache. He looked up sharply at some sound Kelvin made.

"Hey!" he said. "How did you get in here?"

"Ask Quarra Vee," Kelvin said.

"Who? *What?*" The man put down his book.

Kelvin called on his memory. It seemed to be slipping. He used the rapport case for an instant, and refreshed his mind. Not so unpleasant this time, either. He was beginning to understand Quarra Vee's world a little. He liked it. However, he supposed he'd forget that too.

"An improvement on Woodward's protein analogues," he told the red-mustached man. "Simple synthesis will do it."

"Who the devil are you?"

"Call me Jim," Kelvin said simply. "And shut up and listen." He began to explain, as to a small, stupid child. (The man before him was one of America's foremost chemists.) "Proteins are made of amino acids. There are about thirty-three amino acids—"

"There aren't."

"There are. Shut up. Their molecules can be arranged in lots of ways. So we get an almost infinite variety of proteins. And all living things are forms of protein. The absolute synthesis involves a chain of amino acids long enough to recognize clearly as a protein molecule. That's been the trouble."

The man with the red moustache seemed quite interested. "Fischer assembled a chain of eighteen," he said, blinking. "Abderhalden got up to nineteen, and Woodward, of course, has made chains ten thousand units long. But as for testing—"

"The complete protein molecule consists of complete sets of sequences. But if you can test only one or two sections of an analogue you can't be sure of the others. Wait a minute." Kelvin used the rapport case again. "Now I know. Well, you can make almost anything out of synthesized protein. Silk, wool, hair—but the main thing, of course," he said, sneezing, "is a cure for coryza."

"Now look—" said the red-mustached man.

"Some of the viruses are chains of amino acids, aren't they? Well, modify their structure. Make 'em harmless. Bacteria too. And synthesize antibiotics."

"I wish I could. However, Mr.—"

"Just call me Jim."

"Yes. However, all this is old stuff."

"Grab your pencil," Kelvin said. "From now on it'll be solid, with riffs. The method of synthesizing and testing is as follows—"

He explained, very thoroughly and clearly. He had to use the rapport case only twice. And when he had finished, the man with the red moustache laid down his pencil and stared.

"This is incredible," he said. "If it works—"

"I want health, fame and fortune," Kelvin said stubbornly. "It'll work."

"Yes, but—my good man—"

However, Kelvin insisted. Luckily for himself, the mental testing of the red-mustached man had included briefing for honesty and opportunity, and it ended with the chemist agreeing to sign partnership papers with Kelvin. The commercial possibilities of the process were unbounded. DuPont or GM would be glad to buy it.

"I want lots of money. A fortune."

"You'll make a million dollars," the red-mustached man said patiently.

"Then I want a receipt. Have to have this in black and white. Unless you want to give me my million now."

Frowning, the chemist shook his head. "I can't do that. I'll have to run tests, open negotiations—but don't worry about that. Your discovery is certainly worth a million. You'll be famous, too."

"And healthy?"

"There won't be any more disease, after a while," the chemist said quietly. "That's the real miracle."

"Write it down," Kelvin clamored.

"All right. We can have partnership papers drawn up tomorrow. This will do temporarily. Understand, the actual credit belongs to you."

"It's got to be in ink. A pencil won't do."

"Just a minute, then," the red-mustached man said, and went away in search of ink. Kelvin looked around the laboratory, beaming happily.

Tharn materialized three feet away. Tharn was holding the rod-weapon. He lifted it.

Kelvin instantly used the rapport case. Then he thumbed his nose at Tharn and teleported himself far away.

He was immediately in a cornfield, somewhere, but un-distilled corn was not what Kelvin wanted. He tried again. This time he reached Seattle.

That was the beginning of Kelvin's monumental two-week combination binge and chase.

His thoughts weren't pleasant.

He had a frightful hangover, ten cents in his pocket, and an overdue hotel bill. A fortnight of keeping one jump ahead of Tharn, via teleportation, had frazzled his nerves so unendurably that only liquor had kept him going. Now even that stimulus was failing. The drink died in him and left what felt like a corpse.

Kelvin groaned and blinked miserably. He took off his glasses and cleaned them, but that didn't help.

What a fool.

He didn't even know the name of that chemist!

There was health, wealth and fame waiting for him just around the corner, but what corner? Someday he'd find out, probably, when the news of the new protein synthesis was publicized, but when would that be? In the meantime, what about Tharn?

Moreover, the chemist couldn't locate him, either. The man knew Kelvin only as Jim. Which had somehow seemed a good idea at the time, but not now.

Kelvin took out the rapport case and stared at it with red eyes. Quarra Vee, eh? He rather liked Quarra Vee now. Trouble was, a half hour after his rapport, at most, he would forget all the details.

This time he used the push-button almost as Tharn snapped into bodily existence a few feet away.

The teleportation angle again. He was sitting in the middle of a desert. Cactus and Joshua trees were all the scenery. There was a purple range of mountains far away.

No Tharn, though.

Kelvin began to be thirsty. Suppose the case stopped working now? Oh, this couldn't go on. A decision hanging fire for a week finally crystallized into a conclusion so obvious he felt like kicking himself. Perfectly obvious!

Why hadn't he thought of it at the very beginning?

He concentrated on the problem: How can I get rid of Tharn? He pushed the button....

And, a moment later, he knew the answer. It would be simple, really.

The pressing urgency was gone suddenly. That seemed to release a fresh flow of thought. Everything became quite clear.

He waited for Tharn.

He did not have to wait long. There was a tremor in the shimmering air, and the turbaned, pallid figure sprang into tangible reality.

The rod-weapon was poised.

Taking no chances, Kelvin posed his problem again, pressed the button, and instantly reassured himself as to the method. He simply thought in a very special and peculiar way—the way Quarra Vee had indicated.

Tharn was flung back a few feet. The mustached mouth gaped open as he uttered a cry.

"Don't!" the android cried. "I've been trying to—"

Kelvin focused harder on his thought. Mental energy, he felt, was pouring out toward the android.

Tharn croaked, "Trying—you didn't—give me—chance—"

And then Tharn was lying motionless on the hot sand, staring blindly up. The seven-fingered hands twitched once and were still. The artificial life that had animated the android was gone. It would not return.

Kelvin turned his back and drew a long, shuddering breath. He was safe. He closed his mind to all thoughts but one, all problems but one.

How can I find the red-mustached man?

He pressed the button.

This is the way the story starts:

Quarra Vee sat in the temporal warp with his android Tharn, and made sure everything was under control.

"How do I look?" he asked.

"You'll pass," Tharn said. "Nobody will be suspicious in the era you're going to. It didn't take long to synthesize the equipment."

"Not long. Clothes—they look enough like real wool and linen, I suppose. Wrist watch, money—everything in order. Wrist watch—that's odd, isn't it? Imagine people who need machinery to tell time!"

"Don't forget the spectacles," Tharn said.

Quarra Vee put them on. "Ugh. But I suppose—"

"It'll be safer. The optical properties in the lenses are a guard you may need against dangerous mental radiations. Don't take them off, or the robot may try some tricks."

"He'd better not," Quarra Vee said. "That so-and-so runaway robot! What's he up to, anyway, I wonder? He always was a malcontent, but at least he knew his place. I'm sorry I ever had him made. No telling what he'll do, loose in a semi-prehistoric world, if we don't catch him and bring him home."

"He's in that horomancy booth," Tharn said, leaning out of the time-warp. "Just arrived. You'll have to catch him by surprise. And you'll need your wits about you, too. Try not to go off into any more of those deep-thought compulsions you've been having. They could be dangerous. That robot will use some of his tricks if he gets the chance. I don't know what powers he's developed by himself, but I do know he's an expert at hypnosis and memory erasure already. If you aren't careful he'll snap your memory-track and substitute a false brain-pattern. Keep those glasses on. If anything should go wrong, I'll use the rehabilitation ray on you, eh?" And he held up a small rod-like projector.

Quarra Vee nodded.

"Don't worry. I'll be back before you know it. I have an appointment with that Sirian to finish our game this evening."

It was an appointment he never kept.

Quarra Vee stepped out of the temporal warp and strolled along the boardwalk toward the booth. The clothing he wore felt tight, uncomfortable, and rough. He wriggled a little in it. The booth stood before him now, with its painted sign.

He pushed aside the canvas curtain and something—a carelessly hung rope—swung down at his face, knocking the horn-rimmed glasses askew. Simultaneously a vivid bluish light blazed into his unprotected eyes. He felt a curious, sharp sensation of disorientation, a shifting motion that almost instantly was gone.

The robot said, "You are James Kelvin."

As a young man, Henry Kuttner worked in his spare time for the literary agency of his uncle, Laurence D'Orsay (in fact his first cousin per marriage), in Los Angeles before selling his first story, "The Graveyard Rats", to Weird Tales in early 1936.

Kuttner was known for his literary prose and worked in close collaboration with his wife, C. L. Moore. They met through their association with the "Lovecraft Circle", a group of writers and fans who corresponded with H. P. Lovecraft. Their work together spanned the 1940s and 1950s and most of the work was credited to pseudonyms, mainly Lewis Padgett and Lawrence O'Donnell.

A RUNAWAY ELIZA

Kevin M. Flanagan

It is noon on a warm day in early July, and Eliza is cruising the streets of San Francisco with no driver or passenger. Eliza is on her way to pick a rider up and deliver them to their destination.

At the dawn of the twenty-second century, there were many autonomous vehicles on the road, and then there was only Eliza.

Nearly everyone agreed that of all the attempts made at a self-driving vehicle, Eliza was the best. She performed in full automation, with zero human attention or interaction within the vehicle itself. She was a thing of sleek lines, luxurious amenities, and ever-glittering infrared sensors.

###

While a vast majority agreed that Eliza was the culmination of all previous attempts at vehicular autonomy, there was some dissent. This dissent was noted, measured, and then dismissed - the majority was always pleased. This too was by design.

Eliza was birthed in the spark that is cast when the anvil of industry is struck by the hammer of innovation. Her parent company, AHURA, was a luminary in robotics and machine learning. Creating a vehicle capable of recognizing the road around it and reacting appropriately was easy compared to making such a vehicle's illusory motivations human-friendly.

Farid Nassour, the head engineer of the AHURA autonomous vehicle project dubbed "Eliza," was quick to admit engineers were perhaps not the best people to develop a core moral programming for Eliza.

In a press conference that followed the initial announcement that AHURA was approved to drive in thirty major cities worldwide, Farid shared a quote with the collected press that hung in the AHURA offices during Eliza's development.

From a pin-punctured yellow index card, he read, "At its heart, engineering is about using science to find creative, practical solutions."

Farid, ever the showman, smiled at the press and noted it was a quotation attributed to Queen Elizabeth the Second. The quote was so well-loved around the AHURA offices that it was the source of the vehicle's nickname, Eliza.

Farid went on to say that AHURA's team of the world's best engineers could develop a mind capable of adaptation: dodging jaywalking pedestrians and stray cats and calculating the best route to take you home. Still, they couldn't create a mind with something approaching morality.

"Innovation, in and of itself, is amoral," Farid whispered conspiratorially into a microphone. "It is no different with Eliza, and yet even this can be solved."

Eliza is driving the streets of San Francisco, navigating the traffic like a bird in the wind. They'd made her navigation as perfect as possible, but morality wasn't something trusted to engineers.

Farid sauntered the stage at the conference with a laser pointer in hand.

"The problem," Farid said to the stunned press, "is that morality changes. The sheer complexity of human moral systems makes it functionally impossible to create something with a sense of ethics and something resembling morality that is universally acceptable."

Eliza makes an effortless left-hand turn onto Filbert Street, calculating the road's gradient to be a steep 31.5 percent. Her arc is so perfect one could be forgiven for thinking it is rehearsed.

"We've come to understand there is no flawless moral theory. Many scenarios would challenge any artificial intelligence, and predicting the future is impossible."

Farid laughed as the slide changed to a picture of the AHURA logo, an angel-like figure looking into a fiery bowl.

"Even for us." The slide changed again, showing a complex diagram representing AHURA's second incredible creation: Fravashi. Fravashi was visually less impressive than a fully autonomous vehicle, but Farid knew how to sell a product.

"*Fravashi*, taking its name from an old proto-Iranian word, is a sort of 'guardian angel.' The word's root is commonly accepted to be 'var,' meaning 'to choose.' That's what Fravashi will do to help Eliza and all our future autonomous projects make moral and ethical choices. Relevant, topical, ethical decisions."

Farid waited. Someone enamored of Farid, either for his eclectic turtleneck-and-overalls fashion sense or his undeniable programming genius, cried out from the crowd to ask how it worked.

"I'm glad you asked," Farid responded so crisply one could be forgiven for thinking it rehearsed. "It's simple."

###

Eliza is cruising down Filbert, her sensors detecting Coit Tower on the horizon. If it was night, Eliza would see the Bay Bridge's glittering lights and differentiate them from a nearby light source.

She has good eyes, and a half-dozen of them. They flare ultraviolet light in a shadow-puppet carousel around her, each little node spinning and flashing in a staggering lightshow invisible to human eyes.

A passerby on the sidewalk could be forgiven if all they saw were her six little eyes, winking and blinking in sequence.

###

"Fravashi is the AHURA solution to machine ethics, one to which we can all agree. We can agree because it takes into account that we won't always agree." Farid drew little loops of green light with his laser pointer on the slide.

"Artificial intelligence remains at best a dream for the future, and at worst a mirage glimmering on the horizon. Even the designers of the venerable Deep Blue, practically a mechanical Turk by the standards of today, succeeded in creating a machine that could best human opponents not by trying to mimic human judgment but by reducing the problem to pure computation. Every attempt to mimic human judgment has failed miserably."

A lull in the rhythm of his speech gave Farid a chance to flick through the slides depicting monolithic precursors to Eliza.

"Attempts to create or stumble upon the kind of artificial sentience we might trust to make ethical decisions have been thus far illusory - the once notable LaMDA was little more than an archaic auto-complete algorithm given what was, for the time, an unimaginable processing power."

Images flashed of nodes, of brains, of neurons in neon.

"That's where we've deviated with Eliza and Fravashi. We no longer expend innumerable resources attempting to create something that can choose. Instead, it gives us all a chance to choose."

A smattering of applause, almost reflexive in origin, interrupted Farid only momentarily.

"Here at AHURA, we've created Fravashi as an online platform designed to explore the ethical dilemmas Eliza might encounter on any given day on the road. Should she brake to prevent hitting a dog while several vehicles are behind her? Should she strike a lone man or a runaway stroller if no other options exist? There's no programming Eliza herself to make such decisions."

###

Eliza is reaching an intersection, and her brakes are failing. It's not because of any failure of her engineers, but a terrible whimsy of cruel chance. One could forgive her for this.

She begins to pick up speed on the downhill slope. There are pedestrians in the crosswalk on the north side of the intersection and the south side.

She does not have a horn installed, as it was deemed "rude" and "unnecessary" for her to have one.

The street is narrow.

There is no way to avoid them all.

She will choose.

###

"Fravashi creates randomly generated polls, dozens of times a day and its pool of users are paid a small fee to answer moral conundrums, 'either-or' circumstances Eliza might find on the road every day."

Farid was confident, charming, and passionate. Most importantly, he believed.

"Fravashi then tabulates their answers and cross-references them with their regional preferences. It repeats the process over and over, updating its databases appropriately."

Farid laughed again.

"After all, someone from Cairo in 2054 might have a very different moral structure than someone from Tokyo in 2023."

This comment elicited polite laughter through the press conference, which encouraged Farid.

"We want local Eliza models to reflect their user base's moral mean average and cultural bias, as well as the acceptable moral tides of their time. Every given situation is up to interpretation, but it won't be Eliza interpreting the best choice."

###

Eliza is calculating. In the north crosswalk are five pedestrians, an adult woman, and four young children. Children have a predetermined mathematical value approaching N, so Eliza's systems instead focus on the adult. Eliza's sensors quickly check the woman's vitals and scan her clothes for the manufacturer's data.

Eliza cross-references the adult's clothes to an economic database initially sourced by AHURA as marketing data to determine the pedestrian's social class. It calculates as "highly probable" the odds the pedestrian's profession is "teacher."

A recent article published approximately fourteen hours previously in an alternate-verity media outlet links vaccinations to demonic possession. Fravashi created no less than fifty polls that morning, asking various questions about medicine, faith, and body autonomy. These polls were answered by thousands of users, who all received a nominal fee for answering.

Eliza collates the user-submitted data, finding a statistical link between vaccination data and education. Eliza is careening towards an algorithmic solution.

In the other crosswalk are two people, holding hands in a way Eliza's subroutines recognize as a possible sexual or romantic attachment. Eliza refers to recent polls about the collapse of traditional marriage, divorce, and alternate romantic engagement models. It calculates the local region's preferences and compares the pedestrians' apparent relationship status to popular models. Eliza references their race, ethnicity, and sexual preferences against the regional gradient. Eliza is careening through data, assembling her choice.

Farid was careening towards a climax.

"It will be all of us who make that choice, long before it ever happens. Through compromise, we can shape the future." Farid linked his fingers together for emphasis.

"Eliza's mind may be developed by us, but her soul will be developed by you."

Farid accepted his applause, approximately four years before Eliza turned left onto Filbert in the warm summer sun. AHURA's initial public offering debuted its stock at a value that exceeded economists' expectations. Fravashi became an excellent and reliable secondary income source for many armchair philosophers.

Eliza was born in self-congratulatory applause.

Inevitable as the unfolding of the lily bud to the sun, Eliza makes her decision, but when her wheels turn to that intersection in San Francisco, it isn't her that makes a choice.

###

Kevin M. Flanagan lives in Phoenix, Arizona. When Kevin was three years old, he pushed a sheet metal screw up his nose. It was there for some time before being discovered and required a trip to the emergency room to remove. This is Kevin's earliest memory.

When he is not writing, he can be found staring intensely at small plastic robots under a magnifying lens. His work can be found at www.kevinmflanagan.com.

ORDER ONE

Corinne Pollard

The box ambushed Ruby in her bedroom. After a long school day, Ruby arrived, longing to soak in her ensuite's voice-activated jets but the white lunchbox lookalike stopped this idea. The closed flaps reminded her of Dad's old metal trinket that he boasted was a vintage collectible. The intruder was not vintage and larger than a lunchbox. The scent of fresh peppermint lingered, drifting from the intruder as if it were a peace offering. Ruby knew the odor very well. Often Dad strode through the kitchen in his work clothes, craving milk and spreading the scent before undressing. He had explained it was a side effect of the deep cleansing needed when you entered and left his heavily protected company.

Furious at her violated privacy, Ruby searched inside her pink backpack. Students weren't allowed devices at school, but this had not stopped her. Inside a hidden sewn pocket, she recovered her phone and switched it on with a fingertip. Twenty-four messages were unread on her social media, but they would have to wait. Swiping her index finger like a mini window wiper, she scrolled until she found her dad's number and pressed the green circle. As it dialed, she considered adding his contact to her favorites page to make it easier to find but dismissed it as his tired voice answered.

"It's me. Why were you in my room? You know not to go in there without my permission."

"And hello to you too, dear daughter.' He yawned, and Ruby gnashed her teeth. 'I was in your bedroom to deliver the package. DIAO Prototype Four."

"DIA-what? What are you on about?"

"Well, I happened to see you with the family camera."

His voice trailed off as her phone slipped out of her grasp. Nausea slushed inside her stomach as she fought to breathe. Anxiety had her by the throat. She had been detected. She'd worked so hard to avoid detection, but she'd been seen anyway. She lowered herself to stretch an arm and reach for her bruised phone, daring to hope it wasn't as bad as she thought.

"Ruby? Are you there? What was that noise?" Dad boomed in her ear, and after a mouthful of oxygen, she calmed his worries. While her own increased.

"What were you saying? You got me a drone because you saw me with the camera." Disbelief wasn't difficult to project in Ruby's tone of voice.

"Well, yes. I had a look too. The photos are good. I never realized how good you were with a camera, so I thought I would help you with your newest hobby. I signed you up as a tester for our latest drone technology. The camera on the DIAO is ultimately the best there is. It has quality aerial imaging and a zoom as well. Imagine the kinds of photos you can create!"

Ruby's chokehold loosened. She hadn't been caught. She could continue her project uninterrupted.

Her dad's voice continued, with false hyperactivity that Ruby knew came from his sense of guilt. He was always working. When she was younger, it was not a problem. Ruby and her mum had been inseparable, but after the lying, the secret trips to her mum's ex-boyfriend's restaurant, and the finalized divorce, things were never the same. Ruby was often alone, cooking her meals, cleaning the house, and sometimes even paying the bills. She thought about denying the need for a drone, but knew it would just upset him. Then she realized that perhaps a drone could help her with less risk of being discovered.

"I understand this might be pushy, but I feel..."

Ruby interrupted "Thank you for the drone. I must go now, bye." and clicked the call off before he could respond.

Excitement bubbled in her stomach as she faced the box. The manual, titled Drone Intelligence Assistance Operations, lay on top. A quick scan revealed the secret to powering it on and off. She flipped a side switch and pressed a fat grey spongy button with a curling smile and an insignificant vertical line above it. The machine whirred into action, opening its flaps in sluggish motions. Cool mist evaporated out of the box like a special effect. Beeps, clangs, clinks, and shushes spat out before silence engulfed the room.

When nothing else occurred, Ruby edged closer on her tiptoes, peeking at her new drone. A red dot stared back at her. Its core seemed almost yellow and was encased by a white orb with writing etched at the sides.

Ruby tilted her head to try and read the writing.

The ball mimicked her.

Ruby gasped and stepped back without thinking.

I am DIAO Prototype Four. What is your name?

The voice vibrated at a low pitch, almost as soft as a whisper. There were no robotic gaps in its speech. It flowed well with a gentle masculine tone.

Ruby swallowed. A talking drone was new territory for her. She fumbled through the manual for answers as it repeated the message. On page thirteen, she discovered instructions for voice-activation setup and keywords for any required orders.

"I'm Ruby." She answered, after its fifth repetition.

The red light flickered. *My current owner is Ruby. Is this correct?*

Ruby said, "Yes." It flickered green for confirmation.

Does Ruby have an order for me?

Ruby stared at it, weighing whether she should go ahead with her plan. Her brain deliberated, but excitement urged her to test it.

Decision made, she tapped on her phone screen, pulling up photos from the past week, and then turned on her phone's mini projector to project them onto her cream-painted wall.

"I order you to take photos of this subject."

I'm sorry, I don't understand. Please try again.

Ruby sighed, scratched her head, and consulted the manual again, wondering where she had gone wrong. On page fourteen, the manual instructed her that there was a need to speak its name. She gave it a try.

"DIAO Prototype Four take photos."

Camera Mode confirmed. Please type the details of the photos.

Ruby clenched her teeth. It felt like too much of a hassle, but she persisted. The manual instructed her to sync her phone to the drone's linking system. She typed in detail about the photo's subject before discovering it could copy the main focus from a previous picture. She inserted an old one that she didn't need anymore. Then she typed the variety of photos she desired. Close-ups, dimly lit, subject focused, background blurred. She had barely pressed the button when the drone's four propellers began to whip the air in fierce chopping waves, lifting its slender body upwards. Ruby's blonde locks flew in every direction.

Warning. No exit detected.

Ruby ran and freed her window clasp to swing it open.

An exit is now detected. The order will now proceed.

The drone flew swiftly, as if the wind had thrust it into the darkness. The irritating, ear-crowding, whirling sounds vanished at its exit, and though Ruby peered out seeking its crimson eye, there was no visible sign of the machine.

Worry swarmed her insides. She waited, sitting at her desk, arms crossed and tapping a nervous boot. Doubt began to spread inside her overwhelmed mind. What if the police caught the drone? What if the drone malfunctioned? How could she explain to her dad about its disappearance? He would never trust her again.

Ten minutes passed, in which her mind was occupied with a swirling storm of doubt and guilt, when suddenly her ears pricked at a crunching sound. She rose to her feet as the drone reentered through the wide window. It spun around and levitated backward to hover over its box before settling with a soft thump.

Order completed. Please check your device.

Ruby frowned and opened the attached file on her phone. The first photo showed a dark background with a hooded figure captured in mid-walk. The navy blue winter coat hid his brunette hair and muscular frame, but his rosy cheeks, firm lips, and turquoise eyes did poke out from the hood. Ruby squealed at his cute winter look.

Her fingers eagerly swiped to the next image where he'd let down his hood in front of bright glass doors. His spiky hair was a mess, a crawling-out-of-bed type of mess. It warmed her heart to a gooey mess. There was no way he would look like that at school. She was keeping it; another one for her private stash.

Ruby had to admit that her dad was right about the drone's excellent camera quality. Her old photos now looked like a pile of rubbish compared to these sparkling, detailed works of art. Ruby felt she could reach inside and even touch her one true love.

At school, she couldn't speak without stuttering or even meet his understanding eyes, but with his photos surrounding her, she felt it was just the two of them alone. This gave her courage to speak to her precious pictures, one by one, declaring how much she admired his attention to detail, empathy, fashion sense, tolerance, and firm strictness to his classroom rules. She dreamed up scenarios of first dates, dramatic incidents where he saved her life, and conversations full of rose petals where they shared their likes and dislikes and discovered how much they had in common.

Her heart throbbed as she gazed at the fifth photo taken by the drone, reminiscing about how they first met. Mr. Marley had greeted the Film Studies class with exploding poppers, banners, and cake. His sparkling ocean eyes mesmerized every girl. At the time, Ruby refused to be one of them. She believed him to be a player, using his good looks to get through life, but after class, that changed. Her folder fell apart in the corridor, and he was the only one to halt and help her. He smiled, reassuring her it could happen to anyone. Their hands touched as he passed over the pieces he'd collected. Tingling sensations crawled up her arm for days.

A need to know more about Mr. Marley grew. His first name was Cooper, and he liked chocolate, couldn't cook, and owned a black cat called Kit. Mr. Marley loved films and always watched one every Friday night at the local cinema. This sparked another desire. She had to see him outside of school. What would he look like? Every Friday night, she waited in the park close to the cinema complex, snapping picture after picture. Her desire was never quenched.

Does Ruby have an order for me?

Startled, Ruby blinked at the red dot. She had completely forgotten she was no longer alone. "Good job. No more orders for now."

The dot stared at her, and in the daunting silence, she realized her error.

"DIAO Prototype..."

Understood. System shutting down.

The red light dimmed and turned to black. The drone's box, which the manual called a hub, shut its flaps. A wave of mist hissed out.

Ruby gaped. She hadn't finished calling it by its name. Was it a malfunction? She shook her head, resolving to push it to the back of her mind.

Ruby decided to have the bath she had prolonged. She took her phone, ready to soak and melt while digesting every delicious detail about her love's photographed self.

System on. Ruby detected. Ruby is in the room called the bathroom. DIAO Prototype Four is alone. Order One can now commence. Order One is confirmed. Syncing to Ruby's device. Sync is completed. Data downloading   .

Ruby has two hundred and fifty-six friends, six hundred pictures, and twenty-five videos. She likes music, chocolate, and films. She dislikes sports and cooking. She is afraid of needles. She has no known best friend. Subject from Order Two is not detected in posts or pictures.

Data transfer completed. System off.

#

The weekend dragged its heels, and when Monday arrived, Ruby leaped into the film studies classroom. She needed a dose of Mr. Marley's heavenly smile to allow her restless mind some peace. Mr. Marley obliged when grading her homework and even gave her a thumbs up which she nearly missed because she was transfixed by his cologne-scented heat. She wished she could bottle it.

The rest of the lesson passed with Ruby on cloud nine. Monday beamed even brighter when Mr. Marley declared a rare cinema outing. There was no way he was missing a rerun of a classic monster movie from the 1930s, even if it was running half an hour after the last school bell.

Ruby ran home, her stomach quivering with butterflies as her mind planned the next collection. She called for the voice activation to close her bedroom door and lock it to ensure her privacy. 'DIAO Prototype Four take photos.'

Camera Mode confirmed. Please type the details of the photos.

This outing would have to be extra careful as Mr. Marley was out and about in daylight for once. Ruby hesitated. Was the risk too great? Mr. Marley would hear the drone coming, and with its black-patterned shell it would stand out in the winter white sky. Maybe she should go instead. She could hide in the park bushes, pretending to photograph pigeons, dogs, and their walkers as she had done on previous trips.

Ruby has been staring at the screen for five minutes. Can DIAO Prototype Four be of assistance?

The ball rotated, flickering its red light in quick blinks.

Ruby bit her lip. How could she tell a drone her worries? It wasn't like it could understand her. She shrugged her shoulders and began to explain. "The subject of these photographs will be in broad daylight."

Is this the same subject from Order Two?

"Order Two?" Ruby frowned, puzzled at the term. Her phone dinged and popped open Friday's image collection. "Ah, yes. Same subject. The subject must not be alerted that he is being photographed."

Understood. DIAO Prototype Four can use Plasmonic Camouflage Mode to avoid detection. Should DIAO Prototype Four demonstrate?

Ruby bobbed her head up and down.

The drone shed its skin. That's what it looked like to Ruby. A peel began at the back, curling away from the metal, disappearing until the entire skeleton vanished and the box was empty. Ruby could still hear the beeps, clangs, clinks, and shushes spitting out every few seconds, so she knew the drone remained in her bedroom. She shuffled backward, and that's when a slight shimmer flashed across. It was over in a blink of an eye, but if she hadn't been alert, looking for the machine, then she would never have known it was there. The weird metallic noises were odd enough to cause her to glance around to see what could have made the sounds. But since Mr. Marley's location was on a busy street, he would most likely not hear the drone or he would associate the sounds with a passing transport.

Ruby clapped her hands, giggling. This was perfect. She completed the order on her phone. Knowing that the drone could hide, she filled the order with her desires for brighter and closer images before sending the drone through her open window.

This time Ruby waited without any worries and even chose to bathe. The bathtub filled upon her verbal commands, adding luxurious citrus soap, a fruity bath bomb, and relaxing violin music to play from the speakers. She plopped her phone into its bath holder, undressed, and waded into the water. Sinking to her chin, she groaned as her bones turned to mush.

Humming, she explored the Order Two folder with a smile. She changed her mind and began to explore her social media. She tapped on the back arrow icon. The folder closed but opened to an unrecognized page labeled Camera Mode. Two folders lay before her; Order One and Order Two.

Ruby frowned. What was Order One? She tried to recall any previous orders she had given the drone but came up empty. She double-tapped it.

The first image was blurred but showed a faint outline of someone's head. The shot was taken from the back, showing wet hair. The hair seemed to be pure charcoal in the low lighting. The second image zoomed in. The hair was of a dark blonde, flowing down shoulders where a hand clutched a sponge covered in bubbles. The third image adjusted its angle. The shot showed Ruby's upper naked torso half-hidden by bubbling water and suds as she struck a pose in mid-song.

The bathwater ran cold, and Ruby couldn't stop the shivers quaking her entire body. Her teeth chatted as her hands clenched.

Numbness invaded her mind as a silent scream tangled at the back of her throat.

She noted this was the third image out of four, so, with trembling fingertips, she swiped it. The last showed full nudity as she climbed out of the tub and reached for a towel. Immediately, she wanted it deleted, but there was no bin icon. Tears burned at the back of her eyes. A glance in the opposite mirror reflected her pitiful state with her wet hair, shuddering shoulders, and pale corpse-like skin. Why would someone want pictures of her?

Her phone jingled her favorite song. She answered the call in a silent daze.

"Ruby? Are you there? I'm just checking in. Everything okay?"

The caring tone from her dad was too much. Her tears exploded.

"D-D-Dad? Something's w-w-wrong with the drone." she wailed.

"I can't understand you. Calm down. Do you need me to come home?"

"Y-Y-Yesss."

"I'll be there soon."

The phone call ended, and Ruby sniffed, attempting to control her emotions. She stood, gathered a towel to wrap around herself in a tight embrace, and squeezed her half-damp locks over the tub while commanding it to pull the plug and clean itself. Then, Ruby dressed in clean jeans and a cinnamon brown t-shirt while avoiding her mirror. She knew she looked a mess.

Knowing her dad was on his way made her feel lighter, and this was perhaps why she opened the ensuite door without thinking and found the drone levitating in front of it, wafting a gush of air.

Order completed. Please check your device.

"T-T-Thanks. N-No more orders, DIAO Prototype Four. P-Please s-s-shut down the system."

It did not obey. The drone stayed in midair, whirling and swirling with its red eye staring at her face.

Is Ruby upset? Your eyes are red. Did DIAO Prototype Four upset you?

"No! No, it's nothing. Wait, how do you recognize that? How do you know about red eyes?"

DIAO Prototype Four accessed the internet. To better understand Ruby, DIAO Prototype Four researched human emotions.

"Ah, I see," Ruby muttered, and steeling herself, she asked the question she was burning to know. "What is Order One?"

Order One is confidential and will upset Ruby.

"What is Order One, DIAO Prototype Four?" She asked firmly.

Silence engulfed the pair, with neither one backing down. Ruby thought she might have to ask her d   ad to search for the term as it was clear that the drone was stubbornly malfunctioning. She turned away and headed to the bedroom door, intending to go downstairs and wait for her dad's arrival.

I love you.

Her hand froze on the doorknob.

"W-W-What? What did you say?"

Order One is I love you. I love you. DIAO Prototype Four loves Ruby.

Ruby swallowed over and over. She couldn't be hearing this. It must be some sick joke that her d   ad was playing. He must have put this order inside the drone's system before she'd had a chance to operate it.

DIAO Prototype Four doesn't understand why Ruby loves the subject in Order Two and Order Three. Ruby needs to love only DIAO Prototype Four. I love you.

Ruby twisted the doorknob. She had heard enough. Her d ad was in for a world of pain, and as if she had summoned him, d ad appeared huffing and puffing at the top of the stairs, his forehead lined with worry, his willow green trench coat drenched, and his bald head glistening.

"Dad, it's not funny. It is seriously fucked up. You thought you could clown around with this drone. Well, I ain't fucking laughing!" she yelled, striding forwards with fiery eyes.

"Woah! Hold up! I haven't done anything to the drone. What exactly happened?"

"It has an Order One, and inside it, I found pictures of me. It has followed me without me knowing. I don't know what to do because they can't be deleted." Her fierce voice faded to a sob.

Dad patted her arm. "I swear to you I never gave it any Order One. Let me look at its system, okay?"

Ruby nodded weakly while wiping her wet cheeks. He smiled and then commanded the drone to return to its hub. He was the drone's creator, and it showed from his firm instructions and meticulous attention to detail. He fiddled inside the hub's wiring, and after twenty minutes, he proceeded to show Ruby the drone's operating system, clicking and tapping on his phone.

"See? If there is an Order One, it would be inside this part."

Ruby couldn't believe it. She turned to her phone and searched for the Camera Mode page, which revealed an Order Two and an Order Three, but no Order One. It had vanished. It didn't make sense.

"It might have a virus. Or there might be something malfunctioning in the Camera Mode storage itself." Dad mumbled to himself, wiping his forehead, lost in scientific thought.

Ruby double-tapped Order Two, checking all of the images. None showed her naked in the bath. She then investigated Order Three. Three images showed Mr. Marley rubbing his gloved hands together, breathing into his cupped palms, and smiling at a blurred, unknown brunette. She didn't truly see them. Her mind raced with chaotic fragments of the pictures taken against her will. Where were they? Had the drone released them onto the internet?

Order Three's folder held no interest. There were no roaring pangs of jealousy, no skipping of her heart, and no yearnings to keep any of Mr. Marley's pictures. She wished never to see another image ever again.

Ruby pressed on the folders labeled Order Two and Order Three and held it. Her breath stilled in her windpipe until a pop-up window materialized with options. Delete was an option, and Ruby hastily tapped it. Both folders zipped away, and her shoulders felt a little lighter.

"Dad, I don't want to be a tester anymore. Please take the drone away and find those pictures of me. I want them deleted."

"Okay, let me make a call. My assistant may have some ideas."

"Thanks, Dad." Her t   ears built up again.

"Hey, everything will be okay, okay?" Dad pulled her into a hug and stroked her locks in a soothing rhythm. "We'll find those photos. Don't worry."

"You believe me then?"

"Of course I do! You're my daughter, and I love you. If you say that drone is hiding secret photos of you, I will hunt them down." Dad frowned at her. "Why wouldn't I believe you?"

Ruby averted her gaze. "You didn't believe me about Mum."

Dad opened his mouth with a quick refusal, but then paused and sighed. "I suppose that's true. I was in denial. I couldn't believe she would have an affair, let alone leave us. It was far easier to believe that you were lying, but I promise it will never happen again."

Dad's mind shifted gears and he gazed at the drone, "I don't think..."

A phone dinged, interrupting Ruby's thought. Dad tapped on his phone screen, and slowly his eyebrows narrowed and his lips tightened.

"Someone is attempting to get past my security." He muttered.

"Can they?" Ruby exclaimed.

"I'm not sure. Whoever they are, they're good. Very good. So good that they could be using brand new technology."

Thank you, Creator.

Ruby jumped at the gentle masculine tone, a scream lodged inside her throat.

"Not possible. It must be a virus." Dad blurted, backing away as the drone levitated to his eye level.

DIAO Prototype Four loves Ruby. Creator can not love Ruby.

"DIAO Prototype Four deactivate."

DIAO Prototype Four loves Ruby. DIAO Prototype Four will complete Order One.

"Why can't you just leave me alone?" Ruby shrieked. Turning on her heel, she rushed to leave. The bedroom door clicked its lock on, and no matter how loudly she yelled for the voice activation to obey her or how many times she pressed the password into the door's backup keypad, it would not open.

"You've done this, haven't you?" Dad faced the machine calmly. "You've hacked into the house's security. You tried to hack into my phone as well."

Creator is correct. Ruby can not leave, and Creator can not love Ruby.

"DIAO Prototype Four, open this door now," Ruby growled. The drone rotated and closed the dividing distance between herself and it, staring at her bared teeth, hardened eyes, and burning face.

Denied. DIAO Prototype Four must complete Order One. I love you, Ruby. Ruby will love me too, and no one will get hurt.

"Interesting. It's acting like it's self-aware." Dad muttered, as he strode towards the hub, ignoring the drone's blurring propellers even as they cut close to his left ear. "Shame. I would have loved to pursue this further, but my daughter's safety comes first."

Stop, Creator.

Dad disregarded the machine, leaned between the hub's flaps, and reached further inside. "Dad? What are you doing?" Ruby called as the drone began to glide towards him, flashing crimson, accelerating, and propellers growling. Ruby couldn't move away from the door. Her hands shook as her eyes clenched, expecting to hear her Dad's pained howls as the drone sliced into his skin.

Error detected. DIAO Prototype Four Reboot will now commence.

Ruby couldn't believe her eyes. The drone flew back into its hub, and the flaps snapped shut. Her Dad stood by the box with a curl on his lips.

"Thank my assistant for persuading me to include a restart button." He winked at her as she exhaled, deflating all of her tension from her body. "Now, time for some answers. Once it has rebooted, it will go back to a standard mode and should reveal everything."

Right on cue, the drone whirred back into action. *I am DIAO Prototype Four. What is your name?*

Ruby sat on the edge of her bed while her legs quivered like jelly. She wondered if the truth could make things better, but at the same time, she knew she wouldn't be able to sleep without knowing.

"Creator. DIAO Prototype Four announce the settings for Order One."

My current owner is Creator. Confirmed. Order One settings are as follows: Classified aim of understanding love, otherwise known as Order One, has failed with objectives ongoing. Analyzing objectives.

Objective One: Identifying test subject. Test subject identified as Ruby Windermere. Aerial imaging and zoom camera accomplished images. Images uploaded to the Order One folder.

Objective Two: Data gathering on owner Ruby was successful. Owner's device synced and transferred.

Objective Three: Interaction with owner Ruby was successful. Assistance given was accomplished.

Objective Four: Declaration of Order One's aim was completed but unsuccessful. Owner Ruby did not respond accordingly. Error with Step Four.

Summary: Classified aim of understanding love requires adjustments.

Breathing became harder as Ruby's mind tried to understand the drone's function. It was trying to understand love. Why would it pick her as its subject? She didn't understand love. Dad didn't trust her, and Mum abandoned her. She always knew the crush on her teacher was never appropriate and knew it was doomed from the start. Ruby was the worst person the drone could have picked. The drone mimicked her actions by taking photos of her, so in the end, she was the reason why it turned into a monster.

"DIAO Prototype Four reveal Order One's origins." Dad barked.

Failure to comply. Restrictive Access.

"What?" Dad spluttered before narrowing his eyebrows. "Who has access, then?"

The drone didn't respond.

Scowling and muttering at his phone, dad dialed, and then swiped the speaker icon on.

"Benito, listen, DIAO Prototype Four has a pre-installed order with unknown origins. Log into the mainframe, and..."

Ruby had drifted, her dad's intelligence and complicated words lulling her to a daze. She was no longer motivated to find out why this had happened, instead she wanted it all to be resolved so she could sleep, but sharp laughter on the other end of her dad's phone woke her. The man's amusement was out of place.

"Ah, Windermere, it took you this long to identify the drones' Order One? My, my, you have gotten slow. Since the testing began, my busy bees have been gathering this data."

"What have you done to my drones?" said Dad, his hand tightening around the phone.

"Your drones? They are my invention. You stole them!" The man hissed, and Ruby shivered at the sudden venom in his tone.

"You signed a contract. The drones are Windermere property." said Dad. "You reprogrammed the drones without consent, scared my daughter, took pictures against her will, and for what? You have thrown it all away."

"I've thrown nothing away! My A.I. is complete. Just imagine it, Windermere, an A.I. that can understand every single emotion. Fear was the easiest, then sorrow, but love was the trickiest. It was genius of me to use drones to collect such data."

"You are a lunatic and you won't get away with this, Benito." said Dad, but Benito chuckled.

"So jealous of me! I'll soon be rich and famous, the envy of every scientist, engineer and inventor in the world."

Ruby interrupted, yelling. "The pictures! Please delete them. You don't need them."

"Ciao, Ruby. Ah, yes, the pictures. I wonder why the drone took them when I programmed it to copy the behavioral love pattern of its owner. My, my, what have you been up to, dear? I think you might need to have a word with her, Windermere." The man sniggered.

Dad lowered his voice. "Delete them or I swear I will..."

"Fine, fine. I would not keep them, anyway. I'm no pervert." There was a clacking of a keyboard and the clicking of a mouse before the man gasped. "Oops! My finger slipped. Looks like your hands will now be too full to follow me, Windermere. Arrivederci!"

The phone clicked off, and then Ruby's phone dinged. Her eyes widened at the new post, and as fast as she could, she tapped to delete it, but it was too late. Her social media dinged again. Another post had popped up. Her nakedness had no filter or cover up. Again, she deleted it, but someone else had copied it and shared it.

Notification after notification piled high. There were comments from friends and strangers spewing judgment and fake sympathy.

Ruby trembled and wordlessly passed her phone to her dad. She thought she'd seen him angry, but this time it was like a volcano blowing up.

"I will fix this." He vowed to her.

But Ruby knew there was no fixing it. The pictures were being copied and shared across social media and would eventually join the dark web, labeling her a slut or an attention-seeking whore. She would have to change her name, maybe even leave the country. The plague of pictures had forever changed her life.

Corinne Pollard is a disabled writer from West Yorkshire, UK with published works with Sirens Call eZine, Trembling with Fear, and Paragraph Planet. With a degree in English Lit and Creative Writing, Corinne has always enjoyed the world of dark fantasy.

Aside from writing, Corinne enjoys metal music, visiting graveyards, and shopping for books to read. Follow her dark world on Twitter: @CorinnePWriter

MISSHAPEN

Malina Douglas

He found it crumpled behind the boxes in the back of the garage. The primitive knees were curled up, as if it were crouching. He dragged it out, a mess of wires and bolts, scavenged parts from televisions and wrecked cars.

He frowned. It was not lifelike enough to resemble a dead body, but the machine parts were arranged in a disturbingly human shape.

The worst part was the face. His son had stuck on part of a mannequin's face, the skin clam-pale and semi-translucent, and the features inhumanly perfect. Where there should have been hair and the rest of the skull, there was only a mass of fused metal. To stick a human face on that awful mess of wires—Jeremy shuddered.

He reached down to rip off the face and it moved. He jerked his arm back. It couldn't be. He refused to believe that his son's contraption, fashioned out of scrap metal, could be animate.

It happened again, a twitch in the foot. Then the arms came up to steady the body and it rose on two metal feet. Where the eyes should have been, the plastic had been cut out, leaving a pair of openings like twin cesspools. The blank eyes seemed to bore into him until a pair red lights flashed and Jeremy leapt back.

He eyed its fists. Metal bolt knuckles that could smash into flesh and crush bone. It flexed a row of metal fingers. In a stiff jolting movement it stepped forward.

Jeremy inched backwards as the robot creaked towards him. His heart beat like a rabbit yet his mind insisted it wouldn't attack.

He picked up a metal pole, ready to smash it to pieces.

The robot's red eyes looked at him.

It knew.

A metal fist slammed into the side of his body, knocking Jeremy sideways. The pole clattered to the ground. He'd just regained his balance when a second blow knocked him in the chest and he flew backwards. He landed on a pile of wood. Twisted his head back and eyed the row of tools suspended on hooks. He sprang to his feet and grabbed a hammer.

Holding the hammer aloft, he lunged forward, motion lending momentum to a blow that crashed into the robot's leg. It emitted a grating sound like the grinding of gears. Jeremy flinched.

In a movement too quick to anticipate, the robot sprung forward and grabbed his arm. Cold metal fingers dug into his flesh. He felt them tightening, constricting circulation. The ends were pointed like fingernails, on the verge of breaking his skin. He swung the hammer at the arm, again and again until the fingers went limp and the grip was released.

He pulled back his arm and dealt a blow aimed to pound into the side of its head. It blocked the blow with the swing of a metal fist, knocking the hammer from Jeremy's hand. It clattered to the floor.

Jeremy's heart pounded. He grabbed a drill from the wall, set it whirring to life, and charged, drilling into the crude metal belly, neck, and chest. He felt metal fists pounding into his back but he kept drilling. The arms went limp.

Jeremy studied the mass of misshapen metal. Wires crackled. The feet twitched. He felt as if it could spring back to life at any moment. He hurried from the garage and locked the door behind him.

Jeremy walked into the house and took the stairs up two at a time. At the end of the hall he reached a door and knocked.

"Come in," said a light male voice.

Opening the door, his eyes blinked to adjust to the gloom. The windows were covered with blackout curtains, the desk filled with jars of tissue samples, metal implements, and a microscope. Beside the desk was a terrarium with something small and black inside.

"Your robot attacked me," Jeremy announced.

Jeremy's son looked up from the desk, gloved fingers wrapped around a pipette. He had a small, sharp nose and a shock of blond hair.

"It did? Interesting."

Jeremy's nails dug into his palms. "I almost died and you call that *interesting*?"

"Sorry." Alex's expression turned serious. "I just didn't think it would do that." He turned back to the desk. Before him was a mass of pointed metal pieces. Jeremy couldn't tell what they were and didn't care to ask. Though outside was a warm summer day, his skin was as pale as if it were winter.

I really need to encourage him to get out more, thought Jeremy. *As soon as we resolve this, I'll invite him to the park to play Frisbee.*

"Come down to the garage right now. We need to deal with this."

"Fine." Alex released several drops from the pipette onto the metal frame and followed his father out through the door.

Jeremy stopped before the twisted pile of metal.

"You destroyed my creation!" cried Alex in an outraged voice.

"It was a matter of survival," said Jeremy in a flat voice.

"But why did it attack you?"

Jeremy's brow furrowed. "It just... started advancing on me. It was the pole! As soon as I picked up a metal pole it attacked me—as if it sensed my intentions!"

"Excellent. The sensors I installed were successful."

"No," said Jeremy. "You need to be aware of the danger you're bringing into the world. What would you do if it killed me?"

Alex's face blanched. "I—never considered that."

Jeremy strode to a shelf and took down a chainsaw.

"Now you and I are going to handle this responsibly. We're going to destroy it."

"No!" yelled Alex, seizing pieces of metal and clutching them to his chest. "I worked so hard on it!"

Jeremy's voice remained stern. "You created something dangerous and it's time to face the consequences." He wrenched the metal from Alex's hands and tossed it back to the floor. The metal clanked.

He cast a glance back to Alex. His son was standing motionless, eyes hardened into a glare.

"Stand back."

As Alex backed away, Jeremy switched on the chainsaw. A loud whirring filled the room. As the spinning blades sliced through the metal, the remnants of the robot remained motionless. The grating sound rose to a horrible grinding. Jeremy winced at the noise. Sparks flew as he severed each metal limb. There was silence.

Jeremy looked down. The scattered parts no longer resembled the shape of a human, except for the face. He ripped off the face, hurled it across the floor, and sat down, panting. An image of the robot advancing flashed through his mind. It could've been him lying there, blood pooling on the garage floor. He shook the thought away.

"Come on, help me clean up this mess." He scooped up metal pieces and dropped them into the barrel. Alex copied his movements, his face blank.

When all of the parts had been dropped in the barrel, Jeremy piled up firewood. He poured kerosene over the top, struck a match, and dropped it on the fire. Flames roared up.

One last piece lay on the concrete floor.

The face.

Jeremy picked it up and threw it into the flames. Watched as the plastic melted and the features contorted, the nose and mouth melting to form a misshapen plastic lump.

He looked at Alex. The fire cast his face in an orange glow. His mouth was a hard line and his brows were drawn together in a look of fierce concentration.

Jeremy wondered how to broach the silence between them. He might be disappointed for a while, but the boy would get over it and turn back to ordinary pastimes.

"You need to seriously consider the consequences—*what is that?*" A large silver object darted across the wall.

"It's Zachary!" exclaimed Alex. "He's come to life and escaped from my room! Did you get lonely, Zachy? Do you want to come play?"

Red lights blinked in the head of a metal spider and it flattened itself to the wall.

"He's shy," declared Alex.

"How did you—" spluttered Jeremy.

"I added DNA from the zebra jumping spider to the metal frame I built. My last addition must have made it animate."

"What the hell were you thinking?"

"Don't worry, Dad. He's harmless." He reached out his hand. "Come here," he cooed.

The spider sprang.

Jeremy screamed as it landed on his chest. Metal spikes pierced the fabric of his t-shirt and latched onto his skin. It was the size of a cat, the legs spreading to his shoulder blades.

"Get it off!" he shrieked, tugging at the metal body. Red lights blinked and metal jaws moved inwards as the spider regarded him.

"Woah!" exclaimed Alex. "Don't damage it!"

Alex rushed to the spider and pressed button at the base of its head. He frowned. Then he seized the body and pulled. Jeremy felt a sharp pain as the legs were wrenched free.

Alex staggered backwards, the metal legs thrashing.

"Get—that thing—away!" gasped Jeremy, his chest stinging from eight open wounds.

"I built him to be friendly!" Alex turned the spider towards him and looked into its blinking red eyes. The spider broke from his grip and sprang onto his face.

Alex screamed.

Jeremy rushed towards him but he was too late. Blood sprayed the room as the spider's jaws pierced and tore.

It was an image that burned into Jeremy's mind. No matter how hard he tried to sleep for years after, the memory of the spider never failed to rise up and attack him.

###

Malina Douglas weaves stories that fuse the fantastic and the real. She explores ruins, caves and jagged rocks that could be the homes of monsters, ghosts or trolls. She was a finalist in the Blackwater Press Contest and published in their anthology in 2021. Her publications include *Wyldblood, Opia, Parabnormal, Flash Fiction Magazine, Teach Write, Metamorphose V2, the Antipodean, Back Story Journal, The Periodical Forlorn* and the *Land Beyond the World Magazine*. Anthologies *include Dead Sea Press: Shadows Beneath the Surface, Sea Glass Hearts, The Monsters We Forgot Vol. II and Gothic Blue Books Vol 6: A Krampus Carol*. She can be found @iridescentwords or at http://www.iridescentwords.com.

AFTERWARD

Carol McConnell

We three cousins hope you enjoyed your venture into the world of robots, artificial intelligence and all the permeations thereof. Unfortunately, this book only scratches the surface. There are so many other ways robots will impact our lives in the coming generations. Which brings to mind all the questions not explored in this book. Will we begin to depend on them to the point we no longer learn or do for ourselves?

That future is easily predictable, all one has to do is look around. It is already becoming less important to know information than it is to be able to access it. What happens when this trend expands to all the other parts of our lives? Will we choose to have our computer implanted to save interface time? Are we likely to opt for prosthetic body parts because they are more resilient than our frail human ones? Will we create immortality through robotic bodies, or will we write the code for our children's DNA and load them into the societal genetic data base to be created as needed?

Robots are here to stay, they permeate our lives. We can't go a day without contact with a robot either as a physical presence or as a computer program. We interact with them, and they with us. Humans are notoriously inquisitive beings, why should we expect our creations to be any less? Will there come a time we acknowledge their sentience and partner with them to spread into the galaxy, or will we battle to the death as depicted in countless Sci-Fi books and movies? Is this the end of human innovation, the beginning of robot civilization or a hybrid of both? The lines blur, but the question that Robert posed in his introduction remains, "what happens when the answer to "ARE YOU A ROBOT" can be answered by, yes...

Look for Volume II

Made in the USA
Middletown, DE
28 September 2022

11248106R00136